She swung a leg over the bed and nearly stepped on what she thought was a pile of clothes. As her eyes adjusted to the morning light filtering through her window, she realized half the pile was flesh-colored and all of it was lightly snoring.

Speak of the devil.

Kilty.

Brochan had apparently spent the night sleeping on the floor beside her bed like a protective dog, one arm tucked under a crushed pillow, the other splayed above his head, his great back muscles spanning farther than she dared try to step.

Catriona allowed her gaze to run down his spine to the pinch of his waist and his tight, muscular butt wrapped in the plaid boxers she'd bought for him in the hopes they would be enough to satisfy him on his *tartan days*—the days he insisted on wearing his kilt. That woolen thing was so old and worn she suspected it roamed the halls at night, sentient from the mingling of bacteria it had collected over the years. She'd hoped the nice, new boxers would help him with his homesickness for ancient Scotland *and* keep her from having to suffer the stares of strangers as she moved around the city with a kilt-wearing giant.

It's nae a skirt.

She could hear his voice in her head and smiled before wincing at the pain in her lip.

Okay, so smiling hurts. Duly noted.

Broch's tush seemed like the best place to cross the moat of a man, and she stepped over him to tiptoe out of the room, every step triggering a dull throb.

Aspirin. That would be a good place to start.

She made her way to the kitchen to find the bottle of pain relievers in the cupboard and shook three into her palm. She knew two was the recommended dosage, but if ever there was a *three*-aspirin day, it was today.

Catriona eased a bottle of wa⸱ gingerly leaned her backside a swallowed the pills. She closed] breath as her aching ribs would all

D1519205

"Wow. You look like you were hit by a train."

At the sound of the voice, Catriona's eyes popped wide as she dropped the half-finished water. The bottle landed right-side-up and shot a tiny geyser against her shins. She made a fist with her liberated right hand, readying for attack.

Fiona laughed. "Jumpy much?"

A mass of dark hair and a familiar face stared at Catriona from her living room sofa. Releasing her curled fingers, she felt her fear morph into relief.

A sort of relief.

Her sister wasn't who she expected—or wanted—to see in her apartment.

She dropped her forehead into her hand to catch her breath and slow her pounding heart.

"You'd be jumpy too," she mumbled. "Why are you here?"

Fiona's head tilted. "You sound drunk. Are you drunk?"

Drunk? Catriona scowled and then remembered she'd wiped out the Parasol Picture's private plane's collection of tiny booze bottles while trying to soothe her aches and erase the horrors of her trip to Las Vegas.

Could I be drunk?

No...

She didn't feel drunk. She felt confident she wouldn't ache as much as she did if she were. She licked her lip and tasted blood.

Oh right. The football on my face.

"I *wish* I was drunk. My lip is swollen."

Fiona stood and ran her hands through her mane of ebony hair as she walked forward like a catwalk model, lithe and composed. Catriona looked away, disgusted by her sister's *natural sexy.*

Why did she get all the feminine wiles?

Fiona drew close, inspecting her sister's lip. Catriona retracted her neck to avoid bumping noses with her.

"Get your face out of my face," she muttered.

Fiona grimaced. "You look like you had an overzealous pre-Oscars Botox touch-up."

"Thanks. You're not exactly Miss America in the morning either."

It was a lie. Fiona always looked *together*. It was nice to see her a *little* rumpled in the morning. It meant she might be human. A terrible human, but human, nonetheless.

Catriona glanced down to be reminded her water had landed right-side up.

Hm. I couldn't do that again if I tried.

She stooped to retrieve it, groaning with the effort and took another swig from the left side of her mouth.

"Why are you *here*?"

Fiona shrugged. "Daddy tried to kill me, remember? Sean thought maybe I'd be safest here."

Catriona recalled a fuzzy memory of Fiona arriving the previous evening, panting and frazzled and yapping about how their father had tried to kill her and how she'd... *what*? Done something to him...

"Did you say you *stabbed* him?"

Fiona nodded and pantomimed the action. "In the throat. Pen."

"And you think he's dead?"

Fiona shrugged. "Never *dead*. But gone. I hope."

Catriona closed her eyes. There were so many things to deal with in the *real* world. This new reality, where she, Fiona, their father Rune, her adoptive father Sean, and Broch were all supposedly some tribe of time travelers felt like too much to process with what had to be a cracked rib on her right side screaming for attention.

It might be a four-aspirin day.

Something Fiona had said bounced back through Catriona's brain and she cocked her head.

Sean thought maybe I'd be safest here.

"Wait. Since when does Sean care what happens to *you*?"

Fiona shrugged. "Since he realized we're all in this together."

Catriona closed her eyes. "I don't like the sound of that."

Fiona stretched her arms over her head with an

exaggerated yawn that made Catriona open her eyes to see what the noise was about. Her sister wore a familiar t-shirt and it rose to expose her naked thighs as she reached for the ceiling.

My t-shirt.

Fiona motioned to the bedroom. "That moving mountain slept in there with you. You saw him, right? I don't imagine you could miss him."

"I saw him."

"Like a Great Dane. I couldn't have gotten near you if I tried. I got up once to go to the bathroom and I swear I heard him growl."

Catriona nodded in Fiona's direction. "That's my t-shirt."

Fiona scratched at her ribs. "No kidding. Cheap cotton. Itches."

"It's not cheap."

"Trust me. It's cheap."

"It's not cheap—"

"Guid mornin'."

Both women shifted their attention to find Broch standing at the doorway of Catriona's bedroom, still wearing nothing but his plaid boxers, the scar on his abdomen more visible than usual.

Fiona made a *whoof* noise and Catriona glanced at her. It seemed Broch's physical charms weren't wasted on her sister. Fiona might have called him the *moving mountain*, but right now she looked as if she wanted to wrap herself around him like the snake she was.

Catriona eyeballed Fiona as she pointed at Broch's scar. Fiona had stabbed him in another life.

"I don't think you've got a shot with him, Fee, considering you almost killed him," she said.

Fiona shrugged. "Gives him character. He should thank me."

Broch ran his fingers over the scar as he padded into the kitchen. "It itches today."

"It's because of her," said Catriona as he opened the refrigerator to retrieve a bottle of orange juice. "If you spend too much time near her I bet it will open again. We have to get her out of here."

Fiona clucked her tongue. "Jeeze. I'm right here. I can hear you, you know."

"Then take a hint."

Broch unscrewed the top of the orange juice and was about to raise the bottle to his lips when both sisters spoke in unison.

"*Glass.*"

Broch lowered the bottle.

"Richt. Sorry."

Broch opened a cabinet to get a glass and Fiona gathered her clothes from the chair beside the sofa. "Can I at least get a shower?"

Catriona sighed. "Sure."

"And while I'm in there, you think about where I'm supposed to go. I think Sean wanted me to stay here with you until we figure out whether or not Dad is dead."

"He must have forgotten about how your presence agitates Broch's wound."

Fiona glanced at Broch. "Or maybe he thought the big monkey would be in his *own* cage."

Catriona pushed Fiona toward the bedroom, the location of the only bathroom in the small apartment over Parasol Pictures' payroll office. "You're about to be out on the street with no shower."

"Fine, fine. I'm going."

"Dinnae use mah shampoo," Broch called after her as she disappeared.

Catriona moved to the kitchen island. "Why has your shampoo migrated to my shower?"

"Ah didnae wantae lea ye alone with her last nicht, bit ah wantit a shower, sae ah fetched it fae mah abode."

"You couldn't use my shampoo for one day?"

Broch looked at her as if she'd lost her mind.

"Right. Stupid question." She nodded toward his stomach. "How are you feeling. How fast is that thing opening up?"

Broch glanced at the angry scar and finished his OJ as if it were a shot of whiskey. "'Tis fine." He placed his glass on the counter and reached out to cup her cheek, his thumb brushing lightly over her swollen lip. "Mair importantly, how ye daen?"

Catriona shivered at his light touch. All she wanted to do was close her eyes and sleep away the rest of the day curled against his body. She considered telling him, but instead, shrugged and smiled as best she could. "I'm sore. I'll be okay."

"Ye shuid gang back tae yer kip."

"Too much to do. We have to figure out what to do with Fiona, find out if Rune is dead, talk to Sean about whatever happened to him yesterday—"

"Throw her o'er the hall," suggested Broch.

Catriona glanced at her door, considering the guest apartment across the hall from her apartment. She assumed that's where Broch thought Fiona should move, and that he wasn't suggesting they chuck her down the hall—not that she was *against* that idea.

"That's probably still too close to you."

"Nah. It ainlie seems tae itch whin she's in the identical room. Richt noo it feels fine."

He glanced down at his tummy and Catriona did as well, happy for an excuse to stare at his ridiculous six-pack without leering.

"Did they have sit-ups in ancient Scotland?"

"Whit?"

"Sit-ups. Did you do them?"

Broch scowled. "Ah dinnae ken whit ye mean?"

"Nevermind."

Broch smiled, his eyes soft, and Catriona could see in his expression he thought of her as a wounded bird.

"Yer a weirdo, but yer bonny."

She laughed and covered her swollen lip with her hand. "I'm not pretty. I look like beef that's been left out in the sun."

"Na. Ah dinnae see a single maggot oan ye."

"Ew. It disturbs me maggots came to mind for you."

"That's whit happens whin ye leave oot meat."

"I know but—"

Something rattled at the front door and both their heads swiveled. Catriona took a step toward it.

"Wait." Broch came around the island as Catriona peered through the peephole. "Ah said hauld yer horses ye hard-headed wummin."

"It's fine. It's just the FedEx guy."

Broch turned to glance out the window. "'Tis early."

Catriona unlocked her door. "Did you just look out the window to see what time it is by the light? There's a clock on the stove, you know. We need to get you a watch." She opened the door and bent to retrieve the thin white package, her ribs throbbing as she moved. She straightened and closed the door behind her as she pulled the tab to open the package. She'd never pulled a tab so slowly. It seemed she'd torn her Package-tab Muscle.

"Whit is it?" asked Broch.

"I don't know. Papers."

"Whit kind of papers?"

Catriona turned over the sheet in her hand and began to read. She felt the blood drain from her cheeks, an ounce for every sentence she scanned.

"Oh no."

"Whit is it?"

"They can't be serious."

"*Whit?*" Broch snatched the paper from her hand. She reached to grab it back but he held it over his head.

Stretching for it made her body ache.

"It's a mistake," she said.

"Och. Let me read it."

Catriona attempted one last lunge and then grimaced, holding her aching ribs.

"We'll get it fixed. It isn't real."

Broch moved far enough away to read without Catriona interrupting. A moment later he looked up at her, agog.

"'Tis a marriage document?"

Catriona sighed. "Yes."

"This says we're man and wifie."

She nodded. "When we stopped in Vegas for our fake wedding, I forgot to emphasize the *fake*."

"Sae we're married?"

Catriona had stopped listening as she tried to recall every step they'd taken at the Vegas chapel. They'd stopped on the way home from their last mission on a lark.

As a joke.

She groaned, remembering signing papers. "I thought there were too many papers to sign. It should have hit me— "

"Ye did it fer me?"

Catriona heard Broch talking and snapped from her musing.

"Hm?"

"Ye did it fer me?" He moved toward her and wrapped his arms around her, careful not to squeeze her bruised flesh, his chin resting on her head.

He'd been asking to marry her since they'd met. She thought it was *way* too soon, and his revenge had been to refuse to sleep with her, even though the sexual tension between them was driving them both mad.

But if we're married now...

Hm.

She pulled back and stared into his hazel eyes.

"I guess you won," she said.

"Ah ken we both did."

Catriona braced herself, certain they were about to throw themselves at each other and unsure how her battered body would take it. Not that she cared. She'd been waiting to climb this particular mountain for—

"Ew. What are you two doing?"

Catriona tilted to the left to see past the giant in her arms. Fiona stood at the bedroom doorway wearing the previous night's clothing, fluffing her damp hair with her fingers. Her lip curled with what looked like disgust.

Nice timing, Sis.

Broch mumbled in her ear. "We hae tae get rid of her."

Catriona nodded.

"Yep."

CHAPTER FOUR

Rune's tongue touched something dry and granular. Pulling back his neck, he spat and raised himself to his elbows. Dirt rained from the side of his head.

Where am I?

He felt weak and suffered a bout of dizziness as he shifted into a sitting position. Brushing his cheek, he chewed his tongue, summoning as much saliva as he could muster to swish away the grains of sand crunching between his teeth. A pain throbbed where his shoulder met his neck.

He raised a hand to the ache and dabbed at the area with his fingertips.

It felt sticky.

Rune glanced at his fingers and found them dark with blood.

Fiona.

The memory of his wound's origin swirled into his mind's eye like a desert mirage.

My daughter stabbed me in the neck.

He knew the wound would never fully heal. Fiona was a fellow traveler like himself, and while wounds inflicted by average humans disappeared from his skin's long-term story, those donated by fellow travelers never healed entirely. He stared at the metal arm attached to his right shoulder.

Case in point.

Ryft had taken his arm.

What did they call that bastard in this time? Not Ryft...

Sean.

Rune fingered the lumpy scar where Fiona had buried her pen. He suspected she'd nicked his jugular. There was too much blood on his shirt and in the dirt where he'd lain.

Had she tried to kill him on purpose? He'd assumed she'd been scared and lashed out but...

No. She wouldn't try to kill him, would she?

Maybe.

Why had she felt so threatened by her father? She had to know she'd always been his favorite. They'd been so close, once.

Hadn't they?

Rune shook his head. His memory wasn't what it used to be. Sometimes he remembered too little. Other times it felt as if he were remembering everything at once. *Living* everything at once.

He knew he was lucky to still be alive. How had he survived?

A crunchy noise reached his ears, like something sliding across the red gravel around him. Rune turned, careful not to tug the skin near his barely-healed stab wound.

He saw a shoe.

No, *two* shoes.

Two gray-soled athletic shoes sat propped on the ground behind him, balancing on their toes.

How could that be?

One moved.

Ah.

There were *feet* in them. Someone lay on their belly, fifteen feet from his position. One shoe slid away from him, pulled by the leg to which it was attached. The knee of that leg dug into the sand, propelling the body forward, the other leg dragging, still straight.

He heard cars nearby.

I'm still in Los Angeles.

He closed his eyes.

I hate this place.

He'd never been a desert person. Why Fiona had chosen this place to wait for him he'd never understand. Perhaps she'd been drawn by whatever attracted Ryft. Maybe she'd been drawn by Ryft himself.

His mind drifted toward his goal, a quest he knew he had, but he couldn't put his finger on what it was.

I used to have a purpose, didn't I?

He shook his head to refocus and winced at the pain in his neck.

Think.

He needed to concentrate on his current situation. Maybe he could start on *where* he was. Not the year, not the country or the city, but the very plot of blood-soaked sand on which he now sat.

Where am I?

Rune scanned the landscape again, finding only more dirt, scrub brush, and discarded trash.

He decided he'd collapsed in an abandoned lot.

Sand scraped behind him.

Right. The guy with the shoes was still trying to crawl away from him. He heard him breathing. *Wheezing.*

Rune had collapsed, but not before wrestling the owner of those shoes into the lot with him.

He stood and brushed the dust from his pants with his good arm.

The man on the ground looked over his shoulder, his face twisting with panic.

"Get away from me," the man croaked, clawing at the ground, trying once again to make headway in his quest to leave the lot and Rune far behind.

Rune took a step toward him. Though his dark, thick hair and broad nose implied Hispanic descent, the man's skin seemed pale, almost gray. His eyes sat dull and sunken in his skull.

"Leave me alone."

"I can't do that." Rune reached down to press his hand

against his victim's flesh. The man had very little life left. It was a miracle he'd regained consciousness, and doubly so that he'd been able to drag himself a few feet away. Rune knew the man's missing vitality was what had healed his wound. It was the only reason he hadn't been sent spinning through time to be reborn, his wound too grievous to heal.

He would have had to start from scratch.

Rune closed his eyes and siphoned the man's remaining life force. He felt the heat beneath his palm flooding into his veins. The man-made a squeaking noise, one last attempt to protest his fate, before his bodily shell collapsed to ash, mingling with the desert landscape, even his gray-soled sneakers.

A warm eddy of air swirled the man's ashes and sent them dancing farther away than he could have crawled on his own. Rune laughed at the irony.

He stretched his neck and felt the wound.

Better.

Not fully healed, but better.

Good enough.

Rune straightened and his head swam. He reached out to steady himself but found nothing to grab. Dropping to one knee, he took a moment to collect himself.

Maybe one more...

He pushed himself to his feet once again and moved his lanky frame toward a metal fence. Beyond it was the street. He had a flash of himself stumbling down that street, his hand desperately trying to hold back the blood spilling from his throat. He saw the man. He fell on him. Draining him. Dragging him through the hole in the fence he now used to exit the field.

Wrong place, wrong time for the man, but perfect timing for him.

Rune didn't know how long he'd been out. It had been early evening, hadn't it? Now it was morning. Early, but the sun had risen. A teenage girl walked down the street. She looked at him and hurried her step to cross the street away from him, eyes flashing with fear.

Rune looked down at his shirt. It was covered in blood and

dirt.

I forgot.

As he stood watching the girl cross the road he felt a presence behind him. His good arm darted out, his fingers curling around a thin wrist like a mongoose clamping its teeth on a cobra.

"Ow!"

The woman yelped and tried to jerk her arm from his grasp. Her name appeared in his mind. It was all she could think about. Herself. Her safety. Her indignation.

Hello, Maddie.

"Let go of her!" screamed Maddie's friend. She struck him with the side of her fist, a glancing blow that grazed his shoulder and ended clanging against his metal arm. The friend yelped and stumbled back, cradling her hand.

Maddie's attention shifted and Rune's eyes grew wide at the malice of her thoughts. He gaped at her as she struggled to pull from his grasp.

She isn't your friend, is she?

In fact, Maddie hated her 'friend.'

You want her dead.

Maddie's darkest thoughts poured into his brain.

Not me. Why not Dixie? She's an idiot. Not me. Why didn't you grab her?

Rune grinned.

"Her?" he asked.

Maddie stopped struggling. She stared at him, leaning back as he held her as if she were a water skier and he the boat. He could tell she understood that he'd read her most desperate wish—that he'd pulled it right out of her brain.

Kill Dixie. Let me go. You can have her.

She said it in her mind, and he heard her as clearly as if she'd spoken the words.

"If that's what you want," he said, amused by how much pleasure the thought gave her.

He released Maddie's wrist and she fell on her butt with a loud *oof*. Spinning, he grabbed the other woman by the same arm she cradled against her torso, the hand that had struck his metal arm with such force.

"No!"

What's this one's name? He couldn't read this one, but Maddie had thought the name.

Dixie.

Dixie's eyes grew wild as her panic grew. She looked to Maddie for help, the help *she'd* tried to provide.

Rune glanced at Maddie, giving her every opportunity to stop him. She'd scrambled to her feet but remained rooted to the spot. Watching. Standing just out of reach. She wasn't stupid. Best to not press her luck.

She committed to her first thought.

Take her, not me.

Rune summoned all the healing life force he could from the woman now in his grasp. Dixie's flesh went pale. Her features sank, her jaw falling slack as she ceased to struggle. In a moment, she collapsed to the ground, dust swirling away in the desert breeze as fast as it could fall.

Rune closed his eyes and smiled. He felt *amazing*. Fully healed. He raised his good hand to his neck and felt the small jagged scar where his daughter had stabbed him.

Smoother.

He turned to Maddie, who remained there, jaw lolling like a gasping fish's. After a moment she shut her mouth, straightened, and met his gaze.

"Thank you," she said.

The corner of her mouth curled as if she were almost giddy, and then she strode off quickly but never running.

Rune sniffed and watched her go.

I like that one.

She reminded him of Fiona. Back before she was corrupted by her do-good sister and those horrible, horrible Scots.

CHAPTER FIVE

"You okay, Maddie?"

Maddie Barbeau turned to find Jake Hastings staring down where she sat on a picnic bench. She glanced down at her sandwich and realized she'd been picking pieces of bread off it, rolling them into tiny balls, and dropping them.

"Huh?"

"I said *are you okay*? You were staring—" Jake glanced to the left. "—and there's *that*." He motioned to the mess of tiny bread balls in front of her.

Maddie smiled, knowing when she grinned people could see no less than twenty-three perfectly white teeth. Her smile melted everyone. No one could be mad at her when she flashed the pearly whites—she'd learned that early on in life. Her smile was probably responsible for her career as an arts and crafts guru. That, and the fact her projects were the only thing that ever seemed to make her mother take notice. She'd kept practicing until she'd decorated their entire apartment in homemade décor. It looked as if a professional designer had redone the dump.

Not that Mom noticed.

Maddie felt her expression souring and pulled her thoughts away from her childhood. "I'm fine, Jake. Just thinking of a new project for the show."

"Yeah? What're ya thinkin'? Ball bearings made outta

bread?"

Crap. She hadn't thought he'd ask for an example.

Maddie smiled again and tried to look mysterious. "Too soon to say."

He basked in the light of her grin and let it go.

"Okay, but we still have six shows to film and we're running out of your standbys. Keep thinking."

Jake smiled, flashing one lower tooth tucked back behind the others. Coffee stains. But that's why he was *Crafty People's* director, and not the on-air talent, like her.

He stepped away and then turned back. "Hey, you haven't seen Dixie today, have you? Don't you guys usually come to the set together?"

Maddie shook her head. "No. We've bumped into each other in the parking lot walking over here a few times, but we don't carpool."

It was a lie.

I shouldn't have lied about that. She'd probably told people...

"I mean, not much," she added.

"Hm." Jake glanced at his watch and then put his hands on his hips to stare at the ground. "Not like her to be late and I can't reach her. I can only shoot around her segments for so long."

Maddie shrugged and pretended to return to her sandwich. Without the bread to protect her from the mustard, she wasn't sure how to pick it up. She studied it as if it were a puzzle until she no longer felt Jake's presence and then balled it in the paper it had been wrapped in.

Dixie. That's who she'd been thinking about when Jake caught her staring into space. Not the next craft for the contestants to make on their stupid show. Dixie was her bubbly co-host. A blonde airhead with almost as toothy a grin as hers and boobs twice as big. Dixie specialized in woodworking crafts, and with her micro-jean shorts, pink tool belt, and half-unbuttoned work shirt tied at the waist, she'd been stealing the show. Maddie could tell by the way the contestants reacted to Dixie's 'Southern charm' and how they weren't reacting to *her*.

It was Maddie's show. They'd created it for her after she

went viral on YouTube with her crafty life-hacks. The video of the race car track she built for her neighbor's kid out of quick-dry cement and paint *alone* had gotten over five million hits.

She was the *star*.

Then she showed up on set and they trotted out Dixie, all tits and teeth with that drawl and trademark big eye-roll when the contestants didn't live up to their potential... How was she supposed to compete with *that*?

Yesterday had been Maddie's birthday. Craft services provided a cake and she'd blown out the candle thinking, *I wish you'd die* as she smiled at Dixie.

Dixie smiled back.

Idiot.

And then today, that man who grabbed her. He'd known. Somehow he'd *known* she wanted Dixie dead. She could feel him pulling the information from her as if she were reading her own thoughts in *his* head.

Maddie rubbed her wrist where he'd grabbed her, the faint red impression of his grip still visible on her skin.

And just like that, he'd let her go, lunging to grab Dixie instead. Dixie, who'd tried to save her. Dixie, who hadn't run.

Dixie was brave, too.

Good for her.

Look what that got her.

That thing grabbed Dixie and she disappeared as if she were a milkshake and he'd slurped her away until nothing was left but dust.

I did see that. Didn't I?

Dixie turned to dust and blew away.

Even her stupid pink tool belt.

Dust.

The man had been pale when he first grabbed her. When he turned back, after *poofing* Dixie, he was still thin with hollow cheeks and a hawkish nose, but his color looked better as if he'd been hungry and Dixie was a sandwich.

The look he'd given her then—she could tell he understood. That he wouldn't hurt her. For a moment she'd been mesmerized by his admiring stare, but she'd snapped to her senses and left. No use pushing her luck with whatever he was. She'd wished Dixie dead and now Dixie was gone. She *assumed*. She didn't imagine she'd be coming back from *dust*.

It was as if that man had been sent to do her bidding. To make her wishes come true.

Do I have some kind of superpower? Can I wish for anything? Or only death?

More importantly...

Who else do I want gone?

CHAPTER SIX

"What are we supposed to do with Fiona?" Catriona asked Sean. She'd called him two seconds after Fiona broke up her 'honeymoon.'

Ha. Honeymoon. The word in her head made her snicker quietly to herself. Truth be told, she felt a little too...*happy?*

No. Stop it.

Time to make a concerted effort to tamp down her misplaced giddiness.

Grow up, Cat.

The marriage couldn't continue. She'd told Broch it was too soon for them to even *think* about getting married and she'd meant it. The time they'd known each other was practically easier to count in *weeks* than it was in months. She'd look like an impetuous idiot if she *accidentally* married Kilty and then actually *stayed* married to him.

Wouldn't I?

She sneaked a peek at Broch and bit her lip.

It didn't help that he looked so good in those boxers.

Did she *have* to tell him they needed to get the marriage annulled? Bedding him under the pretense of staying married would be wrong.

Right?

Sean huffed on his end of the phone and Catriona jumped, surprised to find herself still talking to him. She felt her face grow hot. She felt like a little girl whose father had walked in on her while she was building a love shrine to the boy with the floppy hair in gym class.

Not that she'd ever done that.

"Tell her to stay there," said Sean. "You'll be out and busy anyway."

Her?

Who?

Oh right. Fiona.

Catriona tried to pierce her sister with a glare. Fiona had Broch cornered, trying to snatch the wedding certificate from his hand.

"But I don't *want* her to stay here," whined Catriona.

"What's that?" Fiona turned at the sound of Catriona's complaining and Broch followed her gaze, allowing the hand holding their certificate to drop.

Seeing the inevitable, Catriona gasped.

"Broch!"

Too late.

Fiona plucked the paper from his grasp and skittered around the sofa as he pawed after her. She slipped behind a chair, nose nearly pressed to the sheet as she tried to read. Before he could snatch back the paper, she'd already lowered it and stood gaping at them.

"You two are *married?*"

"Who's married?" asked Sean from his end of the line.

Catriona stared daggers through Fiona. "No one. It's a mistake."

"We are," said Broch, moving to the phone. "Da, Catriona and ah ur merrit."

"What?"

Catriona strode across the room. "It was a mistake. We had a fake marriage in Vegas when I was all hopped up on pain pills and they misunderstood what I wanted."

Did they, though?

"But 'tis real, richt?" asked Broch.

"Looks real to me," said Fiona.

"It's *not*. I mean, it can't be—you're not even a legal citizen. How could it be?"

"'Tis it, o' nae?" asked Broch, the spot between his eyebrows beginning to bunch.

Catriona could see he was already planning to withhold the honeymoon until she assured him it was real.

Dammitdammitdammit.

Almost three decades without a sister and now that she had one, the wench managed to cause thirty years' worth of trouble every ten minutes.

I'm trapped.

Staying married meant backpedaling on everything she'd told Broch about doing things *right*. Get a quickie divorce and he'd never forgive her—and worse—no honeymoon.

She swallowed. "Well, I mean, it *could* be real...I'm not sure Vegas has the same rules as the rest of the country..."

"I think she wants a divorce," said Fiona, moving to the coffee machine.

Broch's eyes widened. "A divorce?"

Catriona squeezed her eyes shut as if the act could make her invisible. "Will you two shut up for five seconds so I can finish this phone call?"

"You're married?" asked Sean, still understandably confused.

"I guess. Yes. For now. I'll get it cleared up."

Sean sighed. "You two have to figure out what you're doing with each other before you drive me crazy."

"Sure. Absolutely. We're only here to serve." Catriona frowned as she recalled Sean saying something interesting earlier in their conversation.

Tell her to stay there. You'll be out and busy anyway.

"Wait—why did you say we'd be busy?" she asked.

"Busy? Oh, right. You will be. *Crafty People* is missing a host, so I need you to see if you can help find her."

"Isn't that a little below my pay grade? Can't they send a PA to her door? She's probably sleeping one off."

"They already sent someone. They're out of ideas beyond

getting the police involved and we don't want that."

Catriona huffed. "Fine. I was hoping to take a day off. I'm a head-to-toe contusion, remember?"

"Better not to wallow. Keep moving."

"*Healing* is not *wallowing*." Even as she said the words, she knew Sean might be right. The last thing she wanted to do was to close her eyes and see that pit full of dead girls again.

"I'll check in later," he said, clearly maneuvering to get off the phone.

"Can't wait."

They hung up and Catriona let the phone fall to her side. Kilty stood staring at her, the marriage certificate still in his hand. He had an expectant air about him as if he were waiting for answers.

Like I have any of those.

Fiona smirked at her from beside the refrigerator. Somehow she was smiling *and* licking peanut butter off a spoon at the same time.

Catriona pointed at her sister. "You better not double-dip that."

"It's the closest thing to no-carb I could find in your crapfest of a refrigerator." Her gaze darted to Broch and back to Catriona. "So am I buying a wedding card or a divorce card? Does Hallmark make cards for the dissolution of Vegas weddings?"

"They probably make a killing on them," mumbled Catriona, heading for her bedroom.

"Where ye goan?" asked Broch. She could hear his footsteps in pursuit. "We need tae blether aboot this."

"We have a job. Go get dressed."

She held up a hand in an attempt to silence him, but Broch grabbed her wrist and pulled her to him. He murmured in her ear, his warm breath sending shivers down her back.

"Are we merrit or nae?"

Ohyesyesyes...

She felt herself melting into his arms before remembering the ebony-haired headache slurping peanut butter in the front room.

Witch.

She pulled from Broch's embrace and flicked the certificate with her finger. "In the eyes of the law, we are, yes."

"And in the eyes of God?"

Catriona shrugged. "You'd have to ask Him. They had a little chapel, right? Am I remembering that right? I suppose that counts."

He placed a hand on her upper arm, his eyes getting that soft, misty look that always made her melt. "And in *yer* eyes?"

Catriona's attention flicked to Fiona, who had strolled into the bedroom, her face awash with bemusement at the soap opera playing before her.

Catriona felt her cheeks flush with angry heat.

"We have to go. Go get dressed. My face hurts. We'll get all this worked out later."

She walked into the bathroom where she could shut the door. Leaning her back against it, she took a deep breath.

Did I fool myself into marriage on purpose?

She stared at her swollen lip and blackened eye in the mirror.

Ugh.

Who would marry that?

CHAPTER SEVEN

During their walk to the *Crafty People* set, Catriona had expected Broch to talk her ear off. He tended to get excited the same way a three-year-old boy did—a lot of talking, a little running around, and then more talking.

Instead, he strode beside her in pouty silence, which made her feel even worse. It seemed the rush of excitement he'd enjoyed after discovering their marriage had been replaced by deep disappointment.

In her.

Catriona opened her mouth to explain to him, once again, that it was unusual for people to marry within a month or two of meeting each other. It wasn't like the old days when you spotted some girl with childbearing hips and immediately dropped to one knee.

She gently pressed her fat lip against her other, slightly less fat lip.

What's the point?

She'd already tried to explain it to him a hundred times, and no matter what she said, *they were married now.* What did a piece of paper mean anyway? Maybe she could call this marriage a sort of engagement and—

"Can I help you?"

Catriona stopped short as a man with a clipboard stepped in front of her. They'd already reached the entrance to the

Crafty People filming lot. She had little memory of making the ten-minute trek.

She glanced behind her to make sure Broch was still on her heels. He was, his previous pout all grown-up into a deep frown of disapproval as he eyed the paunchy young man blocking their entrance to the lot.

"I'm here about the missing person," said Catriona, realizing Sean had never given her a name.

The man stared down his nose at her and then glanced at his clipboard. "Name?"

"What's *your* name?" she asked, hoping to turn the tables.

The young man pursed his lips. "Greg. I need *your* name to crosscheck it against the list." He emphasized the word crosscheck as if it were a weapon.

"I'm afraid crosschecking isn't the answer. My name isn't on there. I'm Catriona Phoenix. I work for the studio. *You* called me."

Greg scoffed. "*I* didn't call you."

"Not *you*, personally. You, as in *the show*. Someone here called Sean and then Sean called me."

Greg's gaze dropped to his clipboard once more. "Last name of this Sean person?"

Catriona dug her nails into her palms and tried not to lose her patience. Her head throbbed, making it twice as hard not to *lose her mind* on the boy with the inflated sense of importance. *Crafty People* was a new show, inspired by the popularity of HGTV and other 'homey' shows and networks. She knew little about it, which was a good thing. Generally, when she had to pay attention to a show on the lot, something was going wrong.

She spotted a cameraman strolling by with a plate full of eggs and bacon from craft services.

"John!" she called. He turned at the sound of his name. Upon seeing her, his face cracked into a grin.

"Hey, Cat. What are you doing here?"

"One of your hosts is missing?"

John nodded. "Yeah. Dixie. I think they've been looking for her a while now."

She motioned to Greg. "Can you tell him I'm legit?"

John turned his attention to the boy. "She's legit. She works here."

Greg frowned. "She's not on the list. I don't know *you* either, for that matter. How do I know she works here and you're not working together?"

Catriona laughed. "Working together? Why? So I can sneak in and get my macramé plant holder autographed?"

John dipped his head to peer over his sunglasses. "If you don't let her in, you won't be working here much longer. That'll be your tipoff we both work here."

Greg seemed to pale a shade as he turned the clipboard toward Catriona. "Fine. But I need you to sign—"

Catriona was already several steps past him before he could finish his sentence. She headed toward a man sitting in a director's chair wearing headphones, watching something on a small screen.

She glanced behind her to be sure Greg didn't give Broch a hard time. Greg tilted to the left as if to block the Scot and then thought better of it and bounced back to the right.

"Ah nae in the mood," grumbled Broch as he closed the gap between himself and Catriona.

She smiled. At least Broch's displeasure with her could be channeled into useful work-related crankiness.

She approached the man in the chair.

"You the director?" she asked.

He didn't flinch, so she waved her hand in front of his eyes. He pulled off his earphones.

"Yeah?" He stared at her face, peering over his readers, his eyebrows knit. She suspected he was curious about her battered appearance, but after a moment he looked away to make it clear he wouldn't be asking questions.

"I'm Catriona. Sean called me. You have a missing host?"

The man's expression changed and he smiled with what looked like relief. "Oh, great. I'm Jake Hastings." He shook Catriona's hand and glanced up at Broch. "Whoa. Big man on campus."

"Brochan." The Highlander held out his enormous paw and folded it around the small-boned director's hand like a loaf of bread swallowing a muffin.

"You've got someone missing?" asked Catriona.

Jake nodded. "The second host."

"The likable one," mumbled a young woman sitting to Jake's left. His gaze darted in her direction without his head following and he offered Catriona an embarrassed smile.

"Dixie *is* sweet. Pretty. She's got that sex-appeal-without-trying thing. Sexy but women like her, too. It's rare."

Catriona nodded. "Girl-next-door pretty. A Mary Ann."

"Exactly. Only with Ginger's body."

"Ew," said the girl.

From her repulsion at the idea of Jake noticing Dixie's body, Catriona guessed the girl to be his daughter.

"Any idea where Dixie might be? Did she leave any word?"

"No. She just didn't come to work and today was a big shoot day for her. She knew it, and she's not the sort to blow off work."

"Any drug or alcohol issues?"

"If there are, she hides them well."

"Last one to see her?"

"From here, probably Maddie, the other host."

"The unlikable one," mumbled the girl.

Jake twisted in his chair to look at her.

"Why don't you go get me some coffee?"

The girl looked up from her phone, glanced at Catriona and Broch, and then huffed before standing. Her shoulders were so loose Catriona could almost hear her bones jangling as she sauntered away.

Ah, to be young and carefree.

Jake watched her go. "Sorry. My daughter. I've got her shadowing me, working as my assistant, but she's got *opinions*."

Catriona smirked. "At that age, nothing's an opinion. Everything's a *fact*."

Jake chuckled. "Isn't that the truth?"

"She doesn't like Maddie?"

The director grimaced. "She thinks she's fake. Do you know

her? Maddie?"

"Should I?"

"She got famous on YouTube making things out of trash. She's got a real bubblegum, sticky-sweet personality online that clicked with the younger gen, but in real life, she can be intense."

"Intense, how?"

"I dunno. Everything has to be right, you know? Real type A."

"She and Dixie get along?"

"They seem too but..." Jake nodded his head back and forth, seeming to look for the words. "I don't know. You'd have to see them together. Maddie was real sweet to Dixie—I've heard they carpooled, which is why I think she might have been the last to see her—but I'd catch Maddie looking at her sometimes like—"

"Like she's trying to figure out how to make her explode with her *mind*," said the director's daughter appearing behind him with a cup of coffee in hand.

Jake jumped at the sound of his daughter's voice and took the Parasol Pictures mug from her. "Go find something to do."

The girl shrugged and wandered off.

Jake searched for somewhere to set his mug and then, giving up, rested it on his knee. "She isn't wrong. It did look like Maddie was wishing Dixie gone."

"Where can we find Maddie?"

"She should be in her trailer over there." Jake motioned toward a group of trailers sitting at the far left edge of the lot.

Catriona turned to find Broch had moved several feet away to commandeer a large camera. He had it pointed at her.

"Ah kin see the wee holes in yer face," he said.

Catriona turned away. She doubted he'd discovered how to roll film, but the last thing she needed was a permanent record of her swollen lip and every pore on her face.

"*My* assistant," she said to Jake, and he chuckled.

"So you feel my pain."

"I do. Thanks. Anything else you can think to share that could help?"

"No. But if I think of anything I've got Sean's number."

"That'll work."

Catriona glanced over her shoulder and motioned to Broch to follow her. When he didn't move, she put her hand in front of her face and beckoned with her finger. His head bobbed from behind the camera.

"Eh?"

"We're going."

"Och. Richt." He tipped an invisible cap at Jake and followed her toward the trailers.

They traversed the lot, passing a large, brightly lit cross-section of a fake room packed with nine wooden workstations. On the walls hung every tool imaginable and shelves containing bags of glitter, bottles of glue, spray adhesive, construction paper, and other craft-building paraphernalia.

She glanced up at Broch as he strode beside her.

"You liked the camera?"

"Aye. Ye cuid see things far away like a spyglass."

He answered with enthusiasm and Catriona smiled, turning her head so he wouldn't see.

He's forgotten he's mad at me.

They reached the trailer with "Maddie" written on a whiteboard pressed to the door and Catriona knocked. A moment later, an attractive dark-haired woman with bright red lipstick opened the door. Catriona guessed her to be about twenty-five. She had the broad smile and flashy teeth of a person who looked good on camera. Her hair was rolled into a fifties-style hairdo, with a thick fringe of dark bangs across her forehead. All she needed was a red dress with big white polka dots to complete the look. Glancing past her into the trailer, Catriona could see she owned at least one.

"Yes?"

"Hi. My name is Catriona. This is Broch. We're looking for your co-host and we've been told you might have been the last to see her?"

Maddie put her hand on her chest. "Me? I doubt that." She walked down the short flight of stairs to join them outside, shutting the trailer door behind her. Smoothing her oversized black t-shirt over her black tights, she looked up at Broch and flashed him a demure smile before turning her attention back to Catriona. "Who said that?"

"We heard you carpooled sometimes?"

"Oh." Maddie nodded her head as if that explained everything. "Right. I picked her up a few times."

"When was the last time?"

"Yesterday."

"And you took her home?"

"Yes."

"And this morning?"

"I came in by myself this morning. The carpool wasn't a regular thing. Just a way to get to know her, you know? So we could bond for the show and our on-camera relationship would feel *genuine*."

"But it wasn't?"

Maddie's expression flashed with annoyance before shifting to open-eyed confusion.

"What?"

"You said, 'so the relationship would *feel* genuine.' As if there was no way it actually would be, but you wanted to be sure you faked it well."

Maddie laughed and all traces of vexation disappeared from her demeanor. "Oh, no, that's not how I meant it. I meant so we could get to know each other and become friends and then that would show on camera."

"So you considered yourself friends with her?"

"Yes. I mean, we've only known each other for a couple of weeks but, sure. She was swell."

"*Is.*"

"Huh?"

"She *is* swell."

"Right. What did I say?"

"*Was.*"

"I meant *was* swell to me during the friending process."

"Gotcha." Catriona chewed at her lip, wondering what

question she could ask to trigger another response like Maddie's last. The craft star hadn't seemed flustered after being called out for using the past tense. Maybe it was nothing.

Maybe Maddie was a seasoned liar.

"So you don't know where she is?" asked Catriona.

"Nope. I'm sure she's fine. Might have had a call back for another opportunity. Actors hide things like that all the time. You think they've gone missing or caught the flu and the next thing you know, they've left to join another cast."

"Is there any reason to believe she might want to leave this show?"

"No."

"Was her job in danger here?"

"No. I mean, I don't know. We *do* have two hosts. Maybe she wanted to be a solo lead somewhere else. Who knows?" Maddie reached for the knob on the door of her trailer, a move that made Catriona feel as though she'd been dismissed.

Catriona felt Broch's presence behind her and glanced back. The Highlander loomed over her shoulder, staring down at Maddie, his mouth a straight, grim line. His right eye squinted as if he were trying to bore a laser through the woman's head with his left.

"What's up with you?" she muttered.

He grunted and crossed his arms against his chest.

Maddie's megawatt smile dimmed a shade. "Is that all? I have to get ready. I think we're going to shoot around her."

"Yes. Thank you."

Maddie nodded, glanced once at Broch, and disappeared inside the trailer.

"What was up with the death stare?" Catriona asked Broch as they started back across the lot.

"She doesnae lik' her."

"Maddie doesn't like Dixie?"

"Nae. And her smile is lik' a mask."

"In all fairness, around here it's hard to tell sometimes. Everyone's always pretending to be someone else. It's Hollywood."

"Aye. Ah've seen as much. Bit, did ye see she didnae lik' ye implying thay weren't friends, bit whin ye said it plain tae her they *weren't* friends—she smiled even *mair*. She should've been *mair* angry."

Catriona nodded, impressed he'd noticed. She'd seen that flash of annoyance on Maddie's face when she *implied* the women didn't get along, but when she'd pushed on, and *said* their friendship might be fake, Maddie seemed *less* annoyed. She should have been *angrier*. Instead, Maddie dropped a gear.

Catriona suspected she knew why and could tell Broch felt the same thing.

Maddie had had time to prepare.

The first question caught her off-guard, but then she *knew* Catriona was suspicious. She knew better than to be visibly annoyed and raise more suspicion, so she turned on that toothy grin to appease her accusers.

She *was* a practiced liar.

"You're pretty good at this," she said, bumping her hip against Broch's upper thigh.

He grinned. "Aye. And ah ken ye set her up to fail."

Catriona put her hand on her chest. "Me? Would I do that to a studio asset?"

"Ye ken she's hiding something."

"I do."

"Me tae. Ye ken she did something tae the lass?"

Catriona drew her lips into a tight knot and thought about his question.

"I don't know. It's a far leap from jealousy to murdering your cohost because she stepped on your line."

"Stepped oan yer line?"

"Talked over your time to speak. Your line in the play, so to speak."

"Och. Sae whit next?"

Catriona pointed toward craft services. "I thought I'd—"

"—ask the cooks if thay saw anythin'?"

Catriona stopped and put her hands on her hips, narrowing her eyes at Broch. "Did you just step on my line?"

He chuckled and walked on, the bounce in his step betraying how clever he thought he was.

Catriona talked to a few more people on set, but no one seemed to know where Dixie might be. They all seemed to like her more than Maddie, though.

Catriona called Sean.

"No sign of her, no one has a clue."

Sean grunted. "I was hoping she'd show up by now."

"Should I grab her address from the office and swing by her house for a peek?"

"Yes. I suppose so. When you're done with that can you come by here?"

"Where's here? Please don't tell me your house."

"My house. I'll make you dinner."

Catriona groaned. "You'll have to. We'll be on the road for *days* trying to get to you."

"It's less than an hour. We need to talk and I'd rather not do it near the studio or Fiona."

Catriona stretched her aching shoulder.

Does no one realize I might need a day off?

They did need to talk, though. There were way too many time-travelly things going on and she felt as if she was losing track of all the threads. With Fiona hanging around and Rune possibly still in the area, now wasn't the time to fall behind.

And anyway, all she had to look forward to at home was Fiona.

"Fine. What about Fiona? I left her at my apartment, but she can't stay so close to Broch. It triggers the scar she gave him."

"Right. I forgot about that. What about the guest suite across the hall?"

"That's what Broch suggested. He said it stops itching when she leaves the room, so it should be far enough."

Catriona chuckled to herself. In her opinion, no place was far enough away for Fiona.

"Okay. Let's do that then," said Sean.

"Will do. We'll go check out Dixie's place and then swing by your house. Dinner better be *fantastic*."

"You like frozen pizza, right?"

Catriona hung up to call the Parasol Pictures office and retrieve Dixie's address. The co-host lived in a townhouse complex with which Catriona was familiar. A lot of their new actors started there before collecting a few paychecks and moving up—or having their show canceled and moving out. It was always one or the other.

They found Dixie's front door locked. Broch pressed his face to the window and tried to peer past the curtains.

"Are we goan in?"

Catriona shook her head and took a spot beside him. They couldn't see much but what they could spy didn't look like anything they needed to worry about.

"No. We can't just break in. She isn't officially missing yet. She could have just had a family emergency or something."

They walked around Dixie's end unit to the back. Catriona tried the door to find it locked. She was headed back to the car when Broch called her back. He motioned to the door as she rounded the corner.

"'Tis open."

"What?"

She moved back to the stoop and saw the door handle, which had been firmly mounted a moment earlier, hanging loosely from the door by one long screw.

"Did you break that?"

Broch's eyebrows raised high on his forehead. "Hm?"

"You can't do that."

"Whit? T'was open. Ye just didnae turn it hard enough."

"Uh-huh. I see how hard you turned it. It's hanging by a thread."

Broch glanced at it and shrugged. "Ah dinnae ken whit ye

mean. 'Tis faulty. It's a fine thing we discovered the problem fur her."

Catriona pushed open the door and stuck her head inside.

What's done is done.

"Hello?"

Nothing.

They went inside, calling for Dixie every other step. Though the apartment had a second story, it only took them a few minutes to search the entire house. There was no sign of Dixie.

"Coffee pot is still a little warm," said Catriona, placing her hand against it. "There's still droplets on the shower door, and I don't see a purse anywhere—everything says she got ready for work and left as usual."

"Mibbee someone came through her broken door and kidnapped her."

"Don't push it."

He grinned and then knit his brow. "Did she drive?"

"I don't think she had a car. If she didn't carpool with Maddie this morning, we'll have to find out who she caught a ride with."

Broch put his hands on his hips. "Sae, whit noo?"

"Noo, we fix her door and leave her a note telling her where to submit the bill for fixing it."

"Bit then she'd ken *we* did it. How come would we dae that?"

"Because we *did* do it."

"Nah. Ah dinnae ken whit yer oan aboot."

Catriona found a piece of paper and a pen in a kitchen drawer and started writing a note. "We can't let the poor thing think she's been robbed."

Broch shrugged. "Ah dinnae see how come not. She may well be robbed, nae that her door is open."

CHAPTER EIGHT

"How come are we going to Sean's?" asked Broch.

Catriona glanced at him from her spot behind the wheel of her trusty Jeep Cherokee, almost surprised to find him there. She'd been musing about how much her world had changed since he arrived. It all felt like a dream. Or a nightmare, depending on the moment. Her new world had some dark places, but there were sunny spots as well.

Like Kilty.

Am I married to this man?

It had only been a handful of weeks since she'd discovered him, barely conscious, on a movie set at Parasol Pictures. She'd assumed him to be background talent for some *Braveheart* knockoff in production. He'd seemed drunk, lying there with his kilt naughtily akimbo on his truly magnificent hind-end—

"Whit ur ye smilin' aboot?"

Catriona snapped to and straightened the Jeep between the lines on the road.

Whoops. She'd drifted off again for a moment.

"Hm?"

"Ye didnae answer me. How come we're goan tae Sean's?"

Didnae. If they were going to be working together, let alone *married*, maybe it was time to start modernizing his English. For reasons she couldn't explain, she had no trouble understanding him, but she was tired of acting as his translator when interacting with the talent at Parasol.

"*Why*," she corrected.

"Why whit?"

"You said '*how come* are we going to Sean's.' The correct way to say it is *why* are we going to Sean's."

"Did ye ken whit ah meant?"

"Yes, I *knew* what you mean but—"

He shrugged. "Then ah said it perfect."

"Funny. But that's the point, I understand you, not everyone else does. I don't know what to do about that heavy brogue, but maybe we can at least fix the parts that aren't even English."

Broch snorted. "Ah grew up closer tae England than *ye* did."

Catriona pressed her bottom lip against her top until the swollen bit began to hurt.

He has a point there.

She pulled into Sean's long dirt driveway. Why her adoptive father insisted on living in the middle of the desert, an hour away from the studio, she didn't know. She guessed he liked to remove himself from the daily insanity he had to deal with at Parasol. Actors weren't always the best-behaved people.

Shocker.

Catriona parked and leaned into her back seat to grab a bag off the floor behind Broch's seat. He opened his door and walked around to meet her on the driver's side. His gaze dropped to the bag in her hand as she slid from her seat.

"Whit's that?"

She handed it to him. "I ordered it for you."

"Aye? A wedding gift?"

"*No*, it's not a wedding gift. I've had it for weeks."

He tore into the bag, ripping the thick plastic as if it were tissue. From inside, he retrieved a second, thinner plastic bag with a swath of plaid fabric showing through.

"Whit is it?"

"They're swim trunks. I got them in plaid so you'd feel at home."

He ripped open the second bag and slid out the shorts.

"How come ahm ah needin' wee breeks tae swim?"

Catriona opened her mouth to correct his *how come* a second time and then closed it.

What's the point?

Though, even *she* had missed part of that sentence.

"Breeks?"

"Breaches. Trousers."

"Oh. You need *breeks* because you can't keep swimming naked."

"How come?"

He was really pushing it now.

She jerked the box from him and left him holding the trunks. "Because it's weird, okay? You can get away with it here at Sean's pool but anywhere else—you're just going to have to get used to wearing clothes. Sorry."

Kilty grunted and eyeballed the trunks as if they might bite him. "They seem wee..."

"Try them on inside." Catriona strode to the front door of Sean's mid-century desert rancher and let herself inside with Broch behind her still holding the shorts up against his hips.

"Sean," she called to announce their arrival. At his longstanding request, she never called him *Dad*. When he'd found her as a little girl, and kept her like a lost dog, he hadn't been entirely comfortable being thrust into fatherhood. She suspected calling him *Sean* instead of *Dad* had made her seem more like a diminutive roommate than a *child*. The concept of sharing his life with a tiny roommate was easier for Sean to swallow.

"Out here." Sean's muffled voice called from the back patio.

Catriona wound her way through the kitchen and the outer, sliding door. Sean sat in his usual patio chair, a whiskey on the wobbly table beside him. He smiled at the sight of her, but his expression soon shifted to concern.

"Wow. You look worse today."

Catriona smoothed her hair as if putting hairs in place could rearrange her swollen face. "Please. All this flattery will go right to my head."

"I mean the bruises seem larger. Or darker. Or *both*..."

She tapped her lip with her fingertips. "I know. No amount of makeup was ever going to do anything about this."

"You should have visited that group doing the special effects for the monster movie on Lot J. They could have done you right." Sean chuckled at his joke like a proper old man.

"Good idea. I'll swing by there tomorrow to keep from frightening passing children."

Sean turned to look through the sliders into the house. "Where's Broch?"

"He's behind me somewhere. I told him he had to wear trunks in the pool. He might be pouting."

Sean laughed. "Probably a good habit to start."

She sat in the chair opposite Sean and stole a sip of his whiskey. He arched an eyebrow.

"There's more in the house, you know."

She tilted back her head as if exhausted at the thought. "It's so far away."

"Did you see Luther?"

"Luther? Where?"

"Out front? He's coming, too."

"Oh, no. Just us so far."

She stole another sip and Sean waggled his index finger at her.

"Don't drink too much. I've got a job for you two tonight."

"A job? This was a trap? I thought you were making us dinner."

"I am, but I got a call. Konrad Burson's having a wrap party at the *Devil's Warehouse* set and I'd like you to be there as security."

Catriona groaned and searched her memory for more information on the film. Production of *Devil's Warehouse* took place off the main studio lot, so she hadn't heard much about it.

"That's at the auxiliary lot out here, isn't it?"

Sean nodded. "But since I'm hosting Luther, it's handy you're here to run over there for me for a couple of hours."

"Hm. See, I was thinking how handy you'll both be out here

so *you* can go work security."

Sean chuckled. "Nope. That's not how I see it at all. Lucky Luther and I are the bosses."

"Is that the movie about the serial killer from a few years ago? The one who strapped a bomb on his last victim and took out the emergency crew?"

"Uh-huh. The press called him *Pinky*."

Catriona pointed at Sean. "Right. Because all the bodies they found were missing a pinky finger. I remember now. Yikes. So it's a slasher film?"

"Not exactly. It's told from his son's perspective."

Catriona recoiled, remembering details from the news and how she'd felt bad for the killer's son. "He made the kid watch, didn't he?"

"So the story goes. Pinky's dead of course but I met the kid—Marlon. Parasol hired him as a consultant on the film. Him and the cop who killed his father."

Catriona grimaced. "*Awkward.*"

"You'd think, but they've become friends. Soto, the officer, saved Marlon."

Catriona nodded. "I guess that's true."

"Konrad says he's a good kid, considering everything he's gone through. He even cast him to play himself."

"*There's* a marketing stunt."

"I'm sure that had a lot to do with it."

"So what do we need to do?"

"Konrad's going to run the party on set, like a sort of haunted house, but he tends to overdo things, and creep fests like these draw out the weirdos. News has already leaked online."

"Leaked via Konrad, no doubt."

"No doubt. I told him I'd like to have some people there."

"And that's where Broch and I come in."

"Exactly."

Catriona pulled out her phone. "I better call Fiona and tell her we won't be coming back tonight."

"She can stay at your place. You won't have to set her up

across the hall."

Catriona rolled her eyes.

Just what I want. My psychotic sister alone in my house.

She couldn't remember if she had anything incriminating lying around her apartment but felt confident if she did, Fiona would find it.

She dialed and Fiona answered.

"Hello?"

"Fiona?"

"You called my phone. Who do you think it is?"

"Yep. That's you. Always a joy."

"What do you want? And what am I supposed to do here in your hovel? I'm so bored I'm about to watch reality shows *I'm not in.*"

"We won't be back tonight, so you have the place to yourself."

"What's that supposed to mean? You make it sound like being trapped in your sad little apartment is like winning the lottery."

Catriona pulled the phone from her ear and took a deep breath.

Patience.

"Just stay there. We don't know if Rune is still around and if he is, he's looking for the daughter who stabbed him in the neck. You're safer there than in your stupid-expensive, nouveau riche penthouse."

"You *wish* you could be nouveau riche."

"Sure. Every night before I go to bed it's what I pray for. *Dear God, please give me all of the money and none of the brains.*"

The patio doors slid open and Broch walked out, barefoot and bare-chested, wearing his new swim trunks. They fit him like a plaid glove.

Wow.

Fiona said something else but Catriona didn't hear.

"Look, I'm going. Stay there, or the next time I see you I'll be identifying your body. I already told the guards not to let you out, so don't even think about it."

Catriona hung up before her sister could say another word.

She cleared her throat and called to Broch as he sauntered by.

"They look good. How do they fit?"

Broch's lip curled. "Meh."

Catriona glanced at Sean. "Did they say *meh* in ancient Scotland?"

He took a sip of his whiskey. "All the time. We invented it."

Broch strode to the steps leading into the pool and walked in with the confidence of Poseidon returning to the sea. Plunging in, he swam underwater to the opposite side, flipped, and returned to the shallow end to stand, pushing his wet shoulder-length locks from his eyes as if he were starring in a high-end cologne commercial.

Ridiculous.

"I have some clothes for you and Broch to wear to the party," said Sean, seeming less impressed by Broch's figure.

Putting Broch *in* clothes was the last thing on Catriona's mind.

She nodded as Broch turned and winked at her, the skin of his muscular torso glistening in the sun's dying light.

I'm married to that?

Doesn't seem so awful...

And then he had to go and open his mouth.

"Did she tell ye we're merrit?"

Sean lifted his whiskey. "That's right. Could I get a little more information about that?"

Catriona dropped her chin to her chest.

Here we go.

She decided to keep the explanation simple. "The fake marriage we had turned out to be real."

"You're serious? You're legally married?"

Broch spoke before diving under again. "Aye."

"I think so. On paper," Catriona corrected, speeding up her speech in the hopes of explaining before Broch resurfaced. "I'll get it figured out. It's a mistake."

"Does *he* think it's a mistake?" asked Sean, motioning

toward the pool as the Loch Ness Monster in the plaid shorts touched the far end and turned.

"We're—" Catriona cut short and shook her head. She didn't want Broch to hear her talking about a quickie divorce and the man was going to have to come up for air soon.

"We're in discussions," she added as he broke the surface.

Sean reached to retrieve his glass. "Well, let me know if I need to buy a gift."

"I'd like *not* to attend this party as my wedding gift."

"Sorry. Fresh out of those." Sean looked at his watch. "Hm. Luther's running late." He picked up his cell phone and made a call. A moment later he set down the phone again and stared over his back wall at the desert landscape, pensive.

"I assume he didn't answer?"

"No." Sean tapped the table with his fingertip. "Something must have come up. You two will have to go soon. Let's get you fed." He stood and walked inside while Catriona watched Broch swim the length of the pool and back before getting out.

She stood and handed him a towel from a weatherproof plastic locker in the corner of the patio.

"Go get a shower. We're going to eat and then we have to work a party."

"Work a party?"

"We're security."

"Och." Broch nodded.

"And stop telling people we're married."

He grinned and kissed her hairline.

"Bit we *are*."

CHAPTER NINE

"I wonder where Luther is," said Catriona as she and Broch walked toward the *Devil's Warehouse* set. Her father's friend and partner had never arrived for dinner, which was more than strange. While Sean was still at the house when they left for the party, she suspected he'd soon be in his precious Jaguar, off to find Luther.

"'Tisn't lik' him," agreed Broch.

"We need to get this party over and get back to L.A." Catriona knew she couldn't make the party go any faster but, somehow, saying the idea out loud made her feel better.

Some of the guests had already arrived. She'd seen paparazzi turned away at the gate, which was a good sign things weren't yet out of control in the name of publicity. No doubt the air above already buzzed with camera-strapped drones, but the prying eyes wouldn't see a thing once everyone entered the windowless building doubling as the film's main stage and party location.

Broch tugged at his tight-fitting collared dress shirt as if it were trying to choke him. "Ah feel lik' a haggis tucked in a sheep's tummy."

"Sheep eat haggis?"

Broch looked at her as if she were a Martian.

"Sheep *is* haggis. Ye stuff their heart, liver 'n pipes intae the tummy casing afore ye cook it."

Catriona watched as Broch licked his lips at the thought.
Gross.

"Haggis is cooked in a sheep's stomach?"

"Aye."

"Blech. I don't even want to know what the *pipes* are."

"The pipes, ye ken." Broch took a deep breath and pointed at his chest. The button nestled between his pectoral muscles popped off and plinked Catriona on the cheek.

"Ow." She glanced down and knew there'd be no finding the button. Konrad had strings of lights dangling from the parking lot to the front door of the building, but the illumination fell far short of sufficient for finding buttons in desert sand.

"Now you've done it. I *told* you not to flex. Sean underestimated your *package*."

Broch huffed and nearly blew another button. "Ah didnae *flex*, ah *breathed*. Pipes ur *lungs*."

"Well, don't *breathe* anymore." Catriona paused to fold down the edge of his shirt to hide the missing button. "We'll go with the sexy deep-V tonight. Hopefully, that look is *in* this particular five minutes before Hollywood fashion changes again."

His gaze traced the curve of her tight-fitting dress. "Ye keek bonny."

Catriona shifted the bodice of her dress self-consciously. It seemed Sean had underestimated her *package* as well. Her breasts spilled over the top like a flash flood of flesh.

"*Keek* isn't a word, it's *look*, but thank you. Now keep your mind on the job."

She heard him mumble to himself.

"Is *tae* a word."

They approached a young man standing at the door. He raised his tablet and Catriona felt her mood darken.

Not again.

"Name?" he asked.

"Catriona Phoenix and Brochan...er..." She'd forgotten they'd yet to christen Broch with a surname. He'd only known himself as Brochan when he arrived. Since then, they'd discovered he was Sean's *real* son, so she guessed Sean had used his last name when adding them to the party list.

"Brochan Shaft."

She heard it the moment the words left her lips.

Oh no.

The young man squinted at her. "Broken Shaft?"

She winced.

I just gave him the worst porn name ever.

When Sean arrived from the past, nearly thirty years before Brochan, he'd been questioned about his last name in a room with the poster for the movie *Shaft* hanging on the wall. He'd panicked and said his last name was Shaft. He'd lucked out. Sean Shaft sounded acceptable. But *Brochan Shaft—*

"—tenstein," she added, pretending she hadn't finished. "*Brochan.*"

The young man's glower grew deeper. "Brochan Shaftenstein?"

She dropped her head into her hand. *Oh my god. This keeps getting worse.*

Catriona took a deep breath and decided to start from the top. "Look, we're security from the studio. Just let us in."

The doorman tapped his tablet with his finger. "You're not on the list. I'm going to have to ask you to step aside."

Catriona dug through her evening bag for the badge identifying her as Parasol Pictures security. Except for her phone, the badge and lipstick were the only things she'd been able to fit in the child-sized purse she'd found in her old bedroom closet.

In the end, she'd had to strap her gun to the inside of her thigh to keep it from showing beneath her condom of a dress.

The doorman peered at the badge as she held it aloft triumphantly, and then shrugged. "I don't know. You'll have to talk to Mr. Burson. Step aside."

Catriona was about to tear into the young man when a booming voice cut her short.

"Catriona!"

Director Konrad Burson appeared on the threshold of the warehouse, arms raised in welcoming, his round belly leading the way. The doorman stepped aside, clearly perturbed his tiny bit of authority had been stripped.

Catriona smiled. "Hey, Konrad."

Nice timing. She stuck the tip of her tongue out at the boy and he scowled.

"Here to save me from myself?" Konrad asked hugging her.

"Somebody has to." She motioned to Broch as Konrad released his anaconda-like grip on her. "This is my new partner, Brochan."

Just Brochan.

Konrad thrust a hand toward Broch. "You're a big one. Ever do any acting?"

"Na." Broch shook his head. Catriona had tried to slick back his shaggy locks with some hair gel she'd left at Sean's years earlier, but his head shake sent wavy strands tumbling front and back. It only made him more handsome, which didn't seem fair.

Konrad waved for them to follow him. "Come on in. The party's about to start."

Catriona and Broch trailed Konrad to a large room set up as a dining hall with two enormous tables in the center. If Henry the Eighth had walked in and taken a seat at the head of the table, Catriona wouldn't have been surprised.

As they entered, a slight, dark-haired young man lingering at the end of one table turned to watch them. Judging by the scraggly hair on his chin, Catriona guessed him to be about eighteen, though his diminutive size made him seem much younger. She recognized him from pictures she'd seen online while researching Pinky's history.

Konrad headed toward him as if he were magnetized.

"Catriona, Broch, this is Marlon Lang."

Marlon smiled and held out a hand to shake. As Catriona took his hand in her own she felt the nub of a missing digit. Watching as he moved to shake with Broch, she saw the boy's pinky was missing.

He caught her looking and held up his right hand.

"Dad needed a spare," he said with a chuckle. Catriona could tell he'd used the line before to break the tension. She imagined life had to be difficult for Marlon, knowing people knew him as the son of a monster. He probably had a hundred ready-made comments designed to put people at ease.

But something was odd about his missing pinky...

"I thought he always took the left?"

Catriona said the words before she could stop herself and then winced.

That might have been rude.

Marlon smiled. "You did your homework."

She shrugged, grateful he hadn't been offended. "It's my job."

"They're security," explained Konrad.

"Ah." Marlon turned to him. "Can I tell her?"

"Go ahead. I'm going to greet the guests." Konrad leaned to Catriona. "This is one of the secrets we're revealing in the movie. You'll love it."

She nodded and returned her attention to Marlon. "If it's a secret you don't have to—"

Marlon ignored her. "My mother was missing her right pinky. Childhood accident." He touched the nub of his finger. "Dad took the left from his victims because they weren't quite *her.*"

Catriona squinted one eye. "So it was kind of romantic?"

Marlon chuckled. "I guess, in a way. Only family loses the right." As he spoke, Catriona thought she saw a flash of pride cross his expression. She imagined the boy's sick father had tried to convince him the loss of his right pinky *was* an honor.

She felt terrible for probing. "I'm sorry. It must have been hard, reenacting what he put you through."

Marlon shook his head. "Cathartic. Helped me get my head around things."

"Really?"

"I know it's hard to believe, but Dad seemed like a pretty normal dad to me, most of the time. Believe it or not, he was a nice guy."

"He murdured eight wummin," mumbled Broch, taking a goblet of red wine from a tray carried by a passing server.

Catriona tried to surreptitiously elbow him in the ribs, and he struggled to keep his glass from sloshing. "Whit? He did, dinnae he?"

Marlon held out a palm, implying all was well. "No, you're right. I meant, when he wasn't doing terrible things, he was a nice guy to *me* until the end. Boring even." He reached into his pocket with his left hand and pulled out his wallet. Opening it, he withdrew a photo of a pudgy, smiling, balding man. A tall man holding a golf club stood in the background.

"Is that Brooks Koepka?" asked Catriona, zeroing in on the man in the back. While she didn't watch a lot of golf, it seemed every time she visited Sean *he* was watching, and she'd come to recognize many of the players.

Marlon's expression registered his surprise. "Good eye. This was taken at the U.S. Open tournament. He was so happy to go— watched it from the moment it started until the end. He went to every event he could."

Catriona looked away and tapped into the photographic memory she'd only recently discovered she had. Sean called it a mini-time-travel, where only her mind journeyed back to a moment and she could rewatch it as if she was there.

In her mind's eye, she found herself sitting on the sofa in Sean's office watching a golfer being interviewed after his win.

"Brooks *won* that," she said.

"He did. Good memory," said Marlon.

Broch leaned down and peered at the photo. "Golf."

"You know golf?" she asked before realizing it would seem an odd question to a person unaware of Broch's time-jumping past.

Broch scoffed. "We invented it."

"You, personally?"

The big Scot rolled his eyes.

She returned her attention to Marlon, who'd already slid the photo back into his wallet. "So your dad did boring dad things like go to golf tournaments."

"And then he murdered wummin," mumbled Broch, as he craned his neck to catch the eye of a server with a tray of mini quiches.

Catriona grimaced and Marlon laughed at her discomfort. "It's okay. Really. I'm used to it. Don't get me wrong, I know Dad was a monster. I keep that photo to remind me of his other side when my thoughts get too dark."

"People are complicated," said Catriona, watching a short, stocky man approach them.

"Who do you have here?" asked the man, slapping a hand on Marlon's back, his eyes never leaving Catriona's cleavage.

"Hey, Sal, this is Catriona and...uh..." Marlon shook his head. "I'm sorry, I forgot your name."

Broch's hand enveloped Sal's as he sidestepped to block the man's death stare on Catriona's chest. "Brochan."

Catriona watched Sal wince as Broch squeezed.

"Quite a grip you got there." Sal flexed his hand as Broch released him.

She stepped forward to shake his hand. "You're Salvatore Soto, the officer who..." She glanced at Marlon. It felt indelicate to finish her sentence.

"The cop who shot my dad and saved my life," said Marlon, once again gallantly breaking the tension. Catriona couldn't help but be impressed.

Soto threw his arm around Marlon, grinning. "Just doin' my job, kid, just doin' my job."

"Your ankle seems to have healed well," said Catriona, nodding at Soto's feet. She remembered feeling a little ill while reading that the officer's Achilles had been sliced.

Soto flashed a dimple in his right cheek. "You can't keep me down." He winked and stared into Catriona's eyes as if they were the only people in the room.

Catriona thought she heard a growl rumble in Broch's chest.

Seemingly oblivious to Broch's ire, Soto raised both hands, as if urging a crowd to silence. "It was crazy. There I was, creeping down that dark, dark hallway. Razor wire to my left. Razor wire to my right. I hear this weird sliding noise behind me and *poing!* there goes my Achilles."

Catriona winced. The cartoonish noise Soto used to describe having his tendon severed didn't help make the image in her head any less horrific.

Soto pantomimed shooting a gun. "That's when I fell, firing where the pain came from." He shrugged, his perpetual grin failing him for the first time since his arrival. He waved his hand and muttered the rest of his tale. "Then that horrible stuff with the bomb outside."

"You were lucky," said Catriona.

Soto nodded. "I only wish my partner and the others had been so lucky. I want to tell their story now. That's why I'm here."

An awkward silence fell and Marlon scanned the now crowded room. "Well, I guess I better mingle. Nice to meet you both."

Soto sprang back to life as if someone had flipped his happy switch. "Me too." Soto took Catriona's hand in his own. "Nice to meet you." He glanced at Broch and held up an index finger, warding off a second handshake. "You too, big guy, but I'm not making that mistake again." With a final wink at Catriona and a slap on Broch's arm, he headed into the growing crowd with Marlon.

As soon as they left, Catriona flipped her wrist to smack Broch in the chest with the back of her hand.

"Behave yourself, will you?"

"He likes ye," said Broch.

"Who? Marlon?" He's just a kid," said Catriona, knowing he'd meant Soto.

"The wee man. Ah'll tie him into a Celtic knot."

Catriona laughed. "I'm sure he didn't mean anything. He's a hero. Be nice."

Broch grunted.

A commotion rose behind them and Catriona turned in time to see the doorman stumble forward and sprawl to the ground as if someone had pushed him.

Two men dressed in what looked like black, unmarked S.W.A.T. uniforms closed the doors behind them. One spread his legs, standing sentry. The other held up an M16 rifle.

"Everybody listen up!" screamed the other.

CHAPTER TEN

Rune stood outside Maddie's house, watching her watch television. The one-story Craftsman wasn't an impressive home, but in the Los Angeles market, a single-family proved she had some earning power.

If she owns it.

Maybe she rents.

I wonder how much rent—

Rune dropped his chin to his chest and pinched the bridge of his nose.

It seemed his mind wandered to the strangest thoughts these days.

Who cares about Maddie's rent?

She worked at Parasol Pictures. *That* was the important part.

Rune felt it when he touched her, saw flashes of the Parasol logo, again and again, and knew she saw it every day on her way to work. He couldn't say he'd been able to decipher what she *did* at Parasol, though. He assumed she was an actress, but the images he'd pulled from her mind—scissors, glue, paper, and little flat wooden sticks—none of that made any sense.

But none of that mattered. What mattered was that she had access to the studio where *all* his enemies seemed to spend their time. Even his daughter worked there.

He felt the scar on his neck and thought of Fiona.

Traitorous spawn.

Maddie could slip him inside the studio lot. Once in, he could kill them all.

Maybe then I can sleep.

When he closed his eyes at night he could feel their presence. His skin vibrated and itched. It was as if he were allergic to them.

They had to go. He couldn't have them in the same time stream as himself. He didn't want them *anywhere*, especially in the time where he found himself now.

Where he felt his calling.

This feels like the right place.

Maybe his calling was simply to kill *them*.

They were so misguided. They hadn't *evolved* like him. Sure, he had a vague recollection of inspiring good in the people around him, but what was the point? All that wishy-washy inspiration made mankind *weaker*. When he awoke to the realization his natural ability to inspire the best in people was counterproductive, his gut reaction was to kill *everyone*.

Every person on earth.

But that urge passed, coming, raging like a fever and then breaking like one.

When his anger subsided, he was able to see things more clearly. More *calmly*. If he had been making the human race *weaker* by coddling them, couldn't he make them stronger with tough love?

He'd been misguided, but that didn't mean *everyone* had to die.

The realization was a tremendous relief. Having to *kill everyone* on his to-do list had inspired quite a bit of anxiety.

Everyone was a *lot*. It could take him *eons* to rid the planet of humans.

As his new consciousness evolved, he realized his mission wasn't to *kill*, it was to *toughen*. It was easier to inspire *mistrust* than anything else. He made people think about *survival of the fittest*, where *fittest* was always *themselves*.

That didn't mean they *were* the fittest, of course. Often

they weren't. But if they weren't, then they'd die trying to prove they were, so it worked out in the end.

Easy-peasy pumpkin breezy.

Rune shook his head.

Stop it. Why do I think such silly things?

He returned to his thoughts. Everything he wanted to accomplish was at risk with Sean and his son hanging around, inspiring the *best* in people.

They had to go.

So did Fiona, now that she'd turned on him. He'd thought she'd be a partner.

Rune took a deep breath and bopped his lips together, making a string of popping noises.

He was sorry about her.

Maybe if she spent more time with me and less time with them?

He gasped.

That's it.

If they could influence her down the wrong path, how hard could it be to influence her into understanding she was more powerful on *his* team?

"I could talk to her. Make it clear. That would be worth a shot," he mumbled to himself.

Rune looked up from where he'd been studying the toe of his shoe, deep in thought.

What was I doing?

The glow inside the Craftsman caught his attention.

Oh, right.

He walked across the street and knocked on the Craftsman's door. There was a click as the knob turned.

"Hello, Maddie."

Maddie stared at him through the cracked-open door, lock chain still attached. Her eyes had opened wide.

Before he could say anything, she slammed the door shut with a yelp.

He frowned.

Why does everyone always have to make everything so

difficult?

"Let me in." He could hear the boredom in his tone. He hoped that wouldn't make it easier for her to ignore him.

"I'm going to call the police. Go away."

Rune rested his cheek against the door.

"You saw what I can do, Maddie. Do you think the police can stop me?"

Silence.

"Let me in."

"You'll kill me."

"Do you think I *can't* kill you from out here?"

He couldn't. At least not that he was aware, but she didn't know that. It made him a little giddy how much clearer his thoughts were becoming. The fury of his glorious transformation had given way to clarity.

Look how clever I am now.

"I just want to talk." He could barely get the words past his lips he was grinning so wide.

"How can I trust you?" she asked.

He cleared his throat.

Good point.

"You can't. But if I wanted to kill you, don't you think I would have done that earlier?"

Logic. She can't argue with that. So clever.

Maddie opened the door again, the gold lock chain still hanging just below her eyes.

"What's in it for me?" she asked, clearly fighting to keep her quavering voice steady.

There's my girl.

"I think we can help each other. I've already helped you once, didn't I? That's how much I admire you. I did that for *you*. And what I need you to do is, *pfft*." He flicked the air with his finger to show how inconsequential his request would be. Featherweight. Nothing. He could see the white feather he was flicking. He wasn't sure if she could. At least she didn't follow it with her eyes as it bounced up and then fluttered to the ground, scooping through the air back and forth like a rocking cradle.

Where did the feather come from?

It didn't matter. She got the point.

Maddie unlocked the chain and opened the door. She stood to the side like a rabbit, frozen in place, hoping the fox wouldn't notice her as he entered.

He smiled politely and entered. The house was neat, if sparsely decorated. He spotted a gray sofa and sat on it.

"Sit," he said, patting the cushion beside him.

She swallowed and took a seat in a matching stuffed chair nearby.

"If I sat that close to you I'd have to turn sideways and...we'd just be too close to focus."

He shrugged. "Fair enough."

"What do you want?"

"Very little. You saw the feather."

"What?"

Rune sniffed. "Nothing. I need you to get me into Parasol Pictures. You work there, correct?"

She nodded.

"You can hide me in the trunk of your vehicle and we can—"

"I can't enter the lot."

"Hm?"

"I park in the outer lot and then walk through security."

Rune's lips pinched. "Could you request a pass?"

"No. Only the high-ups get to park inside."

"Even after I took care of your rival? You're not powerful enough?"

Maddie scowled. "No. It didn't change my standing at all. I just don't have to share the limelight."

"Hm. Maybe you could pretend I was your father?"

Maddie's lip curled. "But you're not. You don't look anything like him or me."

"Ah, but *they* don't know that."

"They'll ask to see your I.D. Do you have I.D. with my Dad's name on it?"

Rune felt his mood darken. Perhaps Maddie wasn't as

useful as he thought she would be. She certainly wasn't very bright.

"Who are you?" she asked, fidgeting in the silence between them.

His attention snapped to her. "I don't kill you for five minutes and you think you can ask me *that*?"

She stood. "I'm sorry—"

"I'm *kidding*. Sit down."

She raised her hand to her mouth to cover a nervous giggle. Rune smiled. *Now I'm funny too. Not only clever but funny.*

Maddie sat. "I—"

"Shh. I'm thinking." Rune put his hands on either side of his head and rested his elbows on his knees. There had to be something she could do. He needed to walk onto the lot, unmolested, free to do what he needed to do.

Maybe she could help him find the people he needed to kill *outside* the lot?

"Do you know about a large Moor working there?"

"A Moor?"

"A Moor. A man of dark complexion."

"A black man?"

"Yes. Though very dark brown would be a more accurate representation."

Maddie frowned. "Could you narrow it down? I mean, there are a lot of black men at Parasol."

"He works with Ryft and his dreadful son."

"Ryft?"

Rune huffed. "I'm sorry, I'm making a mess of this. My thoughts are sometimes here and sometimes long ago. *Sean.* He goes by Sean in this time."

Maddie's lips pressed tight, her features scrunching into a ball in the center of her face. "Sean *who*? Do you have a last name?"

"He's the guard of the studio. Very good with a sword, both broad and rapier, judging by his style. He works with a large Moor and drives a green car, smaller than most—"

"Oh, *Sean*. You mean Sean and Luther. They run Parasol's

security."

"Yes! Is Luther his son's name?"

"Luther is the black man. Big."

"Right. That's the one. So you know who I mean."

"I do now, yes."

"Do you know where Luther lives?"

"No." Maddie glanced behind her. "But I could probably find out. I could Google him."

Rune stared at her, unsure if *Google* was a good thing. "Would that alert him to our quest to find him?"

"Googling? No. He wouldn't know."

"Okay. Do that."

Maddie stood and went to a small black box sitting on her dining room table. She lifted the lid and it glowed as she tapped on the bottom half of it.

Computer. Laptop.

The words bounced through his brain and he nodded, happy to see them.

With her right hand, she moved something around the top of the table and he saw the lit portion of the computer jumping to display different images and text. Finally, she grabbed a writing utensil and wrote something on the back of an envelope.

"Here," she handed him the envelope. "This is where he lives."

Rune read the address. "Can that computer tell you where *everyone* lives?"

"It depends."

"On what?"

"I need information. First and last name at least, some idea of where they live. And even then, not everyone."

"Excellent." Rune stood. "I'm going to take care of something. Sean will be next if you can find where he lives for me while I'm gone?"

Maddie frowned. "So now I'm your secretary?"

Rune shrugged. "If you like."

"I don't *like*—"

He glared and her agitated tone softened. "Sure. I'll find out where Sean lives. Do I get another favor then?"

Rune blinked. "Maybe. What do you want?"

"I don't know yet."

"Well, you think on that. I'll be back."

As he reached for the door Maddie called out.

"Are you going to *kill* Luther?"

He paused and glanced over his shoulder. "Yes. Does that bother you?"

Maddie shrugged. "No. It doesn't do anything for me either way."

"Everything in your head is about *you*." Rune grinned. "I love that."

CHAPTER ELEVEN

Broch took half a step toward the gunmen who had crashed the director's party and felt Catriona touch his arm.

"Don't," she murmured.

"We're going to spend a little time together tonight," shouted the larger of the two armed men over the din of the confused crowd.

Broch's hand grazed Catriona's hip. "Fall back in tae the crowd."

"You're kidding, right?"

She scowled and he knew asking her to hide and stand down would never be an option.

Everythin' is a negotiation with this wifie o' mine.

"Ah dinnae want ye getting hurt."

Catriona's voice lowered to a hiss. "I was doing this job before you were even in this *century.*"

Broch sighed. He loved Cat's fire, but her presence did complicate how he was going to stop the armed men at the door.

"Hey," one of the men snapped, waving a gun at them. "You two, shut up."

"Oh *you*," Catriona waved a dismissive hand at the intruder. "I don't need to hear it from you, too."

The man's face twitched, his shock at her reaction to his threats rendering him dumb.

His partner's attention shot to Catriona. "Lady, he's

serious—"

Catriona kicked off her heels. "If you think I'm going to stand here and let another man boss me around—"

"Hey! Are you hearing us?" The first man took a step toward them.

"She's drunk," said the second.

Catriona ignored them to tug on Broch's sleeve.

"Are you even listening to me?" she asked, her tone somewhere between anger and tears.

She winked with the eye the uniformed men couldn't see from their vantage.

Och. Clever girl. Ah ken whit yer up tae.

He raised a hand and glowered at her. "Wifie, shut yer mouth afore ye feel the back o' mah haun."

Catriona turned her head as he watched her squelch a laugh. The line he'd used he'd heard watching *Braveheart*. Catriona thought the film would make him feel at home and it did. He'd watched it six times.

He felt his cheeks grow hot at the memory. It still made him uncomfortable that she'd caught him crying over the murder of William Wallace's wife...

Bit t'was sae sad—

Catriona tugged on his shirt and brought him back to the present.

"Oh, *big man*. Does it make you feel tough hitting women?" She swung at him, punching his chest with the side of her fist.

Ouch.

He grabbed her by both arms and roared. "Ye shrew!"

"Hey!" The smaller armed man stepped toward them and, without taking his gaze from Catriona, Broch grabbed the end of the man's rifle and jerked it from his hands. Abruptly changing direction, he swung the butt of the weapon, splintering it against the side of the man's head. It broke into long thin strips and he held the flimsy piece remaining in his hand, fascinated.

That's odd.

Catriona hiked up her dress and jerked her gun from the lace holster on her thigh.

Broch's tongue clicked against the roof of his mouth.

That micht be the sexiest thing ah've ever seen.

Catriona trained her weapon on the remaining gunman. The man dropped his rifle to the floor, threw up his hands, and yelled out.

"Konrad!"

The sound of the weapon sounded hollow as it struck the floor. Broch looked at the hunk of rifle remaining in his hand and realized it was made of a material Catriona had introduced him to soon after his arrival.

Plastic.

"Whoa, wait, whoa, whoa." Konrad pushed his way through the crowd toward Catriona.

"Cat, stop, put down the gun."

Catriona scowled at the hunk of broken plastic in Broch's hand and lowered her gun. She turned to Konrad as he appeared beside her.

"It was a stunt," she said matter-of-factly, but he could see her anger simmering behind the deceptive serenity of her words.

"I didn't sign up for this," said the standing uniformed man, staring at his fallen friend.

Konrad panted, out of breath. "Yes, it was a stunt. They're actors." He turned and held his hands over his head. "They're actors, everyone. False alarm. A little theatre gone wrong. Nothing to worry about. I had a little adventure planned for you, but it appears I forgot to tell the studio's security team."

A ripple of nervous laughter ran through the crowd and the piped-in music returned. The crowd murmured and returned to their cocktails.

Catriona rubbed her temples. "Forget the security team. Now it's going to involve the studio's *legal* team."

Konrad looked at the man on the ground. "Did you kill him?"

Broch leaned down and slapped the unconscious actor's face. The man groaned.

"Na." Broch grabbed the man's hand and hoisted him to his

feet.

Catriona studied the cut on the side of the man's forehead. "You're okay. It isn't bad."

The man put his hand over the wound, scowling at Konrad. "You didn't pay us enough for this shit."

Konrad grimaced. "I'll make it up to you."

A woman screamed from the back of the room. "There's a man on the floor in there!"

Konrad glanced in that direction and then caught Catriona's eye. "A third guy is coming from there."

Catriona sighed and tugged Konrad's sleeve. "With me."

Broch, Catriona, and Konrad made their way through the crowd until they reached the panicked woman on the opposite side of the room. She stood outside a door painted to look like part of the wall. Being cracked open had ruined its camouflage.

"It's okay, it's all fake," said Catriona to the woman. She tapped Konrad's arm. "Tell her."

The woman continued. "But I *really* think he's dead. I peeked in there after the man took the girls—"

Catriona spun to face Konrad. *"Took the girls?"*

Konrad offered a lopsided grin. "He was supposed to take Jessica and a random."

"Jessica?"

"Jessica Scout. The actress who plays the second victim."

"So she's in on this stunt?"

He nodded.

Broch opened the false door. A man dressed in black assault garb lay on the ground of a thin hallway.

He squatted down and felt the man's neck with his fingers.

Nothing. He pressed harder, thinking he must be wrong, but found no sign of life.

"He's dead." His fingers moved to a hole in the chest of the man's padded jacket. The area around it was damp. "Stabbed ah'd say."

Standing, he felt something sticky on the fingertips he'd used to balance beside the man. They were stained red. Squatting again, he located a small pool of blood beside the man.

The man's hand rested on it like an island.

He lifted the dead man's wrist to show Catriona the pinky had been snipped clean away.

Catriona gaped and turned to Konrad. "Is *this* part of your stunt?"

Konrad shook his head, his eyes wide. "No. I swear. This isn't me."

Marlon appeared and pushed past the others to peer inside the door. Broch watched the blood drain from the boy's face as he spotted the actor's mangled hand.

"Close the door," said Catriona.

CHAPTER TWELVE

Rune stopped walking and stretched his neck.

He had a plan.

Thanks to Maddie's directions, he was nearing Luther's house. He remembered the big man now. He'd been there when Sean took his arm. He'd been easily dispatched with a gun, but thinking back on the incident, Rune realized he'd sensed something odd about him.

Luther was one of *them*.

He was sure of it now.

The previous day, he'd watched Luther arrive at work and stared at him through the studio lot gate from his spot across the street.

Luther had turned to look in his direction as if he could sense him.

What if he knows, even now, that I'm on my way?

He'd assumed Sean and his son were the strong pair. That's why he'd decided to practice on Luther.

But what if the Moor isn't the weak link?

Rune didn't like phystical confrontation, but he had to get rid of the people radiating that inspiring energy. It was as if he and the Scots were magnets with opposite polarization. Having them in town pushed him out.

He didn't want to leave. He'd worked out Hollywood was the perfect place to settle down. If he could find a way to influence the messages being broadcast to people all over the world...

The thought made him giddy.

But first, *Luther.*

Headlights headed in his direction and Rune squinted at them. The car began to slow, rolling to a stop in front of him on the opposite side of the street. The window lowered and a man hung his arm out.

"Hey."

Rune cocked an eyebrow.

What's this?

He took a step forward, feeling drawn to the man. The driver had tan skin and straight brown hair, cut as if someone had placed a bowl on his head. The front was clipped, and the sides above his ears were shaved.

Even with his limited knowledge of fashion, Rune couldn't help but think the haircut was ugly to the point of being grotesque.

"We passed the other day," the man called to him. "On the street."

Rune scowled, offended by the man's impertinence. "Passed? And now you think that means I want to talk to you?'

The man smirked. "Oh, you want to talk to me alright. I can help. I know what you are. It's what I am too."

Rune chuckled. "I doubt that."

There is only one of me.

The man took a deep breath. "You used to care about the people around you. You made them better and they didn't appreciate it."

Rune's eyes widened.

Hm?

The man continued. "And then you stopped caring. You started giving people what they *wanted* instead of what they *needed,* even if that meant their ruin. It was crazy for a while during your transition, but now you're feeling better. *Stronger.*"

Rune's jaw had creaked open as the man talked, and it took him a moment to shake away his shock.

"Who are you?" he asked.

"I'm the reason you're in L.A. I think you were drawn to me."

Rune shook his head. "I came here for my daughter."

"Fiona."

Rune tucked back his chin, surprised to hear his daughter's name fall from the lips of a stranger.

The man huffed. "Look, we both want the same thing and we can work together."

"Really?" For the first time, Rune noticed how large the arm hanging from the car was. The driver wasn't a tall man, but he was powerfully built. The very opposite of him.

Maybe the impertinent interloper *could* be helpful.

"Do you know Luther?" he asked.

The man frowned. "I do. You want to take him out first? That's a good idea."

"There's Catriona," said Rune. The name sounded funny on his tongue.

"Whatever, dude. We can compare notes. Let's do this. Get in."

Rune eyed the car. The style was one he'd heard referred to as a *muscle* car. He walked around the back of it, thinking it would be harder for his new friend to run him over backward.

Always thinking.

When he reached the other side he pulled at the handle of the passenger door, but it didn't budge.

"I've got the doors welded shut. You gotta crawl in through the window," explained the man.

Rune frowned. "Why would you do such a thing?"

"So they don't fly open. I do some crazy drivin' sometimes."

Rune lifted one skinny leg as high as he could, swinging it up and dropping his heel on the edge of the window. Grabbing the roof with both hands he slid himself forward, clinging there as he carefully raised the second leg and slipped it inside. After a few wobbles and a fair amount of grunting, he found himself sitting in the car next to the driver.

"If you're going to be chauffeuring me, we're going to have

to find another car," he muttered. That was ungraceful and unacceptable."

The man shrugged. "I make it look cool."

"Hm." Rune sucked his tooth with his tongue. "What's your name?"

"Joseph."

"You know where Luther lives?"

"I do."

"Okay, Joseph. You have my attention." Rune nodded. "Let's go."

CHAPTER THIRTEEN

Catriona, Broch, Marlon, and Konrad slipped into the hidden hallway and closed the door behind them to hide the dead pretend commando from the guests. Catriona illuminated her phone's flashlight. The glow in the darkened hallway made her feel as if they were a coven of witches gathered over a human sacrifice.

I'll be happy when this freaky night is over.

Broch's expression remained grim as he stared into the darkness. Somewhere in the maze-like warehouse, a killer was on the loose, and they needed to find him before he claimed another victim.

Catriona glanced at Marlon. The young man's haunted eyes remained locked on the hand of the corpse. Or, she suspected, on the space where the man's pinky should be.

Catriona turned her attention to Konrad, whose invasion stunt had probably added ten years of therapy to poor Marlon's future.

"Tell me everything you know," she said.

Konrad sighed, looking glum. "Like I said, this guy was supposed to pull Jessica and a random guest in here, and then Jessica would lead the guests through the maze. He'd stay here and look threatening until Jessica returned to take another guest. You get the idea."

"Once someone talked to Jessica, they'd know it was a stunt

and take a tour of the maze set with her."

"Right."

"What about the forty-odd people out there who didn't talk to Jessica yet? The ones who thought there were armed men at the door ready to kill them?"

Konrad's jaw worked but nothing intelligible emitted. "Wha...well, they, uh..."

Catriona held up a hand to silence him. "Let me help you with this one. *They'd be in a blind state of panic.*"

"It was *supposed* to be thrilling."

"There's a difference between *thrilling* and *terrifying.*"

Konrad shrugged. "Not always. Especially now when people are so desensitized—"

"Please, spare me the social commentary. We've got a room full of guests and a killer on the loose. I'll read your dissertation later."

Her face hot with anger, Catriona was about to launch into a speech about how Konrad's history of irresponsible party games was why Parasol Pictures sent her and Broch in the first place, but she stopped herself. She needed to stick to the crisis at hand. Two women were god-knows-where having who-knew-what done to them. They had to *move.*

"Okay. *Think.* Jessica would have gone through here, right?" She hooked a thumb toward the dark hall behind her.

Konrad nodded.

Catriona took a step farther into the hall and tapped a wire spiraling down the wall. Feeling a prick, she gasped, whirling to face Konrad.

"You hired men with fake guns to force your half-drunk party guests through a maze covered in razor wire?"

Upper lip lifting with what looked like genuine horror and surprise, Konrad stepped over the dead man's feet to tap the point of one of the barbs. His jaw dropped open.

"These were *fake.*"

Marlon leaned forward to feel the wire, his expression resembling Konrad's surprise. "It *was* fake. All through shooting. It was never real."

"Is yer faither alive?" asked Broch.

Catriona looked at him.

That's it.

The odd tickle in the back of her brain, Broch had put into words.

Could Pinky still be alive?

Marlon shook his head. "*No.* That's impossible. Soto shot him dead. They took him away." Marlon's voice fell to a whisper. "I had him cremated to be sure."

Konrad put a hand on the young man's shoulder. "It's okay, Marlon. This is just some copycat sicko."

Catriona glanced at her phone. "I've got no reception. Does anyone?"

Konrad shook his head. "It's not just this hallway. It's the whole place. There's no reception on the lot."

"Is there a landline?"

"Outside in my trailer, I have a sat phone."

Catriona's eyes fell to the body at her feet.

"Did you get any threats during production? Any crazy letters?"

Konrad barked a laugh. "I could paper the walls of the grand hall with the insane stuff that showed up during production. Pinky had quite the following."

"Great. What about the guests? Who are they? Anyone we should suspect?"

Konrad shrugged. "The cast, some press, some industry people I wanted to impress—"

Broch leaned down to whisper in Catriona's ear.

"We need tae git the fowk *oot.*"

Catriona snorted a laugh. "No kidding. I'd like to get the f—"

"*Fowk.*" He repeated. "We need tae get the *people* oot o' 'ere."

"Oh, *folk.* You're right. Yes. First things first." Catriona clapped her hands together. "Konrad, you and Marlon get everyone out of here in a calm and orderly fashion. Use your sat phone to call the police. Call Sean too—the studio's going to want to stay ahead of this publicity disaster."

"Um…" he hemmed.

By the glow of her phone, Catriona watched Konrad squint one eye as if he'd suffered a gas pain. By now, she knew that meant he'd done something else stupid, yet to be revealed.

"What now?" she asked.

"They chained the front doors. It was part of the storyline."

"What?"

"This guy…" He motioned to the man on the floor. "He locked the door behind the other two and then came through the maze to get here."

Catriona gaped. "Did it not occur to you at any point what a terrible idea that was? The fire hazard alone—"

Konrad pouted. "In hindsight…"

She turned and flashed her light in the direction of the razor-wire-covered hall. It continued for as far as the beam could travel.

"You're telling me through *here* is the only way out?"

Konrad nodded. "The place is like a fortress. The real building only had two doors and we wanted to keep it that way for security."

Security. That's rich coming from you.

Catriona put her hand over her mouth, thinking. She took a deep breath and expelled it slowly.

This is bad. At least one of them would have to go through the maze and open the doors from the outside, while the rest of them kept the guests from wandering or, heaven forbid, trying the doors. If someone tried to leave and discovered they were locked in, the whole place would erupt in panic.

"We've got a real dead guy and real razor wire. Two women are missing. What other things might have become *real* in the belly of this mess?"

Konrad scratched his head as if it helped him think. "Not much. I mean, the real Minotaur in this maze was Pinky."

Broch motioned to the man on the floor. "Someone is deid. Thare micht be a Minotaur."

Catriona looked to Marlon for input.

"Dad didn't build a bunch of elaborate traps. There were

some false doors, a couple of access hatches like the one he used to cut Soto, but nothing *super* sneaky."

Dad. Catriona sniffed at the use of such an endearing term to describe a notorious serial killer. *Dad*, who happily mutilated women the way other Dads played golf.

And Pinky loved golf, too.

It was all too weird.

She pointed to the door. "Konrad, Marlon, you two go out there. Calm everyone down. Tell them everything up to this point has been part of your moronic *vision*. Give them food. Tell them stories. Do whatever you have to do. We can't let the guests panic and storm the exits. If there's someone in here pretending to be Pinky, we can't let him pick off the party guests one by one as they make their way through the maze."

Konrad frowned. "I can't feed them."

"Why?"

"The food was coming from the trailers outside."

Catriona felt a blip of hope. "Any chance the caterers will figure out something is wrong and call the police?"

"No caterers. I bought a bunch of food. I was going to send my assistant out to get it."

"And your assistant is where? Outside?"

Konrad shook his head. "He's in the party somewhere serving drinks."

Catriona frowned. "Just out of curiosity, what did you do with all the money the studio gave you to cater this thing?"

Konrad glanced down at the body. "I hired the actors."

At a loss for words, Catriona lifted her hands in the air and dropped them to her sides. "Give them *booze* then. Just keep the guests *calm*. Get your actors with the fake guns to stand in front of the doors. Don't let anyone near *either* exit."

Konrad and Marlon nodded.

Catriona pointed her phone's flashlight down the hall. "We'll find the missing girls, get out and unchain the hall door from the outside. Marlon, is there a trick to this maze? A path we should take?"

He shook his head. "It isn't a true maze. It's just a path in and out. Do you want me to lead you?"

"No. Can't risk a studio asset. You guys go. But Marlon, I do have one favor to ask."

"Yes?"

"Don't let Konrad do anything else *stupid*."

Marlon looked at Konrad sheepishly.

Konrad stretched a hand toward the door and then paused. "Cat, I was thinking maybe we don't have to tell Sean—"

Catriona closed her eyes and shook her head. "You know the studio's going to have to fire you for this nightmare, right?"

Konrad pressed his lips together. "Yeah. I suppose you're right."

CHAPTER FOURTEEN

Sean raced his Jaguar down the desert road toward Los Angeles. Something wasn't right, not even counting the bullet-sized hole in his hood, left by Rune during his attempt to kill him. He hadn't died, but it had taken weeks to return the Jag in working order. The poor old girl still looked terrible.

Bastard. Just because I lopped off his arm...

His *near*-death experience, compliments of Rune, had sent Sean spinning into the past. Luther had brought him home. Luther, his best friend, who'd never mentioned *anything* about his ability to time travel, showed up in eighteenth-century Scotland as if they'd bumped into each other at the supermarket.

Not that he wasn't grateful. The past held nothing for him anymore. Now his life was in twenty-first-century Los Angeles, where he could protect his son and adopted daughter.

But Luther could have said *something* over the decades they'd been working together.

I should have known.

Luther seemed unfazed when Sean admitted he remembered living in ancient Scotland. The big man didn't blink when Rune came after them and then disappeared into thin air after Sean separated his arm from his shoulder with a sword.

Why did I think Luther was just really laid back? How stupid am I?

It didn't matter anymore. Now, he could get some answers. Clearly, Luther was the only person who knew anything about Sean's family's strange relationship with time and space.

The dinner was supposed to clarify everything.

But Luther didn't show up.

Luther would never blow off a dinner invite without good reason. And with Rune unaccounted for, Sean couldn't sit at home hoping for the best. Catriona and Broch were safe playing bodyguards at Konrad's party, so when his tenth phone call to Luther went unanswered, he hopped in the Jag.

Forty minutes later, he pulled to a stop in front of Luther's modest bungalow not far from the Parasol Pictures studio. No lights shone inside. Sean glanced at his watch. It was a little after nine. It seemed early for his big friend to be in bed, but *he* seemed to go to bed a little earlier every year, and Luther was even older. Maybe a lot older. Who knew how old his time-traveling friend might be?

Sean stepped out of the car and eased his door shut so as not to alert anyone lurking inside. He checked the front door and found it locked. Moving around the side, he made his way into the backyard.

The back kitchen door was wide open, motionless in the still night air.

That's not good.

Sean pulled his gun from the holster he'd thrown on before leaving home and crept toward the entrance.

The porch steps creaked beneath his feet.

Sticking his head inside, he whispered.

"Luther?"

The house remained silent. He took another step inside.

"Luther?"

Luther's house was old, built long before open concept living had become the norm. He didn't see the mess in the living room until he'd cleared the kitchen.

The old oval coffee table had been flipped over. Glass lay shattered on the wide plank hardwood floors. A chair had been spun sideways from its usual position.

There's been a struggle.

Flipping on the light switch, Sean saw no sign of blood.

That's good, at least.

He checked the other two bedrooms and the bathroom, finding no sign of further disturbance but no Luther either.

Returning the way he came, Sean stood staring out the kitchen door into the backyard.

Luther and someone had struggled in the living room and then, *what*? Did someone carry him out the back door? That would mean two people... No single man could have moved big Luther very far.

Did someone find a way to subdue him without spilling a drop of blood?

Doubtful.

He eyed the open door and noticed the hinges seemed worse for wear as if someone had jerked them out of the frame.

Maybe it wasn't a *struggle*.

Maybe it was a *chase*.

Sean stood on the small back porch, scanning his surroundings. Luther's home sat flanked by other, nearly identical homes, all separated by fences of various heights and types.

If someone had been after Luther and he'd chosen to run rather than fight, where would he go?

Sean moved to the fence line and spotted the indentation of a large bare foot in the dirt of Luther's garden. The enormous print *had* to belong to Luther. Nearby, he saw another print, this one a shoe, something between a sneaker and a dress shoe. He tried to remember what Rune had worn on his feet the last time he saw him but came up with nothing.

This is where Catriona's memory trick would come in handy.

The last time he saw Rune, Sean was trying to run the ghoul down with his Jag as the bastard shot at him. Checking out Rune's footwear had been low on his priority list.

Tucking his gun back into his holster, Sean mounted the fence and hopped to the other side, the neighbor's back porch light providing enough illumination for him to see.

He landed and crouched to study the earth. The ground was too dry to find good prints, but he spotted an area that appeared more trampled than the others.

This way.

Sean continued in that direction until he reached the street and then put his hands on his hips.

Cement made tracking considerably harder.

Did Luther cross the street or run down the sidewalk?

He glanced to the right and spotted a large white building several blocks away.

Ah ha.

He knew that building, and Luther did too. Parasol Pictures rented it as a warehouse for storing spare movie set props.

Luther would have run there. He knew the passcode to get in and he knew the layout of the building. It would make a great place to hide.

Sean broke into a jog.

CHAPTER FIFTEEN

Alone in the hall, Broch and Catriona stared down at the dead man lying beneath the beam of her phone flashlight. Catriona grumbled about the limited brainpower of studio people.

Broch rubbed his head, mussing whatever remained of his slicked-back 'do.

"The evening's gaun exactly as *ah* expected. Ye?"

Catriona chuckled. "We've got to get after those girls, but help me check this guy's pockets. He might have a key for unlocking whatever he's used to seal the front door."

They felt through the man's flak jacket and pants until Broch produced a small silver key.

"Git it."

"Good." She replaced her gun in its clandestine holster and tossed her purse on the floor far enough from the body to avoid any blood. "We better start before my phone battery dies."

Catriona pointed her flashlight down the hall and they left the low din of the party behind, careful to avoid the reaching razor wire.

Twenty feet in, they heard a woman's muffled scream and both froze, waiting to catch the sound of another in the hopes it would give them a direction, but no other calls came.

Catriona started forward again and Broch reached out to grab her arm.

"Mind yerself. Be wise. It cuid be a trap."

Catriona nodded. Kilty had a good point. Marlon didn't think his father's place had much in the way of hidden pitfalls, but maybe this new 'Pinky' had a unique vision.

Following a hard right turn, Catriona noticed a break in the razor wire. She ran her flashlight's beam across the wall and found a round hole where a doorknob might be. She motioned to it.

"It's some kind of pocket door, though I don't know if putting our fingers in the hole to slide it open seems like a great idea."

"Ah'd keep yer haunds close by," agreed Broch. "Staun back."

Catriona stepped back to make way. She didn't know how easily the door would slide, and Broch had a considerable strength advantage. It would be better to open the door quickly, and not be caught struggling with it.

On a quiet three count, Broch heaved the door to the side and they both spun away from the entrance, so as not to be sitting ducks for whatever lay waiting inside.

All remained quiet.

They craned their necks to peer into the room.

Inside, beneath the eerie dull glow of a red, bare bulb, a woman in a sparkly silver dress lay on a cot against the wall.

Catriona hustled to the woman's side. The victim's right hand hovered in the air as if pinned there, and as she knelt beside the cot, Catriona saw the woman's wrist hung ensnared by a cuff bolted to the wall. She'd been gagged. Her eyes were closed and her body was still.

Too still.

As Catriona's fingers touched the edge of the cot she felt something wet. Raising her phone, she squinted at what she'd taken to be a thin scarlet choker around the woman's throat. Her shoulders slumped.

"Her throat's been cut."

Broch looped his fingers around the woman's left wrist and held up her hand. Her pinky was missing.

Catriona stood. "She's blonde. Jessica Scout has dark hair,

so this has to be the guest she took."

Broch grunted. "That means Jessica cuid be in oan it."

"Not out of the realm of possibility. I don't know much about Jessica. She's new to the studio with this project."

Another scream rang out somewhere deep in the warehouse and Catriona jumped, goosebumps running down the length of her arms.

Get it together, Cat.

She set her jaw and did her best to appear calm.

"Whoever did this can't be far."

"Aye."

Every nerve in Catriona's body thrummed with the urge to head back to the well-lit main hall. Only two days removed from her ordeal in the underground lair of a different maniac, she was finding it hard to quell her panic. She'd rather be staring down the barrel of a gun under the desert sun than lost in a dungeon.

"Let's keep going or this asshole will pick off people at the party all night," she said aloud, more to bolster her nerves than Broch's.

Even in the grotesque red light of the bulb, Catriona could see Broch's expression soften as he brushed an errant strand of hair from her face.

"When hae we ever failed?"

She smiled. "You know, sometimes I think you traveled hundreds of years through time just to help me with this horrific job of mine."

Broch chuckled. "Nae on purpose."

CHAPTER SIXTEEN

"Ah see light," said Broch.

Catriona lowered her phone and noticed a dull glow at the end of the black hallway. She switched off her phone to save battery as they entered a large rectangular room and the claustrophobic experience of the hallway lifted. Catriona glanced upward to find a cloth hovering as if a large black circus tent had been erected above the room. Catriona guessed the center of the tent scraped the top of the actual warehouse. There were three doors against the far wall, all painted red.

Nice touch. What about a happy teal? Perhaps a cheery yellow?

Catriona held out a hand to keep Broch from moving toward the doors. "Wait. This is a standard horror movie trope. We have to pick a door and if we pick the wrong one—"

Before she could finish her thought, the three doors flew open, shaking the walls of the makeshift room around them. Three men burst forward as if shot from cannons. Each wore black and held a katana sword, their faces covered but for their eyes. They stopped, each a few feet from their doors, posing with swords at the ready.

Catriona jumped back a step and raised her fists. As she and Broch stood in their fighting stances, locked in some strange stare-off with the three men, she couldn't help but laugh.

"What is this *Enter the Dragon* crap?" she asked aloud.

She felt as if she'd made a wrong turn at Comic-Con. Their attackers were trying *so hard* to look like ninjas.

Unfortunately, the swords looked real enough.

Catriona slid her cell phone into the bodice of her dress for safekeeping. Cleavage always made a handy purse. And who knew, maybe tucked there, her phone could deflect a sword from her heart.

The men stepped forward in unison, brandishing their blades.

Broch glanced at her. "Och. *Enough.*"

Before she could respond, he rushed to the attacker closest to his side of the room. There was no reason a man as large as Kilty, in an outfit as tight as his, should have been able to move as fast as he did.

At the last possible second, the ninja being rushed raised his blade to strike. Broch easily dodged the katana and tackled him, pounding into the man's waist as his right hand grabbed the hilt of the blade. Highlander and ninja slammed into the far wall, the man in black crumpling like a doll, limp and seemingly unconscious.

Though they were dressed as ninjas, it didn't seem these men were the most skilled fighters.

Catriona shook her head.

Highlander vs. Ninja. I'll have to suggest that to the studio.

Broch stood, the katana now in *his* hand.

He turned to face the remaining two, who'd frozen in their tracks, staring as their fellow ninja fell. Catriona imagined their jaws were hanging open, but she couldn't be sure thanks to their dark headgear.

She, too, had been caught off guard by Broch's sudden attack and now blinked at her partner's fierce stare as he waggled the katana at the other two. She knew he was handy with a blade.

Holy hell, I'm glad I'm on his side.

She looked at the men.

"You messed up now."

The ninja closest to Broch ran forward. The remaining

assailant ran at Catriona, screaming, katana raised.

Catriona's bemused smile collapsed. She'd been so shocked by Broch's speed that she'd forgotten to pull her weapon.

Crap.

Catriona pushed aside her dress and fumbled for the gun on her leg. The lace holster refused to release. It felt as if a part of the pistol's rear sight had entangled in the webbing. She didn't have time to jerk it free before the man would be on her.

This is going to hurt.

Running out of options, she bowled herself sideways at his legs. In her head, she thought the angle would make it impossible for the blade to hit her, but geometry had never been her favorite subject and she didn't feel great about the decision.

Her already bruised ribs ignited with pain as she felt the man's knee give way in a direction unnatural for that joint. She heard his attack roar shift into a yelp. As soon as she hit the ground she scrambled to her feet, every movement agony, and kicked the man's fallen sword away from him. He rolled in the dirt, wailing as she finally ripped her gun from its holster.

"Freeze!" she screamed, hoping her command would inspire the man on the ground *and* the man Broch had engaged to cease their attacks. She turned in time to see Broch thrust his blade into the last man standing. With only a muffled grunt, the attacker collapsed to his knees and flopped sideways to the floor.

The first ninja remained folded on the ground, sprawled and still.

Broch sniffed, staring down at his fallen foes. He seemed confused.

"Thay didn't ken howfur tae fight."

"I can see that." She stretched her neck to peer at the man Broch had skewered with his fellow ninja's sword. He groaned, his hand clamped over his side as he tried to stem the flow of blood darkening the fabric above his left kidney. She glanced at Broch.

"He'll probably live, but we're going to have to have a refresher talk about stabbing people. You can't just go around

Katana-ing people."

"Och, ah barely scratched him."

"You stabbed me," said the ninja, his voice strained and grunty.

Broch frowned down at him. "Ye wur trying tae *murder* us."

The wounded ninja's body relaxed, his head lolling to the left.

Catriona tapped his foot with the toe of her shoe. "He passed out."

Catriona moved toward the man writhing on the floor behind her.

"Who are you?" she asked.

The ninja had removed his mask and he spoke through gritted teeth. "You broke my knee."

"You're lucky that's all I broke. Have you seen your friend? Who are you?"

The man lifted his chin, doing his best to look defiant. "We're the Disciples of Pinky."

Catriona squinted. "Really? Do you *hear* yourself? Why are you here?"

"Pinky's been reborn. He's teaching us."

"Reborn, how?"

The man fell silent and Catriona kicked his leg. He howled in pain.

"Reborn, *how*?" she repeated.

"I don't *know*. He called to us. Had us come here."

"How did he call to you?"

He didn't answer and Catriona cocked her leg, preparing to kick.

"No, no, wait! The dark web. I set up a page there called The Disciples of Pinky and he found it. He contacted me there."

"So you're all a bunch of sad, lonely serial killer groupies?"

The man grimaced. "We're not *groupies*."

"Uh-huh." She put down her foot and turned to Broch. "That explains why they were such terrible fighters. They're a bunch of murder-nerds."

"Acolytes," muttered the man.

Catriona rolled her eyes. "Same thing. Where's the other girl?"

"I don't know."

Catriona prepared to kick him again and he waved a hand at her.

"I *swear*! I swear. Pinky has her. I don't know. He told us to stop anyone who came through here."

"Did you see him? Who is he?"

"Who?"

"*Pinky.*"

"He's Pinky."

"Pinky is *dead*. Who is this new asshole?"

"I don't know. We didn't see him."

"You just said he told you to wait for us. How? On the phone?"

"He told us to come here and then slid a note under the door." The man nodded to the door farthest to the left.

Catriona shook her head. "Unbelievable. I wonder what's behind door number three."

"It's just a room," said the ninja.

She didn't even have to raise a foot.

CHAPTER SEVENTEEN

Anne Bonny looked up from where she sat at her desk at Parasol Pictures' payroll office. She'd sent the usual employee, Jeanie, on an all-expenses-paid vacation to station herself near Catriona Phoenix and her Highlander boyfriend, on the orders of her own boyfriend, who'd just walked in the door.

Which was strange, because he'd been in New York that morning.

"What are you doing here?" she asked.

Michael heaved a sigh as he shut the door behind him. "The Kairos are falling ill and—"

Anne held up a palm. "Hold on there, Sport. You already lost me. What's a Kairos?"

The moment she'd seen Michael's face she'd felt a heavy, wet, woolen cloak of *dread* drape around her shoulders. She'd spent most of the previous three hundred years—since her transformation from 'famous female pirate' to Sentinel—as a soldier for mankind's mysterious guardians, the Angeli, hunting and rebooting the infected rogues in their midst. Now, the battle was *supposed* to be over. All the infected Angeli had been *fixed*. She was off the hook, job done, with seven hundred years left to enjoy retirement.

Then this mess in Los Angeles. She'd been sent to spy on Catriona and Broch—she wasn't sure why. She hadn't seen much. Catriona went to Los Angeles and came back looking like she'd been hit by a car. A woman who looked a lot like her came rushing in demanding access to her apartment... There was a lot of action, but nothing that said end-of-the-world doom.

She'd been about to ask Michael if she could come home to New York.

But now, here he was.

That didn't bode well. She sensed her retirement growing shorter by the second.

Michael took a deep breath, closed his eyes, and then slowly released it as if he was tired of explaining life to a child.

She let it go.

"Kairos are enhanced humans like you," he said studying his perfect nails. While Angeli only had one *identity*, it didn't stop them from manifesting themselves as the most *perfect version* of that identity. Especially fastidious Michael. He never manifested clothes that didn't cost more than most people's apartments. His hair was always impeccable. And when he wanted a favor from her, he manifested the sexiest little dimple in his left cheek—

Oh no.

There it was.

The dimple.

She groaned and Michael's brow knit.

"What's wrong?"

"Nothing. So, Kairos are Sentinels like me?"

"No. They're more like Angeli when it comes to their duties, but less...uh, proactive."

"What does that mean?"

"It means we make *changes* to keep the world in order. Kairos simply *inspire* people to be better. Think of them as beacons of light. They inspire goodness in the people around them. They're scattered about time and space and shift as needed." He sniffed. "We can't do *everything* ourselves."

"Of course not. Poor babies. And these Kairos have Perfidia now too?"

Anne hated even saying the word. *Perfidia* was the disease

that had ravaged the Angeli, turning some into monsters. Monsters *she'd* had to fight.

Michael shrugged one shoulder. "I'm not sure. It doesn't look good. Something's going on. We've been getting strange reports since about sixteen fifty-three."

"Military time?"

"The *year*."

"And you're just looking into this *now*?"

The Angeli rolled his eyes. "We don't perceive time the same—"

Anne huffed. "Yeah, yeah. You're *special*. I get it. Why don't you have a seat? This feels like it's going to take a while."

Michael took a seat in an upholstered chair.

"I knew this couldn't last," she muttered.

"What?"

"Life without Perfidia."

"Well, it *is* the only reason you exist."

Anne scowled. "That's like telling someone they only exist for leprosy."

"I mean literally, you'd be dead. Remember that little bit where you woke up after being stabbed on your pirate ship? You never would have awoken if we hadn't extended your life to help us defeat Perfidia."

"Fair point. *Still rude.* I thought maybe you and I could be like a normal couple for a while." She heard a tinge of whine in her tone.

"That depends on your definition of normal."

"Hm. I'm not sure either one of us is the person to ask."

Michael smiled. "Perhaps not."

Anne settled back in her office chair. "So tell me more about the Kairos. How many of them are there? Where are they?"

"They're all over. But it's a group in Los Angeles that's caught our attention."

"They're the sick ones?"

"One is, we suspect, maybe more. We don't always know."

"Can't you ask all the other Kairos to check-in? Whoever

doesn't show up is a suspect? Like you did when the Angels started falling ill?"

Michael shook his head. "It's not that easy. They don't know they're Kairos."

"The *Kairos* don't know they're Kairos? How is that possible?"

"They start slow. They have no special powers beyond their sphere of influence, which grows over time. They move around from time to time—"

"Move where?"

"From time to time."

"No, *where*. Like from New York to L.A.?"

"No, from *time to time*. Like from the seventeen hundreds to the twentieth century."

Anne gaped. "And they don't *notice* this? They go to sleep on hay and wake up in a spaceship and don't think, *boy, that was weird*?"

"They don't notice at first. The jump muddles their mind. Over time they start to remember their past lives—it takes longer for them to find their purpose. It's all part of the process. Some pick it up more quickly than others."

Anne scratched behind her ear, musing how confused the Kairos must feel the first time they remember they used to be in another time. *She* suffered moments like that. Living hundreds of years did that to you.

"I might like Kairos. We have a lot in common. We could start a support group. Complain about you people."

Michael scowled. "*You people*? The Angeli are single-handedly responsible for keeping *you people* from destroying yourselves."

"Don't get your wings in a tangle." Anne turned her head and smiled to herself, pleased she still knew how to get Michael ruffled. As arguably the most powerful Angelus, he leaned a tad *arrogant*.

It's a good thing he keeps me around to keep him grounded.

"So how did you hear about the sick one?" she asked.

"An Angel in the area let us know. An actress went missing

and there's some evidence she may have been syphoned."

"Kairos can syphon energy like the Perfidia did?"

"There's never been any evidence of it, but the Angel was able to identify some dust. Human remains."

"Dust? Not the husk of a body?"

"*Dust.*"

"That's different."

He nodded.

"Could they be turning into Angeli?"

Michael barked a laugh. "Don't be *ridiculous.*"

Anne cocked an eyebrow. "Did you forget about Con?"

Anne's ex-boyfriend and fellow Sentinel, Con Carey, had developed Angeli powers.

Michael scowled.

He wasn't a fan of Con.

He sighed. "Fair enough, but it's never come up before. If it *is* some sort of evolutionary leap, I can't stop their evolution any more than I could stop a child from becoming a teenager."

Anne chuckled. "Good analogy. Probably a similar evil." She tapped her front tooth with her fingernail, thinking. "Can I reboot infected Kairos the way I could Perfidia?"

"I don't know. You were created specifically to syphon infected Angeli. Kairos run at a different frequency."

"Do you need to create some kind of new Sentinel? Like me, only set to a different frequency? Or adjust me, maybe?"

"No. You're perfect the way you are."

She grinned. "Good answer. You're learning."

Michael flashed her a smile and then clucked his tongue. "Seriously, developing a new type of Sentinel could take eons, if we could even do it. We don't know much about Kairos. We know they exist and they help us do what we do, but we run independently. We've barely studied them more than a zoologist might study a species of monkey."

"I'm sure the Kairos would love that comparison." Anne rolled her eyes. "So, any ideas?"

"Not so much an idea as a *direction*. The two we asked you to watch—they're unique."

"How so?"

"Brochan is a sort of warrior class we've never seen before. He came into contact with the infected Kairos as a child and I think it triggered something inside of him."

"Like some evolutionary shift for battling the bad guy?"

"That's my theory. He comes from a strong line. His father took the arm of the same suspect Kairos, but it wasn't enough to reboot him back to inspiring good. Even so, I think this warrior might have the ability to help."

Anne clapped her hands together. "Well, then, there we go. Problem solved. Glad I could help. Can I go home now? I'm terrible at payroll. So many *numbers*..."

She stood and Michael shook his head.

Anne flopped back down again and sighed.

"Fine. What do you want me to do?"

"Brochan doesn't know what powers he has or how to use them."

"So *tell* him."

"We don't know either. Though I think a big part of his enhanced strength has been developed to protect Catriona. The female. She might be our ultimate answer."

"How so?"

"We're not sure yet."

Anne scowled. "You know, for such powerful beings, you people—" She paused. "I mean, you *Angeli*, really don't seem to know much of anything."

"I'm starting to realize that." Michael reached out and took Anne's hand in his, his blue eyes staring deep into her own. The dimple on his left cheek deepened.

She leaned back.

This isn't good.

"What are you up to?" she asked.

He smiled.

"They're going to need training."

CHAPTER EIGHTEEN

Catriona kept watch as Broch tore strips of cloth from the fallen ninjas' costumes and used them to dress the stab wound. When he was done, he used the excess to gag and tie the unconscious man to Catriona's already hobbled victim.

He pressed the hobbled ninja's palm into his friend's wound.

"Keep pressure oan it," he instructed.

Broken Knee's eyes widened and he said what sounded like *you've got to be kidding me* as well as he could with a gag in his mouth.

Broch squatted down and patted Broken Knee on his cheek. "Ye'd rather he die?"

The man rolled his eyes and pressed.

Catriona and Broch moved to the far left door to find, as the acolyte had promised, it opened to a room, empty but for a desk and a chair. The surface of the desk was empty, apart from a silver-framed, larger version of the photo Marlon had shown Catriona of his father at the U.S. Open.

Catriona lifted the photo to study it more closely. "Does this seem odd to you?"

Broch cocked an eyebrow. "Aye. Is thare anythin' 'ere that isnae odd?"

"True. But this..." Catriona tapped the frame.

"Mebbe he's been keeking *Dungeon Decorating* on the

HGTV." Broch laughed at his joke. He'd been smitten with house shows as of late. They served as a primer of modern conveniences for him and as far as Catriona could tell, now he wanted *all of them.*

She smiled and rolled her eyes to demonstrate she'd heard the joke before getting back to business.

"This photo struck me when Marlon first showed it to us. Some sort of blood sport I'd buy, but golf seemed *civilized* for a guy whose hobby was snipping people's pinkies."

Broch huffed. "There's nothin' civilized aboot golf. Ah played. It made me wantae wrap mah club aroond someone's neck."

Catriona closed her eyes and tried to remember watching the U.S. Open with Sean. She found herself sitting on Sean's sofa in his office at Parasol. Golf played on the small television. Sean sat, tilted back in his office chair, feet on his desk, watching.

There must be something here.

Behind Sean hung a calendar. Staring at it, she could *feel* it was June sixteenth, a Friday. Golf generally ran from Thursday to Sunday, so that meant the tournament had run from the fifteenth to the eighteenth.

Eyes still closed, she talked her way through the timeline, recalling the facts of Pinky's dark history.

"Pinky's fourth victim disappeared from her daily jog the evening of June thirteenth."

"Aye. Sae?"

"They found her dead on Sunday the eighteenth."

That's it.

She opened her eyes and held up the photo. "That's the exact time Pinky was hundreds of miles away at the U.S. Open. How did he kidnap and kill a girl *here*?"

Broch shrugged. "He teuk her, murdered her, keeked some golf and then came back to dump her body."

Catriona shook her head. "That *could* work, but when they found her, her body was fresh like the others. He always alerted the authorities to where they could find his victims *moments* after he'd dumped them."

"She hadn't been deid while he was gone." Broch swept his hand through the air, motioning to the room around them. "He kept her chained and *then* killt her when he returned?"

Catriona shook her head. "I don't know. That's risky. I have another idea. How about *it wasn't him.*"

"Whit wasnae him?"

"*Everything.*" She thrust out the photo. "See? This rebuilt warehouse is supposed to be accurate, but why would Pinky put a photo of *himself* at a golf tournament in the middle of his *own* torture maze?"

"Sae the eejits like these can worship him?" Broch jerked a thumb in the direction of the ninjas.

"Maybe. But it seems unnecessary. Those idiots were already ready to kill for him."

Broch tapped his lip. "Tae put the wummin at ease? Mak' thaim think he's a good man who loves golf and then *snip.*" Broch pantomimed clipping off his pinky with shears.

Catriona shook her head. "I don't think so. I think this photo is special to *Marlon.*"

"Marlon?"

She nodded. "I thought it was weird how eager Marlon was to show me this photo. Then here it is again where the cameras won't miss it. He's *bragging.* He's telling the world *he's* the one who killed the girls. Just like a kid, he ran out and grabbed a victim while his dad was away."

"*Girls?* All o' thaim?"

"*All of them.* I bet the girls' disappearances *all* coincided with golf tournaments. Easy enough to check."

Broch scowled. "But the wee cop shot the *da.*"

"Soto shot the man he saw stuck in the wall and assumed that's who cut him. But think about it, why would some sick mastermind get caught in his own maze? Maybe he couldn't pull back in through that little hole because Marlon prevented him. Marlon *wanted* the world to think his father was responsible."

"Och. Tae clean his slate."

"Exactly. But he *wants* someone watching this film to see this photo and figure it out. He's teasing us. *Daring* us to figure it out."

"Bit then he'd git caught."

"I bet he plans to be long gone by the time the movie's released."

Broch put his hands on his hips. "Shuid we gang back tae the front room and grab him?"

Catriona took a moment to consider the idea. "No. I don't think he's there."

"Ye ken he's in here."

Catriona frowned. "He knows *now* is the time to pick us off, in the maze he knows best. Before we open the doors and ruin his plans."

CHAPTER NINETEEN

Catriona left the small red-doored room to reenter the larger rectangular area and Broch followed.

Doors one and two remained open following the ninjas' dramatic entrance, both leading to darkened halls. Broch was about to ask Catriona which hall she'd like to try first when he heard what sounded like whimpering.

He cocked his ear toward door one. "She's 'ere."

With Catriona holding her phone flashlight aloft behind him, Broch hustled down hall one as fast as he dared until a door stopped his progress. He tried the knob.

"Locked," he whispered.

Placing his ear against the door, he heard the whimpering noise again. He took a step back and threw his shoulder against the door. It gave way easily, the frame splintering around them.

A dark-haired young woman perched on the end of a cot, her mouth gagged. She jumped as they entered, screeching, but her arm, chained to the wall behind her, jerked her back to the cot.

"Jessica?"

At the sound of a woman's voice, Jessica stopped thrashing, her wide, red-rimmed eyes shiny with fresh tears. Catriona removed the gag and Jessica's body shook, her teeth chattering with nerves the moment the cloth left her lips.

"*Ohmygod*, I can't believe you found me. He heard you coming. You saved me. He was just about to—"

She motioned to a pair of shears on the ground.

Sobs rose in Jessica's throat and Catriona put an arm around her. "Who did this?"

"It was *Marlon*. I thought he was kidding at first but—"

"*Yes*," hissed Catriona, pumping her fist.

Jessica blinked at her.

Catriona winced. "Sorry, I'd guessed Marlon was the one."

Broch snorted a laugh and then returned his attention to the girl.

"Whaur did he gang?"

Jessica's brow knit. "What?"

"Where did he go?" translated Catriona. She shot Broch a look, which he translated as *See? I told you you need to work on that accent.*

With her free hand, Jessica pointed to what looked like an open vent at the bottom of the wall across from her cot. Broch looked at that hand and then the one pinned to the wall, relieved to confirm she still had all her fingers.

Catriona's eyes widened. "He went through the *vent*?"

Broch squatted and peered into the hole.

"You can't fit through there," said Catriona. "These low tunnels must be how he sneaked around, that little creep. Slithering like a snake." She turned her attention to the cuff around Jessica's wrist. "We have to get her out of here."

Broch tested the chain spanning from the cuff around Jessica's wrist to the wall. He gathered the chain near the plate and, blocking the girl with his body, gave it a yank. It ripped free.

"The walls ur lik' paper."

Catriona motioned to the door. "Take her back to the dining hall."

Broch scowled. "Whit aboot ye?"

She glanced at the vent and he shook his head. "Na. Na. Yer nae goan in there wi'oot me."

"I can fit. You can't. Having you here does me no good."

He glowered at her. "*Na.*"

"Listen to me. You're getting her out of here, and I'm going after Marlon."

"Wait 'til ah git back."

Catriona shook her head. "I can't wait. He'll be long gone."

Jessica tugged at Broch's shirt, the chain hanging from her wrist jangling. "*Please.* I have to get out of here. Did you already save the other lady?"

Broch glanced at Catriona and she shook her head, almost imperceptibly. Broch easily translated that look as well.

Don't tell Jessica the other girl is dead.

He looked down at the actress.

"Ah'm aff tae git ye oot first."

It wasn't a lie.

"Go with him," said Catriona.

The girl stood, wobbly on her shaking knees.

Broch knew what he had to do, as much as he couldn't bear the thought of leaving Catriona behind. He had to get the girl to safety. He froze, wishing he had a twin so he could send him out with the girl and he could stay with Catriona.

Na.

He couldn't split himself, but he wasn't leaving yet.

Nae until ah dae this.

He took a step toward Catriona.

"Kiss me, wifie."

Catriona's brow knotted. "What?"

"Ah'm askin' ye fer a kiss. Dae ah hae yer permission?"

"Um..." Catriona glanced at the girl. "Is this really the time—"

"Aye or na?"

She nodded. "Sure. Yes."

Broch leaned down and pressed his lips to hers. She slid her hands along his sides and gripped him tightly to her. He thought he could feel her shaking, but didn't know if it was his kiss or her plan to follow Marlon that was responsible.

He liked to think it was the kiss.

With a final press of his lips, he pulled from her grasp and turned to scoop the frightened girl into his arms. His gaze met Catriona's once more.

"Ah'll be back."

She tittered.

"You sound like Arnold Schwarzenegger."

He had no idea who that was.

CHAPTER TWENTY

Anne left her post at Parasol Pictures, leaving the office empty. Everyone would have to deal with their own payroll issues today. Michael had provided her with an address and left to run some Angeli-business errand. Apparently, this new address would be her home until they figured out what was going on with the Kairos.

Yay.

She spotted a familiar face walking toward her as stepped outside. Jeanie, whose place she'd taken, had a husband who worked on the lot as well. Naturally, he'd needed to go on Jeanie's vacation, too, so Anne had replaced him without Michael's help.

"We've got a mission," she said.

Her ex, Con Carey, strode toward her with his trademark bowlegged swagger. Thanks to a Perfidian attack, Con had lost the use of his corporeal form for over a hundred years, but now that he had his flesh back, it seemed he hadn't forgotten how to puff his chest. He'd probably swaggered as a ghost, too.

"Aye?" he asked. "Did I see—"

She nodded. "*Michael.* Yep. He's here."

"Did ye tell him I'm here?"

"Not yet. I didn't want to ruin his day."

Con laughed.

"Come on," she said, heading for the parking lot. "He got us a house."

Con chucked the shovel he had resting on his shoulder to the side of the payroll office and followed.

"I guess that means we'll be staying a while?" he asked.

She nodded.

"Yep."

Anne drove them to a large white home not far from the studio. Con grinned as they pulled into the driveaway.

"Now this is more my style," he said.

Anne agreed the upgrade would be nice. They'd been staying at a hotel, and while the place wasn't a *dump*, it would be nice to stay in a proper home.

Anne used the code Michael provided her to open the door. Inside, she found the Angeli had left her another surprise.

"*Jeffrey.*"

Her assistant, Jeffrey, stood in the large modern kitchen, a jar of something in his hand.

"They didn't have the kind of jelly you like—" Jeffrey scowled at Con. "What's *he* doing here?"

Jeffrey wasn't a fan of Con either. That was the one thing Michael and Jeffrey had in common.

"I could say the same to you," said Con strolling to the large sliding doors in the back of the house to stare out at the massive square pool.

Anne took a moment to gape at it as well.

This is definitely an upgrade.

She returned her attention to Jeffrey, who'd resumed putting away groceries. Just having him to cook for her again would be *amazing*.

"Michael flew you in?" she asked.

Jeffrey nodded. "Yes. Though I don't know why. Los Angeles is the *worst*."

"Agreed," said Con, looking at Anne. "So what's the dirty Angel got us doing this time?"

Anne sighed. "We have to train the same people we were watching."

"Train them to do what?"

"Fight. I guess."

Con scowled. "Fight who?"

"I'm fuzzy on the details. Her sister, maybe. Something's up with her. The father they've talked about." She sighed. "I planted bugs in their apartments, but I haven't listened to everything yet. I supposed I should do that now."

"Sounds like a plan," said Con, pulling his shirt over his head. "I'm going to hit the pool."

CHAPTER TWENTY-ONE

Catriona watched Broch and Jessica leave before lowering herself to the floor and peering into the tiny tunnel.

Her stomach twisted into knots. She'd forgotten how much she hated small spaces.

This is possibly the dumbest idea I've ever had.

The screen of her phone warned it had fifteen percent power left.

She sighed. "Great. Perfect timing."

Turning on the flashlight, she shimmied into the vent. Phone in one hand and gun in the other, she used her elbows as pikes to drag her body through the tube.

Progress proved awkward with no free hands to help. Unwilling to tuck away her gun, she took a moment to balance the phone in her cleavage. The soft glow between her breasts illumined the path before her and she continued forward, singing Neil Diamond's *Heartlight* in her head with adjusted words to distract herself from rising claustrophobia.

Turn on your boob light...let it shine wherever you go...

That's when she saw it.

A wire had been strung across the vent. She put down the gun and pulled the phone from its breast nest to get a better look. The wire hung from the ring of a grenade, which perched at the top of the duct, held tight by duct tape.

If she hadn't turned on her *booby-light*, she would have

triggered the *booby-trap.*

That little bastard.

Stuffing the light back into her dress, she untaped the grenade and moved it to the opposite side of the vent. Gathering her gun, she held her breath and slithered on her side past the balled wire.

Catriona's nerves strummed in her chest. She pushed her thoughts toward happier moments—those moments before she'd been stupid enough to crawl into the vent.

That kiss.

The kiss had made her insides woogy.

That was better than this bull—

Her eye caught something in the distance.

Hold on. What's that?

Catriona identified a *glow* at the end of the tunnel and turned off her flashlight to keep from announcing her presence as she worked her way toward the edge.

The vent dumped into a hallway much like the first they'd encountered. Flat black paint covered the surfaces and razor wire coiled down the walls like ivy.

Grateful to be out of the tube and to release the pressure crawling put on her aching ribs, she stood and stretched. An impossibly dim bulb hung from the ceiling, allowing her enough light to keep her flesh from being sliced to pieces as she moved. She could also save her dying phone battery by turning off the flashlight.

Holding her gun ahead of her, Catriona crept forward, a step at a time, searching for Marlon and the exit. She wasn't sure which she wanted more. Odds were good Marlon had left the building. Not a *terrible* thing. If she could get to Konrad's trailer and call the police, they might be able to cut him off on his way out of the desert.

That would mean mission accomplished and she wouldn't have to do the capturing. The cops could find Marlon and handle that part later.

Catriona had taken less than ten steps when she heard a faint scraping noise behind her. The synapses in her brain burst like fireworks and she pictured Soto talking to her earlier in the evening.

I heard this scraping noise...

Catriona jumped straight into the air with both feet.

Glancing down, she caught a glimpse of a scalpel sweeping beneath her. Marlon had slid himself through a hole in the wall at ground level, his upper torso visible, much as she'd pictured Pinky when Soto told his tale.

The scalpel in Marlon's hand arced up, trying to slice her, even as she rose into the air. The whites of his eyes flashed as he strained to reach her. Before he could readjust, she landed hard on his wrist with her heel. Her other foot found the cement floor, providing her much-needed balance.

She heard the scalpel clatter to the ground.

Marlon yelped in pain. She kicked him hard in the face and pointed her gun at him.

"Don't move."

Marlon's opposite hand whipped out of the hole and she nearly fired before seeing him grab for his already bleeding nose.

"Bitch!"

Catriona dipped down and pushed the scalpel far from his reach with her fingertips. He shifted, attempting to wriggle back into his hole.

"Oh *hell* no."

Catriona dipped down to clock Marlon on the side of his head with her gun. The blow stunned him long enough for her to grab him by the armpits and jerk him into the hall. She roared as pain exploded across her injured ribs.

Once Marlon was out, she stepped away from him to point her pistol from a safe distance.

He scrambled to his feet and whirled to face her.

It seemed she hadn't hit him as hard as she'd hoped.

Sneering, he wiped his bleeding nose on his arm.

"What now?" he asked.

She continued to hold him at gunpoint, her heart racing, a muscle in her back aching from pulling his weight through the hole with such a sudden and awkward yank.

"Your father was at the PGA Open when the fourth victim was kidnapped, killed, and dumped," she said.

Marlon grinned and leaned back as he put his hands on his hips. "You got it. No one else did. I'm impressed."

"You used your father as a patsy. Was he *ever* involved?"

Marlon laughed. "My father? He was a *mouse*."

"And you're a monster. Congratulations. Let's go."

Marlon shook his head. "Where? I won't lead you out of here."

Catriona glanced behind her. The dark hallway continued. She realized her work was far from over. She'd have to lead Marlon at gunpoint through the maze—hopefully, before another booby trap blew her up, or the little creep scurried into another hidey-hole—

A cracking sound snapped behind Marlon and he ducked, arms covering his head.

Catriona stepped back.

What now?

A black dress shoe thrust through the ceiling. It appeared and disappeared several times in rapid succession as large chunks of the plywood ceiling tore away and rained to the ground behind Marlon.

Catriona stared.

That's my shoe.

Broch's face appeared in the hole that had been created. A moment later, he dropped from the ceiling to the ground. No sooner did he hit the floor than he straightened and struck Marlon full-fist in the face. Marlon fell back, his head landing at Catriona's feet.

She tapped his head with her bare toe. He didn't move.

"He's out."

Broch grinned. "That wis mah plan."

"Couldn't fit through the vent so you went *over the top*?"

"Exactly. We shuid hae tried that sooner. Easy traivelin oan the framework up thare."

He scooped up Marlon and tossed him over his shoulder

like a sack of flour.

"Let's git oot o' 'ere."

CHAPTER TWENTY-TWO

Two of them.

Luther hadn't seen that coming. He knew about Rune. That skinny freak was hard to miss. But this other dude—he was short, thick, and fast. He'd been able to get to the warehouse's second-floor window in time to watch the two of them coming toward him, down the street, the small one running, something in his hands, some kind of bow.

Is that a crossbow?

It had been some time since Luther was last chased by a man with a crossbow.

Behind the squat man came Rune, striding like Ichabod Crane was late for a date.

Luther patted his hip. Luckily, he'd still had his work keys in his pocket, which included the keys to the spillover warehouse. He'd locked the door behind him but if they were determined, it wouldn't take them long to get through. It would take them a while to find their way to the second floor, though. The warehouse was enormous and cluttered, and the door to the stairs that led to the second level was tucked behind a large papier-mâché dragon. Well, it was *now*. It had been the largest, lightest thing he could get his hands on and he'd pulled it across the entrance as he closed the door behind him.

There was a second staircase in the back, but they wouldn't see that unless they circled the building and spotted it from the outside.

Luther glanced down at his empty hands.

How could I not grab my gun?

It had all happened so fast. No sooner did he spot Rune than the little one was coming after him, running down his hallway like a bull. He must have slipped in through the bedroom window.

He'd had two choices. Run, or stop and fight the bull, hoping his hands would be clear by the time Rune made it into the house.

Back at the house, the little man's trajectory had led him directly between Luther's position in the kitchen and where Rune would be entering through the unlocked front door. One last glance at the look on the little one's face and Luther had known the kid wouldn't go down easy. If Rune had a weapon he'd be a sitting duck.

So he ran. Burst through the back door and started running, cursing at himself for not anticipating the attack. He'd been late heading for Sean's and his mind had been on that.

He *hated* being late.

Luther leaned against the warehouse wall. Across the room, he spotted a large wooden bar once used in a western shoot. The bar would make a good shield, and its central location made it an ideal spot to keep an eye on both entrances. It was also near the window. If he had to, he could jump out. If he dangled there, he was pretty sure there was a small overhang above the door downstairs. It might break his fall. He'd have to remember to grab that ledge and hang. Jump too far out and he'd miss the overhang and impale himself on the fence. Squiggling like a pinned bug wouldn't be the best way to go.

The only light came from an old security system mounted near the ceiling. It illuminated the eyes of the fiberglass creatures positioned around the room. Every sort of prop was stored in the building, but it seemed all the strange, big-eyed ones had ended up on the second floor.

Luther heard a thump and then another.

They're knocking through the door downstairs.

Another thump and then a crash told him the door had been breached.

I need a weapon.

Luther began moving through the room looking for something he could use. He found a cache of swords behind a suit of armor. Not real, but stiff enough to do some damage.

Not bad.

It wasn't like he was going to find any guns. A half-assed sword would have to do.

Luther picked the heaviest one and swung it back and forth. It had been a while since he'd used a sword. He and Sean used to practice with swords from the sets, playing, but they hadn't for years. They'd gotten older and lazier. No real reason to keep up their sword skills in modern America. The chances that Star Wars-like lightsabres became the norm in the future ware highly unlikely.

"Like riding a bike," he mumbled to himself.

Time wore on as the noises downstairs betrayed his pursuers' growing impatience. They couldn't find him and hadn't noticed the door to the second floor yet.

A movement caught his eye. Luther turned as the door leading to the outside creaked open.

How? He'd checked and that door had been locked.

They'd breached the *downstairs* door. He hadn't heard them try the second floor entrance.

Then, he heard a rough voice call his name from downstairs.

That has to be the little one.

He looked at the second-floor door.

This must be Rune.

Luther crept forward to hide behind the door as it opened.

A nose appeared, followed by a forehead and a patch of white hair.

Luther had been about to stick his visitor in the gut when something struck him.

White hair?

Rune didn't have white hair.

Luther reached around the door and grabbed the visitor by the chest to jerk him inside.

He felt the tip of a gun poke into the soft spot beneath his chin where his jaw bone split.

CHAPTER TWENTY-THREE

Broch and Catriona leaned against her truck as the EMTs carried a body bag from the warehouse. All she wanted to do was go home, but they needed to wait for the police to finish questioning them.

Konrad wandered over.

"The publicity—"

Catriona shook her head. "Don't get excited about the press. A woman and one of your fake troopers died, Konrad."

"Mebbe a ninja," muttered Broch.

"Hopefully not." Catriona had already resolved to tell the troopers *she'd* stabbed the ninja so they wouldn't look too deeply into Broch's identity. They'd made him a fake I.D. but it wouldn't hold up under scrutiny. But, if she was going to confess to stabbing someone, she didn't want to end up in jail, either.

Konrad wrinkled his nose. "You're right. Sorry."

"I'm sure you're still going to be fired."

"You think? This was Marlon's fault. Not mine."

"I dunno. Bad decisions were made. *Really* bad decisions."

"What if the movie does well?"

Catriona sighed. "There's a chance the studio won't remember how stupid your stunt was if ticket sales triple."

Konrad grinned. "That's what I'm thinking. I mean, it's not my fault the kid was crazy."

"The families of the deceased might not see it that way."

"Shit. That reminds me. I have to call my lawyer."

"And your insurance," called Catriona as Konrad headed toward his trailer without another word.

"Whit an eejit," muttered Broch.

"Welcome to Hollywood."

"Ah wish ahd come back tae Scootlund instead o' this devilish place."

"But then you wouldn't have met me."

Broch put an arm around Catriona and her body filled with warmth as if someone had poured a soothing elixir over her aches and pains. She snuggled against him.

This is nice.

"True. Ah tak' it back."

"You're like some kind of natural aspirin," she mumbled.

"Eh?"

"Nothing."

Catriona spotted a police officer approaching and stepped forward to shake his hand, slipping out from beneath Broch's arm as she moved. Instantly, her body ached again.

So weird.

After an interview that seemed longer than their time in the maze, they were cleared to leave.

Catriona tried Sean for a third time as they walked to the Jeep but got no answer. "Let's get back to Sean's. I can't reach him."

"He's mebbe asleep."

"Probably." Catriona yawned. "Lucky guy."

They drove the twenty minutes back to Sean's house in exhausted silence. Once back, Catriona went to Sean's bedroom and rapped lightly on the door.

"Sean?"

She poked her head in.

The bed was empty. She opened the door more fully and stepped in to check the en-suite bathroom. He wasn't there.

"Sean?" she called down the hallway.

"Nae in his kip?" asked Broch.

"No."

She heard the patio slider open as she checked the spare room and living room. By the time she'd re-entered the kitchen, Broch had returned from outside.

"He's nae outside."

"Oh, duh, his *car*."

Catriona jogged to the door that led to the garage and flipped on the light.

The Jag was gone.

"He left. Do you see a note anywhere?"

Broch's head swiveled and he leaned forward to snatch a piece of paper from the kitchen counter.

"Here."

Catriona glanced at it.

Went to see Luther.

She sighed. "Good. I guess Luther couldn't make it because of car trouble or something, so the mountain went to Muhammad."

"Eh?"

"It's an old saying."

Broch rolled his eyes. "Ah ken whit ye *think* yur sayin'. But it goes, 'If the mountain will not come to Muhammad, then Muhammad must go to the mountain.' That makes Sean *Muhammad*, not the mountain."

Catriona stared at him. "How do you know that?"

"T'is Francis Bacon."

"If you say so. But how do you know *that*?"

Broch frowned. "Ah had schooling. Ah remember things, too, ye know." He tapped his skull. "It's nae just a rotten potato up 'ere."

"Can you see things that happened before in your head like me? Relive them in detail?"

Broch shrugged. "Nah. Ah dinnae ken sae. But ah remember written things better than most."

"Hm. I didn't know that." Catriona leaned against the counter and felt her knees beginning to weaken. Part of her wanted to grab Broch and kiss him for being so damn sexy and smart, but a much larger part of her screamed for sleep.

"We should go to bed."

"Aye. Ye've black under yer eyes."

"I do?" Catriona dragged a finger beneath each eye to find mascara on them. "Was I like that the whole time?"

"Much of it."

"Why didn't you tell me?"

Catriona moved to the bathroom and washed her face. She grabbed one of Sean's t-shirts from his room to use as a sleeping shirt and pointed Kilty to her childhood bed.

Another good reason not to jump him right now. This is just weird.

"We can sleep here. Luckily, I had a queen mattress as a kid so it won't be too bad."

He slid into bed and she slipped in beside him. Broch pulled her against him to spoon, his flesh warm in the chill of the sheets. Again, she felt a heat ooze through her body and her aches evaporated.

"You feel good," she murmured, barely able to keep her eyes open.

"Sae dae ye," he whispered. "Wifie."

She swallowed. She'd almost forgotten about the accidental marriage.

What am I going to do?

Overwhelmed with worry, she closed her eyes and pushed it all away until tomorrow.

CHAPTER TWENTY-FOUR

"Sean," Luther hissed, as the tip of Sean's gun settled against his chin.

Sean unclenched his jaw and lowered his weapon.

"That's a good way to get shot, Luth."

Luther huffed. "*You* were the one in trouble, sneakin' up on me—"

"I'm not sneaking up on you, I'm *looking* for you, jackass. There are two men downstairs."

"Two sounds right."

"Who are they? I saw one through the downstairs door who looked like Rune."

"Yep. It's Rune and somebody I don't know. Little guy, built like a bowling ball."

"What are you doing in here?"

"Seemed like a place I could lose them. I'm not the greatest runner these days. Couldn't go on forever before they caught me."

Sean put his hands on his hips. "How long have you been here?"

"You mean how long until they find me? They've been running around down there for a while. They'll come upon the door leading up here soon enough. I got it hid behind a papier-mâché monster."

"You were supposed to be at my house hours ago."

Luther grimaced. "Oh, *excuse me*. I'm a little busy trying to not get killed."

"Point is, you couldn't have been hiding up here for two hours."

"I was already late, okay? I admit it. And then this."

"You should *call* when you're going to be late," muttered Sean.

Luther shook his head.

Sean put his hands on his hips and looked around. "Anyway, is this door and the hidden one downstairs the only two ways up?"

"Yeah. Pretty sure. I chased a boy from that kid show they shoot on seventeen once. Spent over an hour looking for that brat in here."

"Which kid?"

"The one with the pug nose."

Sean clucked his tongue. "I knew that little bastard was up to something."

"Yeah, he is. Dealing to some of the other kids and a few of the adults, too." Luther heaved a sigh. "You should know something."

Luther's heavy tone caught Sean's attention and he looked at him. "About the kid?"

"No. I'm not going to be here much longer."

Sean scoffed. "What are you talking about? At the end of the world, there'll be nothing left but you and the cockroaches."

Luther shook his head. "It's time for me to go. It's your turn."

"My turn?"

"It's why you're here. You came here to take my place when I move on."

"Here in this warehouse?"

"Here in this *time*."

Sean walked toward the door leading downstairs to put his ear against it. "What are you talking about? Where are you going?"

Luther grinned. "I'm movin' on up the food chain."

"Could you make an ounce of sense, please?"

"I'm becoming an Angeli."

"A *jelly*?"

"*AN-jell-ee*"

Sean frowned. "Is that some sort of cult?"

Luther's low chuckle, so familiar and reassuring, almost made Sean forget the hunters downstairs.

Luther made sure the door leading outside was locked and then turned back to Sean.

"In the beginning, we *inspire*," he said.

Sean raised his hand to his head to rub his temples. "Oh no. You *did* join a cult."

Luther shook his head. "*No*. Dumbass. Listen. In the beginning, we *inspire*."

"Who? Inspire what?" Sean glanced at the door that led outside. "Can we just go? We could be far away by the time they realize there's an outside door up here."

Luther ignored him. "*Us*. We inspire people who come near us to be better people."

Sean leaned against the old western-style bar and resigned himself to listening. "Yeah, yeah. I figured that much out," he said. "Us time travelers."

"Yes. And some of us get kicked up the line should a spot open up."

"And become *jelly*."

"*Angeli*."

"Right." Sean said *Angeli* again under his breath, trying to get the pronunciation right. As he pictured the possible spellings, he realized the word reminded him of another. "Do you mean *angels*? Are you saying we become angels?"

"I guess. Maybe." Luther ran his hand across his balding head as if thinking on the topic roiled his brain so much he had to soothe it. "I don't understand it all yet. He told me about it but he was in a hurry."

"Who?"

"The voice in my head. It's why I was late for dinner."

"Because you were talking to an *angel*?" Sean sighed. "Oh boy."

"I don't know who it was, but I know the Angeli *make* good happen, whereas we can only inspire it."

"Got it. And I'm here to take your place after you move up?"

"Yes."

"As what?"

"Senior Kairos."

Sean shook his head. "You lost me again."

Luther smiled. "All will become clear."

"If you say so, Yoda. I think you must have hit your head." Sean fell quiet a moment and then looked up at Luther. "Why me?"

"Because you've been doing this longer than almost anyone."

Sean snorted a laugh. "As far as I know I haven't been doing anything at all."

"That's a lie. You know you've jumped through time. You know you *have* to help people. *Have* to. Not *want* to."

Sean sighed. "Maybe. But it hasn't been that long—"

"It's been longer than you think. Every time you jump, you lose some of your memories. Some of your past lives. You have to, or the horrors of all the evil you've tried to stop, the memories of all the loves and children you've lost, would eat you from the inside."

Sean felt his jaw fall slack. He could *feel* Luther was telling the truth and it made his mouth dry.

Who have I forgotten?

He squinted at his old friend. "You're saying I've been alive doing—whatever I do—for longer than I know? That I've had past families I don't even remember?"

"Yes. Me too. Though, mostly I remember now." He smiled. "The memories are good. Even the bad ones are good now."

"What about Catriona and Broch? Will I forget them?"

"Maybe not. They're like you."

"So *they'll* lose family and the memories of those families?" Sean felt himself become agitated. *What curse have I left for*

Broch? Have I passed it to Catriona somehow?

Luther sighed. "Want to know a secret?"

"There's *more*?" Sean heard his pitch rise and covered his mouth with his hand.

Luther leaned toward him and almost whispered the words. "Catriona and Broch are older than you are."

"*What?*"

"She's special. She's a lodestone."

Sean felt like his brain was spinning in his skull. "Luther, I swear—"

"Listen to me. Catriona's a great source of good. Her presence can inspire amazing things. She's going to be very important in the war ahead."

"War?" Sean struggled to find the words. "Does she know this?"

Luther shook his head. "She did. But Rune cut her down too soon in her last life. Before her memories returned to her."

Sean raised his hand to his head, covering his eyes, hoping the darkness would help him make sense of everything. "When is all this happening?"

"Soon. The Angeli have suffered losses. The same disease infecting Rune took them down, too. That's why I'm moving up."

Feeling weak in the knees, Sean squatted, his arms between his legs, eyes locked on the ground. Luther smiled down at him and Sean marveled at his friend's peaceful, *amused* expression. Every word tumbling from Luther's lips made him want to run screaming from the building.

How can he be so calm?

Luther moved to the door to listen again. "Broch exists to love and protect Catriona."

Sean chuckled. "Even I figured that out."

"It's more than that."

"You said she's special...?"

"Yes."

"And he keeps her safe so she can—"

"Protect us all." Luther's lips pressed into a hard line. "I haven't even told Michael all this."

"Michael?"

"He's an Angel. Big shot. He's in town, sniffin' around, trying to figure us out. But it all just sorta came to me. All this *knowledge*." Luther rapped his skull with his knuckle.

Sean looked away, his mind drifting to his children. "Seems kind of lopsided."

"Huh?"

"That Broch *lives* to protect Cat. I mean, does she love him back?"

Luther nodded. "She does. Always. Sometimes it takes longer than other times for them to find each other."

"How long have they been doing this dance?"

"Long time."

"When you say a long time, I imagine that means a *long* time."

"Oh yes, brother. They're like the original Romeo and Juliet."

Sean bit at his lower lip, asking himself how he felt about all this new information.

Is that why I found Catriona? Was everything planned before I even knew—

"They're coming," said Luther.

His words didn't immediately register with Sean. Things clicked when he heard steps on the stairs and Luther ran toward him. The big man pulled Sean with him as he passed, and they dove behind the bar as the door crashed open.

Sean raised his gun and popped up from behind the bar long enough to aim. He shot at the short, stocky man leading the charge into the room. The one who, no doubt, had put his shoulder to the door. With a yelp, the man twisted and flipped backward down the stairs. Rune threw himself flat against the wall to avoid his partner as he tumbled and then bolted toward the window covering his head with his arm. Sean re-aimed and fired again. He caught a glimpse of Rune jerking as if he'd been hit.

"You get 'em?" asked Luther as Sean dropped back behind

the bar.

"Hit them both. Little man fell down the stairs. Rune's by the window."

They waited another moment and then peered over the edge of the bar, craning their necks to see.

Rune had collapsed at the foot of the floor-to-ceiling tinted window occupying most of the eastern wall.

Sean and Luther looked at each other.

"That was easy," said Sean.

"Hm."

They stood. Sean crept to the stairs to check that the bowling ball wasn't returning. Luther moved toward Rune.

Finding the shorter man still crumpled at the bottom of the stairs, Sean turned to join Luther. He saw his friend poke Rune with his foot. "What are you doing? Don't—"

Rune's boney hand shot out to grab Luther's ankle. The big man roared as if Rune's touch burned him and, leaning forward, wrapped his massive hands around Rune's shirt, jerking him to his feet.

"Not on my watch!"

Rune leered and reached for Luther's neck.

Sean leaped forward.

"*Stop!*"

Luther lifted Rune from his feet as if the man were as light as the clothes he wore. Rune clung to him. Unable to throw the man, Luther ran toward the large window. Rune's back struck the glass first, and it shattered against the weight of the two of them.

Rune's eyes bulged wide as the hand once reaching for Luther's neck flailed, searching for something to stop his fall.

Sean saw a flash of red where Rune's fingers clawed at jagged glass.

And then both men were gone.

"*Luther!*"

Sean ran to the space where the tinted window had been, wobbling at the edge to keep from falling. By the glow of the front door's floodlight, he saw Luther sprawled on the cement below, an ever-growing disc of dark red pooling around his head like a demonic halo.

Rune lay not far away at an odd angle. It took Sean a moment to realize he'd fallen half on a loading ramp and half off. His spine hooked like a letter C, his back broken.

A movement near Rune caught Sean's eye. He squinted.

A rat.

A large rodent scurried from beneath the loading ramp to sniff Rune's broken body.

Sean was about to spin away from the window when he spotted Rune's hand whip from his side like a cobra to snatch the rat. He heard a squeak and saw a small flash of light, and then the rat was gone.

Rune sat up, vertebrae popping like corn as he straightened. His gaze settled on Luther before shooting upward to lock on Sean.

He smiled.

Sean felt the blood drain from his cheeks.

"Oh no you don't, you son of a bitch."

Sean raised his gun. The jagged glass poking from the window frame bite the back of his hand. He cursed, and the gun fumbled from his fingers to fall to the ground below.

Rune laughed.

Swearing, Sean ran for the stairs, nearly falling down them in his haste.

Luther hadn't fallen.

Luther had *jumped*, tackling Rune on his way out.

He'd sacrificed himself to save Sean.

Why?

Sean hit the bottom step and rounded the corner of the building.

He stopped.

Rune was gone.

Luther lay in the same position, unmoving.

Sean turned and stared through the front door, looking for the short man who'd been sprawled at the bottom of the stairs.

He'd disappeared as well.

Did he help Rune get away?

Did it matter?

Breaking into a low, crouching jog, Sean ran to his friend's side and grabbed his hand.

"Luther?"

He felt no pulse. He tried in vain to start Luther's heart, but it quickly became clear that no amount of CPR or chest-pounding would wake him.

Luther was dead.

The big man's eyes were closed, but the corner of his mouth had twisted into a coy smile.

As if he had a secret.

Another one.

CHAPTER TWENTY-FIVE

Fiona stared out the window, her chin resting in her palm. She'd gone through her social media accounts and responded to all the fans she could bear. She'd posted some old photos she'd been meaning to add. She deleted some losers and followed some people she hoped could influence other people to follow her.

She'd gone through all of Catriona's drawers and found what her sister *apparently* considered her nail tools, doing her best to smooth some rough edges on her middle and index fingers. She couldn't bring herself to repaint her nails with Catriona's cheap polish. The little jars looked twenty years old and straight from the nearest convenience store.

She'd finished snooping through the bedroom closet when Catriona called to let her know she wouldn't be returning. Her sister told her to stay put under the penalty of death and blah, blah, *blah*.

After that, Fiona tried to leave, only to have the guard stop her. He told her he was under orders to call the police and have her committed for observation if she tried to leave.

Nice touch, sis.

The guard was probably bluffing or repeating whatever nonsense Catriona had told him to say, but she'd *been* to a public mental health facility before and had no intention of going back. If they pulled her records it could take weeks before they let her out again.

Sis would be no help.

She returned to Catriona's apartment and wrote *bored* on a piece of paper a dozen times in a dozen different styles.

While staring out the window and stretching her neck, Fiona caught a glimpse of someone walking past Catriona's apartment on their way to the gate.

Bet they'll let him through without threatening to commit.

She stared daggers at the *free man*, and then something struck her about his hair and gait.

I know him. What's his name, what's his name...

Ah.

Pete.

The studio's resident doctor. She'd tried to talk him into doubling her Xanax prescription once, and he'd been surprisingly difficult to bend to her will.

A studio doctor with scruples.

What's the point of that?

His last name was something that rhymed with No-See-Um, the nickname for the way he kept his mouth shut about the indiscretions of the actors. *That,* she appreciated.

Hello, Pete.

She tugged on the window but it didn't budge.

"Dammit, what the—"

Lock. Duh.

She twisted the lock and tried again. It slid open just as Pete began to disappear from her direct view. She craned out the window.

"Hey, Pete!"

The blond man stopped and turned to squint back at her.

"Hey." He paused and cocked his head. "Are you wearing a wig?"

"It's Fiona Duffy. I'm Catriona's sister."

"The reality show actress?"

Fiona felt her lip twitch. "Just *the actor* is good, but yes."

"Right. I remember you." he added.

Fiona broke into a broad grin.

Don't piss him off, Fiona. He's your ticket out.

"I'm kidding, Pete. You can call me whatever you like, just as long as the paychecks keep coming."

Pete took a few steps forward. "So you're Catriona's sister? Did I know that?"

Fiona lowered herself to her knees so she could stare out the window without having to hunch. "I don't know. Probably not. *We* didn't know it until recently."

"Huh." Pete looked down and rocked from heel to toe. "I haven't talked to her lately. She's been...*busy*."

"You mean she's been with that giant slab of beef."

He shrugged, but Fiona could tell she'd touched a nerve.

Ooooh, somebody has a crush on Catriona.

She thought for a moment.

That means he's straight. That hadn't been her first guess.

Hope abounds.

"Why don't you come up here and have a drink with me?" she asked giving him her best saucy wink.

He seemed uncomfortable. "Are they there?"

"Who?"

"Cat and Sean Connery-on-steroids."

"No. They're not coming back until tomorrow. It's just me and I'm so *bored*." Fiona tried to lean forward so Pete could get a better look at her cleavage. If she could have, she would have removed a breast and tossed it down to him—anything to gain her ticket out of Boredom Town. "Come on up and keep me company."

"I don't know..."

"Please?"

Peter's head began to nod. "Yeah. Okay. Why not? I was just going to pick up some Chinese."

"We'll order out here. We'll get some wine and order a pizza."

She had no intention of eating carbs but pizza seemed like a thing a man would like.

"That works. Be up in a second."

"The door has a code. I'll come down."

"I know it."

Really. How intimate.

She was about to pull back inside when she realized she didn't have to spend hours talking Pete into what she *really* wanted him to do.

I'm going about this all wrong.

She thrust forward again. "Hold on. You know what? It's weird to be in Cat's place. Let's take a road trip and get dinner. You said Chinese. My treat."

Pete grinned and thrust his hands into his pockets. "Did you just ask me out on a date?"

As if.

"Why not? Down in a sec."

Fiona shut the window and adjusted her boobs to maximum bumpage before jogging to the bathroom to check her face. While in there, she caught a glimpse of a black dress she'd noticed in Catriona's closet.

Hm.

It will probably be too large but...

It was worth it to look her best *and* look as much like Catriona as possible.

Though, in my opinion, those two things are mutually exclusive.

NoSeeUm was her ticket out. If he liked Catriona, she would *be* Catriona.

Fiona slipped into the only pair of heels in Catriona's closet and searched for her keys before realizing she'd *walked* from her place to her sister's after her run-in with Rune.

Dammit. No car.

No matter. The good doctor would have a car. And with him crushing on Catriona and Catriona smote by the Highlander, she could get Pete to do *anything* for her. Wasn't Cat's *sister* the next best thing? Revenge against the woman who'd spurned him—*priceless.*

Fitted as well as possible into Catriona's dress, Fiona strode into the hall and took the elevator down. As the doors opened she spotted Pete waiting outside, his hands still in his pockets.

The payroll office was dark and closed for the night.

Thank god. Something about the redheaded payroll lady made her uneasy. It felt like she was *watching* her.

Fiona slowed before opening the door to appear poised and in control as she made her exit.

Like a pro.

Pete's gaze roamed her body as she made her exit.

Mission accomplished.

"Is that Catriona's dress?" he asked. The words sticking in his throat.

"Hm? Oh, I needed to borrow something. Do you like it?"

"She bought that for emergencies. She's worn it to almost every job she ever had to be dressed up for."

"The same dress?" asked Fiona, horrified.

Pete nodded. "I helped her pick it out."

He sounded wistful.

"So you two are pretty close."

Pete seemed to blush. "Yeah. I mean—"

"Until *he* showed up."

He looked away. "She's been busy."

Fiona put out her hand and traced the back of Pete's ear, letting her fingers trail down his neck. He shivered. Leaning forward, she whispered.

"You're too good for her."

Pete giggled and then cleared his throat. "I don't know about that."

"I do. Come on. Let's go."

Fiona slipped her arm through Pete's and led him toward the gate.

"Where are we going?" he asked.

"I don't care. You can pick it."

"I don't want to take advantage of your kindness."

"Oh please. Take advantage of me. I *want* you too."

Fiona watched for a reaction and spotted Pete swallowing hard.

Too easy.

"So..." Pete seemed to search for a way to break the sexual

tension only he was experiencing. "Did you hear about Dixie?"

"Who?"

"From the new craft show. She went missing."

"Really?" Fiona feigned interest and picked up her pace as they approached the gatehouse.

"Hold it." The gate guard stepped out to block the door as they approached. He pointed at Fiona. "She can't leave."

Fiona eyed the chubby guard with her best glare but he refused to wither. Too full of misplaced pride for the tiny bit of power he wielded.

Here we go.

Pete's brow knit. "Come on Don, what's up?"

"He's my doctor," added Fiona. She slipped her arm out of Pete's to make it seem more likely she was under medical care and not skipping down the yellow brick road.

The guard pressed his lips together into a hard line. "I dunno. Cat said you weren't supposed to leave under any circumstances."

"Cat said?"

Pete's voice changed as he said her sister's name. It sounded as if he'd found out the Queen would be stopping by for tea.

She scrambled.

"My sister meant without a doctor's supervision. But I've got Dr. Noseeum—"

Pete looked at her. "Roseum."

"Right. Dr. *Roseum.*"

Pete leaned close and spoke in her ear. "What's this about supervision?"

She whispered back, careful to be sure her lips brushed his ear. "It's a joke. Catriona told them I was insane and not to let me out."

Pete chuckled. "Really? She's so funny—"

Fiona felt her mood darken. The boy was hopelessly smitten with her stupid sister.

Time to work on the guard—the one staring at her tits.

"Let us through, Dan," she purred.

"Don," said the guard and Pete in unison.

"*Don*. We're going for dinner to discuss my, uh, medication and then I'm coming back. Cat will never know."

Don scowled. "Why do you have to go to dinner for a checkup?"

"My pills have to be taken with food."

Ridiculous, but it was the excuse that popped to mind. Fiona did her best to keep a straight face.

The guard looked to Pete for confirmation, and Pete nodded. "It's okay. I'll be with her the whole time. I'll bring her back."

The guard shrugged and stepped back into his little house. "Go ahead. But if there's any blowback, *you* talk to Cat."

"Will do."

Fiona wobbled a little as she and Pete walked into the parking lot. Catriona's shoes were loose on her feet and had started to rub. It didn't help Pete's car was apparently parked in another state. The lot was big, but it felt as if they'd been walking forever with no end in sight.

"*Where's* your car?" she asked, trying not to sound as impatient as she was. She still had to talk him into driving her to her house.

"It's that one right—" Dr. Pete's face fell slack.

"What's wrong?"

The life in Pete's eyes seemed to dim.

"Pete?"

The doctor dropped to his knees and then face-planted onto the asphalt. Fiona sucked in a breath, horrified at the sound it made.

"Pete —?"

Fiona noticed what looked like a dart sticking from his back, complete with feathers flowing from the back of it as if she'd stumbled into a jungle movie.

"What the—?"

She felt a sharp prick below the base of her neck and reached up to slap it as if it were a mosquito. Her fingertips brushed the side of something hard, but she couldn't reach it.

Her spine seemed to give way as if the tension support holding up the structure of her body had collapsed. She folded her legs to drop straight down and avoid landing on her face like Pete.

It still hurt when she hit the ground.

Fiona threw out her hands to protect her head. She felt the sharp bark of skin tearing from her elbow as she slipped into darkness.

CHAPTER TWENTY-SIX

"We hae tae gang."

"What?"

Catriona opened her lids, but it was as if her eyeballs had rolled back in her head and she couldn't get them straight. The world flashed in staccato bits. Someone sat beside her on the bed, shaking her shoulder.

"We hae tae gang."

Catriona rubbed her eyes until they centered. "*Go.* The word is go, not *gang*. And why? Go where?"

"Back home. It's Sean. He's in trouble. Ah hae tae gang. *Go.*"

Catriona sat up and looked at her watch. It was four-thirty in the morning.

"Did he call?"

"Nae."

"Did *someone* call?"

"Nae."

"Then how do you know he's in trouble?"

Broch took her face in his hands, placing one palm against each of her cheeks until she could see nothing but his face.

"Ah kin *feel* it."

Catriona squinted into his eyes and found him convincing. "Fine. Let me call him."

He released her and Catriona fumbled for her phone. The

cord she'd used to plug it in the night before was too short and as she tried to pull it to her, it ripped from her hand and clattered to the floor.

Spaz. Calm down.

Groaning, she leaned over the bed and scooped it up to try again, hoping to prove the Highlander wasn't psychic. She didn't want to admit it, but she had a niggling feeling something was wrong, too. Her anxiety had started with Luther's absence at dinner and had only grown from there. It had taken the resurrection of a serial killer to distract her. Broch sensing Sean was in trouble now brought all her concerns rushing back.

She heard Sean's voice on the other end of the line and perked for a moment.

"You've reached Sean Shaft. Please leave a message. If this is an emergency—"

Damn.

"Okay," she said, swinging her legs out of bed. "Let's go."

They scrambled into their clothes and jogged to the Jeep. Catriona threw Broch her phone.

"Keep trying him."

She heard the muffled ringing of Sean's phone again and again as she drove, each time ending in the same voicemail message.

"He willnae answer. Cannae ye drive faster?"

"Not without getting pulled over or blowing the engine on this poor old girl." Even so, Catriona pushed the pedal a little harder and heard the Jeep moan with reluctance. She was a trusty old machine, but flying down the desert highway at a hundred miles an hour was more than an SUV with its own AARP card should be asked to do.

Catriona kept her eyes locked on the road and eased to ninety. There were very few cars on the desert stretch of highway so early in the morning. While that was a good thing, it also meant she didn't have taillights ahead to warn her about potential speed traps that would only slow their progress.

On the upside, she felt *amazing*. She hadn't realized it right away, but it was as if all her aches and pains had simply vanished overnight. Falling asleep in Kilty's arms, she remembered having the passing thought she'd probably awake in even more discomfort.

Quite the opposite.

"How do you feel today?" she asked Broch.

"Eh?"

"How do you feel? Especially good, bad, anything?"

"Ah tellt ye, ah'm worried aboot Sean."

"No, not that. I mean how do you feel *physically*?"

He shrugged. "Aboot the same as usual, ah ken. Yer lip looks better."

"Yeah?"

She touched the spot where her lip had been swollen. It felt smooth. Normal.

Hm. So weird.

Maybe Sean was on to something, sleeping in the desert. Maybe the dry air helped bruises heal. Maybe lizards had licked her split lip back together while she slept.

She touched it again, finding it hard not to think about lizards licking there.

Ew. Why do I think things like that?

Forty-three minutes and fifty phone call attempts later, the glowing Parasol Pictures sign rose into view.

"Hauld yer horses." Broch reached out to touch her arm as they entered the parking lot.

"What?" Catriona glanced at him, nearly forgetting to brake before the Jeep hit the guard gate. The tires screeched to a halt. The night guard burst from his booth, waggling his hands in the air.

"Whoa, whoa, *whoa!*"

The guard dropped one hand to rest it on his gun. Catriona pointed at her face, hoping he could see her through the glass.

Easy there, rent-a-cop.

Broch opened his door and jogged away through the outer lot.

Where—

"Where is he going?" she heard the guard ask as she rolled

down her window. He echoed her own thoughts.

She hopped out. "I don't know, but you get your hand off your gun right now or you're fired."

The guard took a step toward her, his expression a mixture of anger and confusion. It wasn't Don, whom she'd asked to keep an eye on her sister the night before. Shift change was at midnight. She didn't know the new guy.

The guard moved his hand from his weapon but maintained his mean expression. "Who are you? Show me your I.D."

"I'm your *boss*." It was a half-truth. Only Sean and Luther had direct seniority over the guards, but she was pretty tight with *them*. "How long have you worked here?"

The guard sniffed. "Three weeks."

Hm. That explained the crappy hours. Catriona supposed she rarely pulled in at three a.m.

"Look, I'm Catriona Phoenix. I'm security for the studio—"

"Catriona! 'Ere! Noo!"

Catriona's head swiveled away from the guard. Broch had stopped fifty yards down the parking lot and now sat on his heel, crouched over something and beckoning to her.

Is that a person?

Catriona gasped.

Sean.

She broke into a sprint.

"You can't leave this here!" yelled the guard behind her.

"Call an ambulance!" she screamed back.

Sean. It has to be Sean. Something's happened.

As she grew closer she saw the sneakers on the body's feet and knew immediately it wasn't Sean. It wasn't until she was nearly on top of Broch that she could see the man's face. He lay on his stomach, nose peeking out beneath a shock of moppy blond hair.

"Pete?"

Catriona kneeled beside her friend.

"Shuid we turn him ower?"

"I don't know. I don't think we should move him. There's

the possibility of spine injuries and head trauma and all sorts of—"

Pete groaned.

"Pete?"

Pete moved his arm to push himself to his side, his tongue darting out to lick at the blood covering his lips.

Broch winced. "Och. His face looks lik' ground lamb."

Pete rolled himself to his butt, propping himself up with one arm. His face was a sheet of dark red from his nostrils to his chin. His nose had swollen to twice its usual size and the ridge down the center had relocated itself to the left. He stared up at Catriona and smiled, the blood between his teeth casting a ghastly hue.

"Hey Cat." He reached up and touched her hair. "I love you."

Catriona recoiled, embarrassed. "Stop kidding around. We have to fix your face."

"What? Why?" He reached up to touch his nose and then jerked his hand away with a squeal of pain.

"Because I think your nose is broken."

"You *think*?" Pete yelled the words, though the movement of his lips seemed to cause him further discomfort. "I must have fallen on it."

"You tripped?"

"Tripped? No, I...Where's Fiona?" Pete turned to look left and then, more slowly, right. He wobbled and repositioned his hands to steady himself as he finally focused on Broch.

"Oh. *You*," he muttered.

Catriona mimicked his visual sweep of the lot, seeing nothing unusual. "What about Fiona?"

Pete coughed and then groaned. "Do either of you have any water? My mouth feels like I've been eating cotton balls."

"Pete, what about Fiona?"

"She was with me. She was going to buy me dinner." He closed his eyes and tilted his head back. "Dinner, dinner, fo finner, banana fana bo binner..."

"Buy *you* dinner?" Catriona did the math and began to nod.

"Oh. You mean she used you to get by the guard."

Pete scowled. "No. I mean *yes*, but I think she likes me."

"Did she pretend she was under your care as you passed the guardhouse?"

He scowled. "Maybe."

"She *used* you. What happened to her?"

"I don't know. I felt something hit my back and then I don't remember anything." He looked around. "Why is everything so wobbly?"

Broch moved around Pete to lift his shirt. He remained quiet as he scanned the doctor's skin. "'Ere. A wee pinprick."

"He's stabbed?"

"Na. Lik' a wee dart."

Pete jerked his shirt down. "Get off me, you big monkey."

Broch stepped away, staring down at Pete with his hands on his hips. "Ah dinnae think he's right in his heid. The wee dart was poisoned."

Catriona scanned the ground.

"Where's the dart?"

Broch shrugged. "They took it back."

"So someone shot him with a dart, he fell on his face and they grabbed Fiona."

Pete frowned. "Who goes around shooting people with *darts*?" He giggled as if he'd told a joke.

Catriona searched the surrounding asphalt for evidence, finding nothing but pebbles and more of Noseeum's blood.

Broch put out a hand to help Pete to his feet. "Git up."

"No. Go away. I have a secret for Cat." Pete slapped his hand away.

Catriona sighed and looked at Broch. "Go to the guard gate and make sure he's called an ambulance. We better get him checked out."

Pete poked his chest. "*I'm* a doctor." He gingerly felt the shape of his nose. "Though I'm not sure I have the balls to straighten this myself."

Catriona scoffed. "Let me save you some time. *You don't.*"

"Thanks for the vote of confidence."

Broch strode in the direction of the guard box as Catriona squatted back down beside Pete.

"Would you let someone who earned their medical degree in the Caribbean straighten your nose?"

He barked a laugh. "Never."

"Exactly. So let's get someone else to do that for you."

He nodded. "Point taken. But ouch, jeeze." Pete took a deep breath as he watched Broch walk away and then turned his attention to Catriona.

"Seriously, why *don't* you love me, Cat?"

Catriona looked away. "Pete, the drugs have you loopy."

He grabbed her arm to regain her attention. "No. They have me *clear*. I realized last night that I have to know or I'll never get over you. We've known each other for so long. Why am I always in the friend zone with you?"

She peeled his fingers from her arm and took his hand in hers. "It's not you. It's me."

He rolled his eyes. "Oh come on."

"Pete. Look at me."

He did, and she felt a wave of nerves as she prepared to tell him the truth.

Why would I tell him this? Do I need to hear it out loud myself?
She pushed through.

"It's me. I'm serious. I'm not capable—" She stopped.

Pete tugged on her hand. "What?"

She took a deep breath and squeezed his hand. "How many relationships have I ruined?"

"With men?" Pete chuckled. "All of them. You're like a love buzzsaw."

"Exactly. And how long do they even last?"

He shrugged. "Days? Weeks?"

"Could it *always* be *their* fault?"

"I—"

"I'll answer for you. No. It's *me*."

Pete's eyes went soft. "But you're *wonderful*."

"I'm not. Not to date. I sabotage every relationship. I can't be happy. I don't know why."

"Are you going to do it to him too?"

He looked past her and she turned to glance in Broch's direction. He was talking to the guard.

She shrugged. "Probably."

She thought about having to tell Broch they needed to dissolve their accidental marriage and something in her chest throbbed with ache. Her eyes began to water and she blinked hard.

She wiped her eyes discreetly, thankful Pete seemed too wrapped up in his drama to notice her tears.

He pulled her hand toward his chest. "But I *know* you, Cat. The others—"

"But that's just it, Pete. I love you too much to ruin our friendship. I couldn't bear losing you."

Pete's shoulders slumped. "Couldn't you just ruin our friendship a *little*? For, like, a week?"

"What?"

"Maybe twenty minutes? Could you ruin our friendship for twenty, hot, sweaty minutes?"

Catriona laughed and pushed his shoulder. "You're terrible."

"Ow."

She helped him to his feet. "So you have no idea what happened to Fiona?"

Pete's attention wandered to the east. "It's morning?"

"Yes. What time was it when you left?"

"Maybe ten? Eleven?"

"Last *night*?" Catriona raised a hand to her forehead.

Fiona's been gone a good six hours.

She could be almost anywhere.

"Have you seen Sean?"

Pete licked his fingers and used the spit to rub the dried blood from his chin. Dark flakes fluttered to the asphalt. "No. Not for a couple of days. Why?"

"Nothing."

Catriona turned as Broch returned.

"He called the ambulance," he said.

"Could it be *Fiona* you sensed in trouble? Not Sean?" she asked, hopeful.

Broch shook his head. "Nae. It was Sean."

Catriona's phone rang in Broch's pocket and he retrieved it to look at the screen.

"Speak o' the devil."

"It's him?" Catriona snatched the phone from his hand and pressed it to her ear.

"Sean? Are you okay? We've been calling—"

"I'm fine. Are you still at my house?"

Hearing his voice, a wave of relief flooded Catriona's body. "No. We're at the studio. Someone knocked out Noseeum and grabbed Fiona."

"I need you at the warehouse. The one down the street from Luther's."

Catriona scowled, finding it worrisome Sean hadn't reacted to her kidnapping news.

"What's wrong? Was there a break-in?"

"No. It's Luther."

"What happened?" As she asked, she heard the bark of a police radio on the other side of the line. "What's going on?"

Sean released a ragged sigh.

"He's dead, Cat. Luther's dead."

CHAPTER TWENTY-SEVEN

Catriona and Broch arrived at the Parasol warehouse moments before the crime techs finished with Luther's body. The big man lay on the ground, tinted broken glass scattered around him like ash, a pool of drying blood beneath his head.

Catriona covered her mouth with her hand and closed her eyes, willing the vision to go away. She had never seen Luther so still. She feared the image of him so broken would never leave her.

When she opened her eyes again she saw Sean standing nearby, his face pale. He spotted them and motioned them over.

"You made it."

Catriona fought back the lump rising in her throat. "What happened?"

Sean stared up at the broken window of the warehouse as he answered. "Rune. Luther tackled him through the window."

"Why?"

"To save me. To save us. Who knows? He was talking crazy before it happened. Like he knew it was coming." Sean pulled Catriona to him and hugged her tightly against his chest. "I'm sorry. I didn't want you to see this."

Catriona grappled with the idea of Luther purposely following Rune through the window. There had to have been another way. "I don't understand. Why would he do *this*?"

"I don't know."

Sean's right hand was covered in blood, much of it dried, some still glistening. On the ground near his foot, a little pool had collected, splash marks spattered on his shoes. She grabbed his wrist to inspect it.

"You're cut."

Sean looked at the gash on the outside of his palm as if he were seeing it for the first time.

"Glass," he muttered, chin thrusting up toward the broken window.

"It's deep. You should get it looked at while they're here. You might need stitches."

He didn't answer and instead motioned toward the parking lot with his other hand. "You two go find Fiona. I don't want you messed up in this.

"But—"

"I have to stay and talk to the cops."

"You can't tell them about Rune." Catriona grimaced as the words came from her mouth.

Duh.

Sean flashed her the withering glance she'd expected. "You're saying I can't tell them there's a time traveler from the past hell-bent on destroying my family?"

She looked up at the window. "Speaking of Rune—did he fall, too?"

Sean nodded.

"Where—?"

"He walked away."

"How?"

Sean sucked his tooth as if he wasn't sure what he wanted to say.

"Near as I can figure? A rat helped him."

Catriona squinted at him. *"What?"*

"I could see his back was broken from up there. Then he grabbed a rat that came sniffing after the blood and..."

Sean trailed off until Catriona couldn't wait any longer.

"And *what?*"

"It was like he absorbed it. Used it somehow to heal

himself. He was gone by the time I could get downstairs."

Catriona stared at him, speechless.

"How is that a *thing*?"

Sean shrugged. "I don't know. What happened to Fiona?"

"She tried to leave my apartment using Dr. Pete to clear the way."

"What's Pete got to do with anything?"

"I told the guard not to let her out. She used Pete as a key."

"Ah."

"From what we could get from Pete, someone shot him with a dart and he passed out. When he woke up, she was gone."

"A *dart*? Like from a tranq gun?"

She nodded. "I guess. The dart wasn't there anymore."

"What time was this?"

"Around midnight? He was fuzzy when we talked to him. Broke his nose, too. Looks like he has a potato screwed onto his face now. We sent him off with the ambulance."

Sean seemed to ponder this new information. "It could have been Rune and his friend. They could have gotten there by then." He motioned to the shattered glass around them. "After this happened, I spent a while looking for Rune before I called the cops. I searched Luther's apartment for clues and followed the path from here to there a few times. I told the cops I found him like this."

Catriona gasped. "Without Rune, they're going to think he jumped."

Sean nodded. "I'm not sure I should dissuade them. Fewer questions."

"But Luther would never—"

"I know. He's got a niece in Florida. I don't want her to think he killed himself."

Catriona fell silent.

"Whit kin we dae?" asked Broch.

Sean put a hand on his son's arm. "Go. I mean it. I've got this."

Catriona snapped from her trance. "Are you sure?"

"Yes. But keep an eye out. There was a short, Hispanic-looking man with Rune. Thick-bodied. I shot him, but he disappeared with Rune. I don't know where he went or who he is."

"But he was working with Rune?"

"Definitely."

Catriona frowned. "Great. Now there's two of them."

On the way home, Catriona gripped the steering wheel, alternating between numbness and anger. She almost missed a red light and screeched to a halt.

"Are ye okay?" asked Broch, catching his forward momentum against the dash.

"No. I'm not. This isn't fair. Why would they kill Luther? I'm going to *kill* Rune."

She turned to glance at her back seat. Two gym bags sat there.

Perfect.

She made a left and Broch looked at her.

"This isn't the way hame."

"We're going to the gym."

"How come?"

"I need it. I need to hit something. If I go home I'm—" She felt the tears coming again and stopped.

"Ye kin hit me," said Broch, reaching over to give her leg a brisk pet.

"Thank you. I'd like that." She sniffed a little sobbing laugh. They'd sparred before and she knew she found striking the oak tree of a man immensely satisfying.

When they arrived at the gym, Brochan held open the door as Catriona stormed through, trying to clear her mind and pretend it was just another day at the gym. If she allowed her thoughts to wander to Luther, she'd start crying, and she had no idea how she'd ever stop.

Catriona nodded to the girl behind the counter and, after a quick change, headed into the kickboxing studio. It was blessedly empty. She set down her bag and retrieved the tape for her hands. Today, she would pound away with her fists, her feet, and everything else she could throw at the bag until she was too tired to cry.

Brochan dropped the makeshift training bag she'd gathered for him beside hers. It was pink, one of her old gym bags, but she knew he didn't mind the feminine color. No one would dare call the giant *girly*, not even if she'd given him a My Pretty Pony bag covered in glitter.

Not if they had any sense of self-preservation.

Broch taped his own hands, and she watched his technique as she finished her own.

"Good job. You remembered. It usually takes people a long time before they wrap that well."

He shrugged and held her gaze. "Whit aboot yer pains?"

Catriona positioned herself in front of the heavy bag, punching and kicking it lightly several times, testing out her sore spots. They seemed healed. What she'd felt sure was a cracked rib now felt fine.

"It's weird, but they're gone."

Brochan punched his bag and it shuddered from the force of his blow. Catriona returned to her workout, wondering whether it would be better to process the loss of Luther *while* she worked out, or better to push him out of her head and keep her pain locked down until she could find time alone.

Neither option seemed ideal.

Instead, she imagined Rune standing in front of her. Skinny bastard. *Bam!* One in the face. He's reeling. *Bam! Bam! Bam!* Repeated blows to the body. He's up against the wall. *Sidekick!* Now *his* ribs are broken.

She saw a flash of Luther's body on the ground, blood pooling beneath his shattered skull. Had it been quick? Had he known he couldn't survive the moment he broke through the window? Had he made sure to push Rune toward the wall to break his back as Sean had described, only to have him get away?

"Catriona. Catriona. Stop. Stop."

Broch grabbed her and pulled her to his chest. She realized she was sobbing—her hot tears dripping down Broch's arm.

So much for not crying.

He held her close to him, her head resting against his massive bicep. The hard muscles in his chest rose and fell against her body. He cradled her like a bird with a broken wing.

That was how she felt. Broken. Her wounds had healed, but she felt weak. Luther had been like a second father to her. The thought of a world without him...

She allowed herself to cry until her nose was stuffed and she couldn't produce any more tears. She felt Broch's lips press against the top of her head.

"It'll be all right," he whispered.

"I'm going to kill him."

"Ah ken."

She sniffed as embarrassment replaced her pain. It was one thing to cover the big man's arms in tears, but she felt self-conscious about the rivers of snot headed in his direction. She pulled back and wiped his arm.

"I'm dripping all over you."

He smiled. "Ah dinnae mind."

Another man had come into the gym, not as large as Broch but *fit*. He was already sweaty from working out in another part of the gym.

"Get a room," he said to them. It was a joke, but he sneered as he said it, catching Broch's eye as if to scoff, *women*.

Catriona looked at him and he laughed upon spotting her puffy eyes.

"Yikes. Breakup?" he asked.

Broch straightened. "Ye best mind yer own business."

"Yeah well..." He mumbled something under his breath Catriona couldn't catch.

Asshat.

Catriona suffered a sharp flare of anger. She wiped her face on her arm.

"You want to spar?" she asked.

The man snorted a laugh, looking back and forth from Broch to her. "*Right.* So you and the hulk can double-team me?"

"He won't be involved."

"Cat—" Broch touched her arm and she flinched away from him, white-hot anger burning behind her eyes.

She couldn't find Rune yet, but maybe this man would do for now.

Rune's proxy shrugged one shoulder. "Fine. Your funeral."

Broch made a small disapproving noise and Catriona shot him a look. "I'll be fine."

He nodded. "Oh, ah ken. Ah juist dinnae ken if yer in the richt mind fer this."

Catriona strode to the equipment area and suited in headgear and sparring pads. The man moved next to her and donned his own, smirking at her as he did.

Oh, I can't wait to smack that look off your face.

After padding up, she moved to the mats to await her opponent.

"My name's Jake, by the way," he said as he took his position across from her.

"I don't care."

He held out his closed fist to bump. "I just wanted you to know what name to call out for mercy." He leered, his gaze shifting in Broch's direction as his voice dropped to a whisper. "Maybe if you're lucky, you can scream my name out again, *later.*"

Catriona smacked her gloves together and then tapped her chest.

"Don't be afraid of him. Be afraid of *me.*"

Jake laughed. "*Whatever.*"

She bumped his glove with her own and dropped back, readying. As she suspected, he attacked seconds after the bump, running at her, flailing his arms like a monkey in an attempt to rattle her. She dodged and circled to the opposite side of the mat, avoiding him easily.

He turned to face her again, grinning.

"You gonna run away from me all day?"

Catriona smirked. "That was my gift to you. A moment to reconsider."

Jake raised his hands again and moved forward, thrusting out his foot in an awkward sidekick. Catriona moved out of the way and spun toward him, striking him in the side of the head with the back of her fist as she whirled past.

Jake grunted and ducked too late, stumbling off the edge of the mat.

He spat a curse as he corrected his balance and hopped back on the mat, pounding his gloves together as if he were psyching himself up for the next attack.

"You sure you want to do this?" taunted Catriona. "You're not very good."

Jake raised his gloves. Moving in, he kicked at her shins and she blocked him with her foot. He thrust forward with his right hand and she deflected. He threw a haymaker, stumbling forward, a victim of his momentum. As she pushed him past her, he stabbed the back of her arm with the point of his elbow.

Catriona turned toward the pain and saw his fist coming, a punch aimed at the back of her head, now about to strike her in the ear.

Cheap shot.

She dropped and punched forward, striking him in the lower abdomen with all her strength.

With a loud *oof!* Jake dropped to his knees, his gloved hands clutching at his stomach.

Catriona had her fist raised, ready to punch him in the head when she heard Broch behind her.

"Cat. Na."

She stood there, fist-shaking in the air, seeing only *white.* Slowly, she felt her control return and saw Jake wincing beneath her. She swallowed and lowered her hand. Jake's face pinched with anger and pain.

"Dirty bitch," he spat through gritted teeth.

"You started it." She strolled off the mat. "I think we're

done here."

"I'm going to report your ass," he said, taking his hand from his stomach long enough to point at her.

"*Whatever.*"

Catriona held out a hand toward Broch, silently asking for help removing her glove. His smirk seemed uncontrollable.

"He deserved that."

"I know. *Ow.*"

As he unpeeled her wraps, she felt a sharp pain run through her wrist.

"Are ye well?"

"I think I might have jammed my wrist on his liver."

Broch took her wrist in his hand and held it tight, acting as a makeshift wrist wrap. He tugged on her, just enough to make her look at him. When she did, he kissed her on her sweaty forehead.

"Yer terrifyin'," he whispered.

She felt her face grow warm. "He picked the wrong day to be a douchebag."

"Ah dinnae ken he gits a day aff."

She laughed. Broch released her wrist and they walked to their area, where she removed her pads and threw her wraps in her bag. As she did, she noticed her wrist no longer ached. She moved it back and forth and side-to-side, searching for the motion that had made it twinge.

Nothing.

Weird.

They gathered their things as Jake moved to his bag without saying a word. As they left, Catriona glanced back. Jake had been watching her, but he quickly looked away.

She smiled.

Her frame of mind had improved. The exercise and the pounding she'd given the jerk made her feel a *little* better about life. It was still a life without Luther, but, maybe he wasn't *dead.* Gone, but not dead. She, Kilty, and Sean had all died, only to appear again somewhere in another time.

She'd come back as a baby last time. Maybe Luther was a

baby now, somewhere far in the future. Some giant baby.

The thought made her smile.

She pushed open the gym door and marveled again that her wrist remained pain-free.

She eyeballed Broch as they walked to the car.

"Whit?" he asked, feeling her gaze on him.

"This might be a dumb question, but do you think it's possible you can heal people?"

Broch laughed. "Whit?"

"All my aches and bruises from my fight with Volkov disappeared after we slept together." She looked away, embarrassed by how she'd phrased her sentence. "I mean literally *slept* together, so close in that little bed."

Broch scowled. "Aye?"

"And just now you grabbed my wrist and the pain went away."

"That's nice tae hear ye ken sae, bit—"

Catriona grabbed at the spot where Jake had pounded his sharp elbow into the back of her tender arm and felt a dull ache.

"Right here. Is it bruised?"

She stopped so he could inspect the spot.

"Aye."

"Touch it."

"Whit?"

"Lay hands on it or whatever. Just hold it."

Broch rested a hand on the spot. "Lik' this?"

"Yes. Hold it for a second."

Broch squinted into the afternoon sun. "This is mad."

Catriona shushed him and waited, unsure how long his magic might take. When she thought as much time had passed as the time he'd held her wrist, she pulled away and clawed at the spot with her opposite hand. She poked and pushed on it, unable to find the bruise.

"It doesn't hurt anymore."

The spot between Broch's eyes bunched. "Aye?"

"Is it still bruised?"

Broch inspected her arm. "Nae."

Catriona took a deep breath. "What do you think that's about?"

He shrugged and held up his hands, his gym bag still hanging across one palm. "Ah dinnae ken. Ah ken ah'm magic."

She chuckled. "I *ken* you are."

As they walked toward the car, Catriona felt as though she had a lot to think about. She didn't want to have to pay attention to the road.

"You want to practice driving?" she asked as they approached the Jeep.

"Oan the road?"

"Yep." Previously, she'd only allowed Broch to drive around Sean's lot and on obscure roads where she didn't think he could run into trouble. Without a social security number, an iron-clad I.D., or any form of identity other than a worse-for-wear kilt, it was risky letting him drive, but he had to know-how.

She threw him the keys and took his bag from him before he jogged to the driver's side like a kid running to the tree on Christmas morning.

She threw the bags in the back and hopped in to sit on the passenger seat.

"Ready?" he asked, grinning as the Jeep roared to life.

"Don't kill me."

"Ah wouldnae dae that."

"That's what all the people who've killed me said."

Broch looked at her. Catriona waited to feel the lurch of the Jeep slipping into reverse, but it never came.

The weight of his stare became too heavy. "What are you doing?"

"Ah dinnae ken if ah kin bear it any longer."

"What?"

No sooner did she say the word, than she saw by his expression what he meant.

He's going to kiss me.

No. More than that. That look said something more.

She felt a trill in her abdomen.

I can't. I shouldn't.

She'd just finished telling Pete how she was going to hurt Broch. It wouldn't be fair—

Broch touched her arm and it felt as if a fire ignited in her veins.

Screw it.

He leaned forward and they grabbed at each other as if they were a meal each had been denied too long.

CHAPTER TWENTY-EIGHT

Fiona opened her eyes to find herself in what looked like the living room of the saddest, loneliest man in the world. Beside her sat a maroon, threadbare sofa, one cushion dark with greasy overuse. Beside it stood a chipped, light blue stool acting as a stand-in for the side table that wasn't there. On that, sat a can of beer.

She tried to raise a hand to rub her eyes, only to discover her arms were bound to her body by a thin but secure rope. She tilted back her head and felt it clunk on the back of the high-backed wooden chair. The chair peeked out on either side of her thighs.

She sighed.

Not again.

Fiona twisted her neck to get a better view of the rest of the room. On the walls sat racks and racks of weapons. Well, *racks* was a strong word for the mishmash of hooks and makeshift shelving, but each DIY project protruding from the wall held a prize. Swords, nunchucks, maces, sticks she assumed were made for the express purpose of hitting people in the face, darts, and plenty of other oddities she couldn't identify.

Because I'm not a psycho.

She noticed what looked like a long, bamboo pole hanging close to the darts and found her attention lingering. The fuzzy memory of a parking lot returned.

The feel of a pinprick.

Sonovabitch.

He shot me with a blow dart.

He. Probably a *he*. But who? It had to be Rune, but as she looked around the depressing bungalow the place didn't *feel* like Rune's house. What little she remembered of him, he'd always been fastidious. Not sloppy. Not *gross*. Not some weird weapons nerd.

Who else would want to hurt me if it isn't Dad?

She hadn't stabbed anyone else in the neck that she could remember.

There is something else.

She squinted, thinking, trying to tie together the loose ends flapping around in her muddled brain.

Ah.

What happened to the doctor she'd used to get out of the studio?

Did Rune kill him?

It didn't matter.

Unless he was in this same sad little house somewhere and could be of use again...

What was his name again?

"Pete?"

She called the name, quietly at first and then tried again and again until she was yelling.

She heard the sound of a door closing and snapped her lips shut, unsure the person coming was the person she was hoping to see.

A moment later, Rune walked into the room.

"Hello, Fiona."

Fiona felt a strange little burst of relief.

It *was* Rune.

That still doesn't bode well, but better the devil you know...

She swallowed and relaxed the muscles in her face until she imagined she looked half-asleep. She hoped to appear still doped, hoping it would give her an edge should the opportunity arise.

Think. Think. What do you say to a man you stabbed in the neck?

She offered him a weak smile. "Hi, Daddy."

Rune smiled back, surprisingly enthusiastically for the attentions of his black sheep daughter. The one who'd stabbed him in the neck.

"There's my girl."

As Rune grew closer Fiona saw a jagged scar on his throat. *Yikes.*

She'd sunk a pen into his neck. Somehow, he'd not only survived but completely healed in a day.

Nice trick.

"How, uh, are you?" she asked. She needed to get him talking so she could read his mood and divine what he wanted to hear. She was willing to say anything to get out of that depressing little room. She couldn't even *imagine* how the walls had gotten to be such a dirty off-white.

What do you name a paint that color? Milky Misery? Awful Alabaster?

Rune moved to sit and then, spotting the filthy state of the cushion closest to Fiona, moved to the next cushion down. He folded his hands in his lap and stared at her, smiling.

"How are *you*?"

Fiona glanced down where her arms would be if they weren't pulled behind her and wrapped in a clothesline.

"I'm tied up."

Rune nodded. "I'm afraid that's necessary for now."

"Why?"

"Because I need you close."

"Why?"

"Because you've been spending too much time with the others and you're letting them influence you."

He doesn't approve of the crowd I'm hanging with. Typical Dad behavior.

"Which crowd?"

"You know."

"No..."

"Ryft, his son, and that girl."

"That girl? My *sister*? Your *daughter*?"

Rune scoffed. "She's no daughter of mine."

Okay...

Fiona forced a laugh. "I haven't been hanging out with them."

"Yes, you have." Rune's hand rose to his neck, his fingers stroking his scar. "You never would have done this to me if you were right in your mind."

"I didn't mean to. You scared me."

"No. It's their influence."

"No, it *isn't*. In fact, I've only been talking to them as a *spy* for you."

Rune's head cocked. "What?"

"I'm infiltrating them. I'm going to, uh..." She fumbled for the phrase she'd once used while starring in an erotic espionage film... "...*collect intel* for you."

Rune seemed to consider this.

"That's very smart," he said after a moment.

"Right? That's what I thought. I wanted to tell you about it but—" Fiona changed direction. "I stabbed you to earn their trust."

"You did?" Rune stroked the scar again. "What if you'd killed me?"

"I knew it wouldn't kill you. I didn't cut through the jugular, did I?" Fiona crossed her fingers behind her back, hoping that detail didn't ruin her excuse. She'd certainly been *aiming* for his jugular but assumed she'd missed.

"You nicked it," mumbled Rune.

"Sorry. Sorry. That wasn't my intention. But you can heal, right? You took care of it." Again, a guess. He had to be able to heal. How else could he explain that scar growing in a day? If she could convince him she *knew* he could heal, maybe he would forgive her.

Rune nodded slowly. "I had to eat a woman."

Fiona grimaced. "I don't want to hear about your love life,

Dad."

"Huh? I *devoured* her. Ate her like a meal."

"What?" Fiona felt a cold rush of adrenaline dump into her veins. She hadn't seen that coming.

Dad eats people?

Rune rubbed at his forehead, avoiding eye contact with her as if he were embarrassed.

"I mean, not with my *teeth*. It's a figure of speech," he added.

Fiona realized her mouth was hanging open and shut it for fear of what might fly into it in that repulsive little hovel.

"Can you explain what you mean exactly?" she asked.

"You *know*. When we pull all the life out of someone and use the energy to heal ourselves."

"Oh. Right. Right." Fiona nodded and looked away, hoping Rune wouldn't see she had no idea what he was talking about. If she had the power to do what he suggested, she would have eaten her idiot assistant to heal her ever-deepening crow's feet years ago.

"And, uh, the woman you *ate*. Figuratively. She's dead now? Literally?"

"Yes. Of course. Dust. Poof." Rune closed his fists and then exploded his fingers outward to pantomime, Fiona imagined, the explosion of *dust* that had occurred after his snack.

"Was it anyone I knew? Not Catriona, by any chance?"

"Huh? No. She was an actress. Works with a girl named Maddie who might be helping me get to Sean and the others."

"Maddie," echoed Fiona, trying to place the name. "Maddie Barbeau?"

Rune shrugged.

Didn't Pete say something about the craft show co-host going missing? Someone with a stupid name...something Southern...Who was that woman Maddie was always complaining about?

"Dixie?" she asked, the name popping into her mind along with the vision of the woman it belonged to. Blonde, big tits. Just the sort of young up-and-comer she hated.

If Dad had to eat someone...

Rune grunted. "I think so. It doesn't matter. Do you name your food?"

"Do I...?"

Rune stared at Fiona, his eyes suddenly shaped by a cruel squint she'd seen before when his mood turned sour.

She smiled. "No. Of course not, silly. I was just thinking I'm glad you chose her. She was—" Fiona was about to say a terrible person, but though Dixie was a lot of things, *terrible* wasn't one of them. Too *nice*, if anything. "She was *annoying*. A goody-two-shoes."

Rune looked up from where he'd been staring at the crumb-littered floor and suddenly leaped from his seat to lay his good hand and his metal hand on her knees. Catriona yipped like a Pomeranian with surprise and fear.

"*Exactly*." Rune stared into her eyes. "You *do* understand. We have to teach these people to look out for themselves. Survival of the fittest. None of this help-our-fellow-man nonsense that only creates *weakness*."

He hissed the last word and pounded her left knee with the back of his good fist. She flinched.

"Ow."

"Sorry." He patted her and then leaned in, his eyes dancing left and right as if he was about to share a secret he didn't want anyone else to hear.

"There's more of us," he whispered.

"Oh?"

"This man." Rune raised a hand and swept it outward.

"The guy who owns this house?"

"Yes. He's one of us. There are many more of us, I think. We're going to turn the tide."

"Yay." She'd been aiming for *supportive* but not too enthusiastic, but she didn't quite commit and the word came out sarcastic.

"I mean *yay*!" she corrected.

Rune put her face between his palms. She tried to recoil but the back of the wooden chair prevented it.

"I know you're not there yet. Not *with* me. You used to be.

For years when I didn't understand my purpose, *you were still there with me.* But you've changed."

"No, I *am* with you—"

He moved his hands down to hold her jaw shut, pinching her lips. "You're *not.* It's all right, child. We have to spend some time together. I need you close until the change comes."

Oh, I don't like the sound of that. I like me just the way I am.

"The change?" She mumbled as well as she could with Rune holding her lips shut.

He released her mouth. "Until you're like *me.*"

"But I am like you, Daddy, already, I mean, I never help anyone..."

Rune returned to his spot on the sofa. He sat and bounced to his feet. Fiona winced as he moved toward her, but he passed to one side. She whooped as her chair tipped back.

Rune dragged the chair to the other side of the sofa, taking a moment to move a pleather recliner with stuffing poking from the seat. He positioned her chair directly beside the sofa and then sat beside her. She understood. That side of the sofa was cleaner.

"There. That's better." He plucked an ancient television remote from the table and the thick-bodied television sitting across from them sprang to life. It was so old Fiona was surprised to see the picture in color and so blurry she could barely make out the people moving across the screen.

No one could see wrinkles when this television was made. I could have been a bombshell into my sixties...

Fiona cocked her head.

What a strange thought to have when my crazy father is probably going to kill me any second.

She looked at her father.

Oh my God. It's working. I'm getting even more self-absorbed.

"So I'll be able to eat people and heal myself?" she asked.

He seemed surprised. "You can't now?"

"No."

Rune patted her knee with his creepily realistic metal hand. She noted he could move the fingers independently. It seemed to work like a normal hand.

"Then soon. Of course," he said.

"Will it make me younger?"

That might not be so bad.

He frowned. "I don't know. I'm embarrassed to say I've only eaten two so far and I'm afraid both times all *that* energy had to go toward not dying."

"Two?"

"Once when you stabbed me and once yesterday after the big black man pushed me out a window."

"Black—*Luther*?"

Rune shrugged one shoulder. "I had to get better so I could come to get you. Joseph had one, too."

"Joseph?"

"My friend. He owns this house."

Lucky guy.

"He fell out the window, too?"

"Sean shot him."

"Ah." Part of her wanted to ask more about what happened with Luther and Sean but most of her didn't care. "You've been busy."

Rune held up a finger. "No. Wait. I've eaten two women and a rat."

"A rat?" Fiona's lip curled.

Oh hell no. Not even for eternal youth.

Rune wrapped his mechanical fingers around her upper arm and pointed the remote at the television with his other hand.

"Do you like cooking shows?"

CHAPTER TWENTY-NINE

"There's a Bentley in the garage," said Jeffrey, sounding morose.

Anne looked up from the pool. She'd been staring at the water, trying to find the strength to start over again with a new, but familiar collection of monsters, when Jeffrey spoke.

"You were hoping for a Maserati?"

"I was hoping for a *driver*." Jeffrey sniffed. "I like the pool, though."

Anne felt certain Michael had set them up in the enormous mansion to distract her from her misery. She had to admit, it didn't hurt. Though part of her still wondered if Michael had *created* these new monsters for her to kill, just to reboot their relationship. While he'd admitted his undying love for her, he didn't always seem super comfortable with being a *boyfriend*.

Anne scanned the pool area. From the built-in outdoor kitchen to the slick wall of water tumbling into the square, dark-bottomed saltwater pool, there proved little she could fault.

A melodious chime filled the air.

"What's that?"

Jeffrey shrugged. "Doorbell?" He remained standing behind her, his head tilted back to the sun like a daisy.

She cleared her throat and he squinted an eye at her. She stared until his brows furrowed.

"What?" he asked.

"Go see who it is."

He rolled his eyes and disappeared into the house.

A minute later, Jeffrey returned looking miserable.

"What's wrong?"

"It's your dipshit ex," he grumbled.

"This is the spot, eh Boyo?" Con said, slapping Jeffrey on the shoulder.

Jeffrey winced and looked at Anne, his expression settling into a stone mask of disapproval. "I'm going out."

"Get some salsa," said Con. "They have good salsa here."

"Get it yourself, you Irish ape," muttered Jeffrey as he turned to leave.

"Poncy prick," responded Con.

Jeffrey left without another word. Con threw open his arms and headed toward Anne like a guided missile.

"Give us a hug," he said.

She grimaced. "Get away from me, you're all sweaty. Where'd you go?"

"I went for a jog. Check out the place. The women—"

"How's Boudica?" asked Anne, invoking Con's girlfriend's name.

Con frowned. "We're, em, not seein' eye-t'eye at the present moment."

Anne chuckled. "What did you do now?"

"*Nuttin'.* Why would you go assumin' our relationship problems are my fault?"

"Oh gosh. I can't imagine. Other than knowing you for two hundred fifty years."

Con dipped his toe in the pool. "That's not long enough to leap to such hurtful assumptions."

"Uh-huh."

Con walked two steps into the water. "So, what's the Angel want us to do now?" He turned his head and pretended to spit as he said the word *angel*. "Guessin' he won't be happy to see me here, as he knows lettin' you get too close to me is bad for him."

"I'm sure he'll be terrified when he hears."

"Aye, no doubt."

Anne stood and walked past Con toward the house. "Did you pick a room far from Jeffrey's? I don't feel like listening to you two bicker the whole time we're here."

"You're no fun."

She grinned. "You know that's not true."

Con threw out an arm to grab her as she passed, pulling her close to kiss her sloppily on the lips, cheek, and neck as she struggled.

"Let go of me, you idiot."

"I missed you, Red. Which room is yours if ye don't mind me askin'?"

"Don't even think about it." She pulled from his grasp and looked at her watch. "I have to find our students. You'll be good?"

"We have whiskey?"

"I suppose. The place seems fully stocked."

Con's infectious grin spread across his face like the sun peeking through the clouds. "Then I'll be quiet as a church mouse."

"Perfect."

Anne went inside and opened two wrong doors before she found the one that led to the garage. Jeffrey had left the mechanical door open and the sun filtered in, illuminating the one remaining car, a black Land Rover.

He must have taken the Bentley. Brat.

She found the keys folded up the visor and headed for Parasol Pictures. She needed to find Catriona and Broch and start their training.

As she headed down the street, her phone rang.

Michael.

"I'm on my way to them now," she said, instead of *hello*.

"There's been a development."

Anne rolled her eyes. "There's always a development. What now?"

"I have someone here they're going to want to talk to. He'll help us earn their trust."

"I'm on my way to the studio. Have him meet me there.

Anything I need to know?"

"Yes. Tell them you're here to help them fight Rune. He'll take care of the rest."

"Okay."

She hung up as she arrived at the studio's large front parking lot and spotted Catriona's Jeep.

Good. The girl is here.

She was about to get out of the Rover when movement inside the Jeep caught her eye. It looked as if people were wrestling inside.

Alarmed she'd arrived during an attack, Anne jumped out of her vehicle and sprinted with inhuman speed across the parking lot, coming to a screeching halt about twenty steps from the Jeep.

She could see inside better now.

There *were* two people, as she suspected, but they weren't wrestling.

They were *kissing.*

Or trying to swallow each other.

It was hard to tell.

CHAPTER THIRTY

Catriona felt as if her blood had been replaced by fiery lust juice.

If that was a thing.

It has to be.

Restrained by the limited space in the Jeep, she was about to *demand* Broch get out of the vehicle and march directly to her bed when she heard a rap on the window.

She and Broch jumped at the sound.

A familiar redhead stood outside the driver's side, smiling, alternately waving and motioning for them to roll down the window.

It took Broch a moment to find the right button, but soon they found themselves face-to-face with Anne, both their chests heaving and Broch's hand placed firmly over his lap.

Not embarrassing at *all*.

Catriona swallowed, feeling half-embarrassed, half-annoyed, and *all* eager to continue with Broch back in her apartment. After all, they were married, right? For now?

I'm going to hell.

"Hi." Anne waved again. She had alabaster, flawless skin, except for the freckles splashed so perfectly across the bridge of her nose. They looked as if Michelangelo had dabbed them there.

Catriona frowned.

Is it me or does she smell amazing?

"Hullo," said Broch.

"Hi, Anne," said Catriona. She realized she was staring and forced herself to talk. "Can we help you?"

"Nope, I'm going to help you." Anne grinned, flashing two rows of perfect white teeth. That's when Catriona became aware the skin around her mouth *stung*, probably thanks to Broch's stubble. The whole area around her lips was probably pink with irritation.

This keeps getting better.

She rubbed her lips with the back of her hand as Anne watched without reaction.

Is she some kind of alien sent to this planet to make me feel like an ogre?

I'm here to help you with your predicament," said Anne.

"What predicament?" Catriona needed both hands to count all their predicaments, but Gorgeous Annie wouldn't be likely to know any of them.

Anne shared another one of her reassuring smiles. "Can I buy you two lunch?"

"We were aboot tae get lunch," said Broch, always excited to hear food was forthcoming. Catriona glared at him.

How could he not sense how strange Anne was acting? Why would the payroll clerk ask them to lunch?

Catriona pushed past the siren song of Anne's calming demeanor and shook her head. "Is there something wrong with our paychecks?"

Anne's smile slipped away and Catriona sensed the nature of her visit had changed.

"I'm here about Rune," she said.

At the sound of that name, Catriona's blood tingled. The lust hormones dissipated, replaced by what felt like seltzer.

"How—"

"Explanation is what lunch is for."

Catriona swallowed. "You work with Rune?"

"Quite the opposite."

Catriona glanced at Broch. He was staring at her, his expression telegraphing, *whit are ye waiting fer?*

She always imagined his expressions had an accent as well.

Catriona opened her mouth and found she lacked the energy to deny the woman her lunch date.

"There's a Mexican spot around the corner. Is that okay?"

Anne nodded and pulled a phone from the pocket of her skort. She texted someone and slipped it away as Catriona and Broch exited the Jeep.

"Lead the way," said Anne, holding out a hand. "I have to make a quick call."

Catriona and Broch left the studio parking lot and headed toward Señor Chips, walking side-by-side with Anne behind them on the narrow pavement.

"How does she know about Rune? Why are we going to lunch with this woman?" mumbled Catriona as they walked.

Broch clucked his tongue. "Ah'm nae sure. She's—ah cannae—" He seemed to struggle for the words and Catriona nodded.

"I know. Me, too."

She glanced back to find Anne still following them, as expected. She smiled.

Catriona smiled back.

Why is that?

They took a seat on the back patio of Señor Chips in the corner, farthest away from a couple happily chatting about the differences between Modela and Carta Blanca beers.

"What do you know about Rune?" Catriona spoke the moment Anne's butt hit the seat.

Anne crossed her hands in front of her on the table. "I know he's causing you problems."

It took Catriona a moment to shake the initial shock of Anne's intimate knowledge of her life.

Anne suddenly looked up, past Catriona.

"There you are," she said.

Catriona turned as an enormous and very familiar black man sat in the empty chair beside her.

Luther.

"Hey, firecracker," he said, smiling. He reached out to take Catriona's hand and she snatched it back as if he were made of acid.

"Who are you? What is this?" She looked at Broch, who sat smiling at Luther's doppleganger as if nothing in their universe had changed.

"What are you smiling about?"

"'Tis Luther."

"No it's *not*. We saw his body." She turned to Luther. *"We saw your body."*

"It's him. Ah kin tell." Broch stood and Luther did the same. They embraced in a loud, clapping hug.

When they were done, Luther looked down at Catriona.

"You got one for me?"

Catriona found herself unable to speak.

Luther touched her cheek. "It's me. I promise."

Tears welled in Catriona's eyes.

"But how—"

"I'll tell you the story." He nodded to Anne. "Or she will. Either way, hug me."

With one final hesitation, Catriona stood and threw her arms around him.

He feels like Luther. Smells like him.

"I thought you were dead," she said, squeezing him to her. She no longer cared if it was an elaborate trick on them. It felt too good to have him back.

"I wouldn't leave you for long. You know that."

After a long hug, they returned to their seats, Catriona still feeling shaky. She rested her head in her hands, one clamped on each side of her skull.

"Someone explain."

"Hola! I'm Jason. How are you all today?" The server bounced to the table as if his shoes were made of superballs. Catriona could tell by his accent he was from the Midwest, and he was handsome enough she guessed he wasn't a waiter, he was an aspiring actor. When he wasn't acting, apparently he was going to be the *best darn waiter Senor Chips had ever seen.*

"Ah lik the carne asada, here, with the flour wrap thing," said Broch to Anne, helpful as always.

Catriona sighed.

We're sitting at a table with a payroll temp and a dead man like it's nothing.

"One carne coming up!" said Jason scribbling on his pad like a monk transcribing an auctioneer.

"You got a soft steak taco, right?" asked Luther.

Catriona blinked at him.

Luther always orders steak tacos.

Catriona put another mark in the *It's Luther* column.

"Sure do. You want corn or flour tortillas?"

"Flour."

Catriona mouthed the word with him, knowing what he would order.

He looks like Luther.

"Is that what ghosts eat? Steak soft tacos?" she asked.

"I've got a friend back at the house who could tell you what ghosts eat," murmured Anne as she looked over the menu. Then more loudly, "I think I'll take the crispy pork belly taco. Flour please."

"Will do. And you?" Jason looked at Catriona.

She smiled. "I'll take a sangria in a bucket as big as my head."

"So that would be the large..." mumbled Jason, scribbling. "Any food?"

Catriona couldn't fathom eating. "Not right now."

"Okay, I'll be back with some chips."

Jason bounced off again.

Catriona locked her attention back on Anne and Luther.

"Please tell me what's going on now?"

Luther nodded. "I'm gonna say this as blunt and quick as possible."

"I'd appreciate that. You're probably due back at the morgue."

Luther laughed.

Sounds like Luther's laugh.

He plowed ahead. "There's a group of beings—the Angeli. They're guardian angels for *everyone*. With me so far?"

Catriona had fifteen questions formulating but decided to let them go as Jason appeared with three glasses of water and a sangria glass as large as a fish tank. He placed it in front of her and she lifted it with two hands to take a deep drought.

Thank you, Jason, you strange, wonderful, bouncy creature.

She finished and sat back. "Sure. Guardian angels. Why not. Go on."

Luther continued. "A while ago, some of the Angeli started getting sick with a disease called Perfidia."

Anne's hand shot out and tapped Jason's arm as he passed on his way to the far table.

"I'd like five shots of Irish whiskey."

Catriona blinked at her.

Yikes.

She already felt the warmth of the sangria running through her veins. Was Anne trying to one-up her? Was this meeting some kind of drinking competition?

"So this disease killed the angels?" she asked, trying to get Luther's story rolling again.

Anne shook her head.

"No. It made them stop protecting humans. They started *syphoning* them, like energy vampires, to keep themselves from rotting away."

"Ew." Catriona took another sip and nodded at Anne. "Are *you* human?"

"Yes. *Enhanced.*"

Catriona snorted a laugh.

No kidding.

Anne side-eyed her and then continued. "The Angeli enhanced me to help the Angeli with their rogue angel problem. I've been doing it for hundreds of years. I'm Anne Bonny."

Catriona scowled. "Like the pirate?"

Broch's eyes opened wider. "You're a *pirate*?"

He looked like a little boy who'd just met the real Peter Pan.

Anne nodded. "Yep. The actual Anne Bonny."

Catriona scowled and took another gulp of her drink.

For crying out loud, could this woman get any cooler?

She looked to Luther, who sat, bemused, his arms crossed against his chest.

She was looking to a dead man to help her debunk a three-hundred-year-old pirate.

Jason arrived and placed a plate in front of each of them. They took a moment to shake hot sauce on their food and then Anne spoke.

"My job has been to reboot the infected Angeli. We're thinking you might be able to do the same thing with Rune. I'm here to train you."

"Reboot?" asked Broch.

"I start them over. I don't *kill* them, though it looks like it. They disappear and come back, cured."

Catriona plucked a tortilla chip from Broch's plate. "Sean already rebooted Rune. He came back just as bad." She turned to Luther. "And what does all this have to do with you?"

Luther grinned. "I got a raise."

"A raise?"

"I've been bumped from Kairos to Angelus."

Catriona scowled. "What the hell's a Kairos?"

Luther pointed at her and Broch. "You are. Sean is. I was. Now I'm one of the Angeli."

Catriona sat back and dabbed her mouth with her napkin.

"This is all insane, you know that, right?"

Jason bounced back to the table and deposited Anne's five whiskeys before her. She shot one back before he set down the second.

Catriona stared down at what was left of her ruby-red sangria, fruit floating at the top, and then looked back at Anne's shots lined neatly before her. Her cocktail looked like the Playskool version by comparison.

Anne pushed a shot in front of Broch, Catriona, and Luther. The remaining glass she kept for herself and held it aloft.

"Here's to defeating the infected Kairos. Cheers."

"*Cheers.*" The others picked up their shots and downed them.

"Ah prefer Scotch," said Broch, smacking his lips.

Amy Vansant

Anne smiled. "Duly noted."

Catriona wiped her mouth as her throat began to burn.

Insane.

She took another sip of sangria to cool the sting.

CHAPTER THIRTY-ONE

Fiona threw her hands toward the television as if she wanted to choke it. "You can't use a *stainless steel* pan for salmon."

"Idiot," agreed Rune.

Fiona found watching television with her father surprisingly relaxing. She'd decided to stop dreaming of escape and instead settle into her captivity. Not only could she consider it a vacation from her life, but it was the best way to learn more about what Rune was up to and how it might benefit *her*. It seemed he had powers she was hoping to gain herself and there was no way for her to learn them beyond apprenticeship.

Maybe he's a genius. Maybe he's crazy.

Potato, potahto.

The never-ending house and cooking shows had allowed her mind to relax and wander. She'd begun thinking about her career from a different perspective. For one, she realized it was silly of her to refuse roles like the 'crazy aunt' in a Hallmark Channel movie. She'd played the vamp in sexy thrillers and reality shows for so long she'd forgotten she had *range*. Being with Rune was helping her come to terms with aging. She felt as if she were growing up.

Maturing.

Really, her father had given her a gift, forcing her to spend time away from Hollywood and its oh-so-judgmental gaze.

Maybe she could even play the mom of a *teenager.*

She sucked in a breath at the thought.

Baby steps.

Sure, her ankle itched a little where Rune had attached the cuff. At the end of a long chain, another cuff clamped around an ancient radiator. She'd never seen cuffs like them before, and couldn't dream what they'd be used for other than keeping someone on a long leash. It crossed her mind that the same person who'd bought all the weapons mounted to the walls *had* to be the same person who'd bought the cuffs.

Didn't anyone ever ask what he was up to? It was like walking into Home Depot and buying rope, duct tape, trash bags, lye, and a shovel.

Somebody had to do the math.

She had yet to meet the owner of the dismal little hovel she now called home. Luckily, her father was equally disgusted by their accommodations. He assured her that once her assimilation was complete, they would move. In the meantime, he'd suited up in gloves and a homemade trash bag hazmat suit and cleaned the only bathroom until it smelled like a hospital ward. For that, she was forever grateful. He'd also run out and bought clean sheets, which he used to cover the greasy sofa and everything else offensive to their eyes.

Dad was a nice guy under all the humans-need-to-be-destroyed diatribe.

And really, who could blame him for being a little bitter? There he was, encouraging people to be kind to their fellow humans for *years*, centuries maybe, and they just kept starting wars and killing each other with pollution and greed.

Who wouldn't get exasperated?

She'd never liked people anyway. She'd been warming up to Catriona, but as Dad said, that was because she was hanging out with the wrong crowd. Catriona and her band of soft-hearted idiots were a bad influence on her. They were making her *soft*. Rune was here to clear her mind and, damn, if she didn't feel clearer.

"You know, I think you're right about people. They don't need to be coddled. They need to *fight* to become stronger," she said, echoing one of the lines he'd been feeding her during their time on the sofa.

"Exactly."

"I think you can unclip me from the radiator now."

Rune patted her knee. "Not quite yet, I think."

Fiona pouted. "What if I promised to go wreck Catriona's world?"

Rune looked at her. "Who?"

"Catriona. My *sister*." She huffed. "Why do you pretend you don't know who she is?"

"I don't know what you mean."

Fiona eyed him. "I can't figure you out."

There was a rattling in the back of the house and a moment later, a squat, tan-skinned man appeared at the hall entrance. He stared at Fiona, a laptop tucked under his arm, his thick features pulled to the center of his expression.

"How's she doing?" he asked.

Rune smiled. "Very well. Making wonderful progress." He motioned to the man. "Fiona, this is Joseph. Joseph, this is my daughter, Fiona."

Joseph grunted.

Fiona raised her hand to the back of her neck. "You're the one that shot me with the dart."

He nodded. "Si. Rune insisted we give you another chance."

"But you don't like the idea?"

"No."

Gosh, Joseph, tell me how you really feel.

Fiona clicked her tongue against the roof of her mouth and mentally put Joseph on her *list*. Little man had to *go*.

She glanced at her father. She could tell from his expression they were on the same page, but that for now, Joseph was somehow useful.

Fine.

Joseph moved to the reclining chair, now covered with a sheet. He plucked at the sheet, glanced at Rune, shrugged, and sat to open his laptop on his lap.

"I've had a tremendous response," he said.

Rune arched an eyebrow. "How many?"

"At least a hundred."

"Keep up the good work."

"A hundred what?" asked Fiona.

Joseph's mouth hooked to the right. "None of your business."

She glowered at him. "As long as I'm chained to your radiator, it absolutely *is* my business."

Rune agreed. "You can tell her. What can it hurt? In a day she'll be assimilated or eliminated."

Fiona's head swiveled.

Wait, what?

Joseph took a deep breath and forced it out as if bracing himself for a great confession.

"Using shortwave radio, Internet chat rooms, and email I've contacted a large number of people like us, all over the country."

"Like us?"

"Time travelers who have changed our minds about our core mission."

"Our core mission to help people?"

Joseph seemed surprised she knew. "Right."

"All these people are time travelers, too?"

Joseph nodded.

"How do you know?"

"They said so."

Fiona nodded. "Riiight."

So that's one percent time travelers and ninety-nine percent crazies.

"What are you asking them?"

Joseph scratched his cheek. "I asked them to come here."

"Why?" Fiona straightened. *He's calling every nut in the country to our doorstep.* She glanced at the cuff around her ankle. *I have to get out of here.*

"They all worship Rune."

Fiona looked at her father.

"I was one of the first to see the truth," he explained.

She nodded. "Ah. You're the O.G."

He blinked at her.

"The Original Gangster."

Rune shrugged.

Fiona moved on, returning her attention to Joseph. "But, do you think that's a good idea? Bringing them all here?"

Joseph wriggled in his chair as if agitated by her questions. "Rune and I decided. We're going to build an army."

"In Hollywood?"

"What better place? We'll take over the media here, and then we'll expand."

Rune shook his closed fists in the air like an over-sugared toddler. "I'm thinking D.C. next. We'll take over politics."

"Which should be easy once we have Hollywood," added Joseph.

Rune pointed at him with a long bony finger. "Exactly."

Fiona chewed on her lip, thinking. "Okay. I see where you're going with this. But, to play devil's advocate, what if they're lying?"

"Who?"

"The people you're contacting. What if they're lying about being like us. What if they're just *crazy*?"

"Ah," said Rune. "But what if *we're* just crazy."

Now it was Fiona's turn to blink at her father. He stared back, his eyes wide.

Oh boy.

"Dad, are you under the impression you just made a point?"

Rune lifted his chin and looked away from her. "Don't be rude."

Joseph folded his laptop and leaned forward, scrutinizing her from head to toe. "She hasn't gone through the change yet."

"No, I don't think so," agreed Rune.

Fiona groaned and scratched her ankle. "How can you tell?" She asked as off-handedly as possible, hoping to catch them off-guard.

Please tell me it's as easy as asking them. I'm an actress. Give me the script and I'll play the part.

Rune tapped his chin. "Well, when I started changing, I felt a bit lost."

"How?"

"I started losing time, finding myself in places I didn't remember going."

"Me too," agreed Joseph.

Rune perked. "See? That's the point I was trying to make. We're all crazy, until we're *not*."

"Until we're crazy like a *fox*," added Joseph, grinning.

"And you're better now?" asked Fiona.

Both men nodded, and then Joseph seemed to have a second thought. "It took a few years—"

"Decades, I'd say," corrected Rune.

"Yeah, maybe, but then you can see *everything*."

Fiona gaped and looked down at her cuff. "Decades? If you think you're keeping me chained on this filthy sofa for *decades*, you've got another thing coming."

I'd go right from crazy aunt parts to grandmothers.

She shuddered at the thought.

Rune wrapped a gangly arm around her shoulder and pulled her against him. "No, no. We'll let you go once it starts. Then we'll keep an eye on you to make sure the change is easier on you than it was on us."

"You won't be alone like me," mumbled Joseph.

Fiona grimaced. "But what if I already feel like you do?"

"Without the transition period?" asked Rune.

"What if I've *already* had my transition period?"

Rune seemed gobsmacked. "Is that possible?"

"I felt lost during the eighteen hundreds. A little loose cannon."

"Oh yeah?" asked Joseph. He seemed less disdainful of her for a moment.

Rune tilted his head, ogling her as if she'd appeared before him for the first time. All the attention made her feel like the cool girl at the party. It was an experience both familiar and missed.

"I never considered that you might have already gone

through the change," said Rune.

Fiona nodded as earnestly as possible.

Or maybe I'm just smarter than both of you and don't have to lose my mind to change my mind.

A touch of suspicion crept back to Joseph's countenance.

Time to put some effort into the little one.

"I'm fascinated by your plan, Joseph. Tell me, what are you planning to do with all these people when they show up?"

Joseph leaned back. "Um..."

Rune slapped the tops of his thighs with his palms. "We'll have some meetings—"

Fiona stopped him. "See, that's what I thought. We're going to need a house."

"We *have* a house," said Joseph.

Fiona laughed. "This isn't a house. It's an episode of Hoarders waiting to happen."

"This is *my* house." Joseph's voice rippled with irritation.

Whoops. This is no way to earn Joseph's trust.

Fiona rushed to backtrack. "No, I'm sorry. I wasn't clear. This is a fine house for a *few* people, but we need a *compound*. Somewhere we can keep our army and do things right."

Rune's eyes lit. "That's a fabulous idea."

"It's a pretty good idea," admitted Joseph. "But who's going to pay for it?"

"I'm a famous actress. I can get us money. Sponsors, even."

"Maybe some of the new people are rich," suggested Rune.

"Maybe," agreed Fiona, though she didn't think the sort of nutballs beating a path to Joseph's door were likely to be rolling in dough.

But who knew?

"And who's in charge of the entire operation?" she asked.

"I am," said Joseph and Rune simultaneously. They looked at each other.

"I mean both of us," said Joseph.

Fiona smiled.

I don't think so.

CHAPTER THIRTY-TWO

After lunch, Anne insisted they all come to her house, promising Sean would be joining them. As if on cue, Sean called Catriona's phone to confirm the mysterious meeting he'd been asked to join involved her and Broch.

"We're going, too," she confirmed. She was about to tell him about Luther when Luther raised a finger to his lips, mouthing *Shhh*.

She grimaced, knowing it would kill her not to spill that particular can of beans.

Sean continued. "She wanted me to come to Señor Chips but I couldn't get away that soon. Is that where you are?"

"Yes."

"Who is this woman?"

"The woman who replaced Jeanie at payroll for vacation."

"Replace Jeanie? What are you talking about?"

Catriona looked at Anne.

Had she just walked in and taken Jeanie's place?

She put her hand over the phone.

"You didn't kill Jeanie, did you?" she asked.

Anne laughed. "No. She's on an all-expense-paid vacation with her husband."

"So you replaced them both?"

Anne nodded. "Me and a friend."

Catriona sighed.

Fantastic security.

"We're going to have to talk about security," she said into the phone.

"*What—?*"

She could tell from Sean's tone he had no patience for a mysterious meeting with strangers today. Not only had he spent the morning identifying his best friend's body, but she doubted he'd slept for close to forty-eight hours. She longed to tell him about Luther, but the big man kept his eye on her.

She grimaced. "Just go to the address. You need to hear this."

He huffed. "This is all I need today. Hey, cough if this is a trap."

Catriona remained silent.

"Is she there? Is she listening?"

"It's *safe.*"

I think.

Sean sighed. "Fine. See you in a bit."

She hung up before Sean could ask any more questions and frowned at Luther.

"You're *killing* me."

"Someone already killed me today. It's only fair." He laughed as they peeled away from the table.

Catriona and Broch returned to the Jeep with plans to follow Anne and Luther in her Land Rover.

"What do you think?" asked Catriona as soon as she and Broch were alone. Feeling she might have overdone it with the schooner of sangria, she'd let him take the wheel once more. The seat was already back in his position anyway.

"Ah trust her," he said without hesitation.

"Really?" She looked away and watched Anne slip into her car. "Is it because she's pretty?"

"Nah. Ah kin tell she's blethering the truth. Cannae ye?"

"No. I don't seem to have a nose for things like you do."

He leaned forward to kiss her. "Mebbe that's why ah'm here. Tae show ye the way."

She kissed him back and he shifted the Jeep into reverse.

"She is pretty, though," she added.

"Nae as bonny as ye," said Broch.

Catriona smiled.

Good answer.

They drove into the Bird Streets area of Hollywood, tight on Anne's tail. After pulling through two enormous golden gates, they parked in an impressive, paved circular drive while Anne pulled into an open garage beside a Bentley.

Catriona hopped out of the Jeep, craning to see the whole of the mansion splayed out before them. Expensive cars. Huge house.

I guess the pirate life really does pay.

Luther and Anne joined them in front of the oversized doors.

"This place is gorgeous," said Catriona as they entered the mansion. The airy, modern interior seemed pulled directly out of a magazine.

Anne nodded. "That is one of the perks of working with the Angeli. They always go first class."

A thin man in jeans and a light blue t-shirt appeared, looking both surprised and displeased.

"Guests. With no warning. Wonderful," he murmured.

Anne nodded toward him. "That's Jeffrey, my assistant. He's a bit snotty but he means well."

"Is he a pirate?" asked Broch.

"Nope, just a cranky, regular old human."

Jeffrey sneered playfully at her. "I'm not *old*."

A chiming noise filled the room and they all looked skyward, searching for the source. Jeffrey strode past them toward the door.

"It's the doorbell," he said, rolling his eyes to show he didn't approve.

He opened the door to reveal Sean standing on the doorstep.

"Hi, I'm here to meet—" He looked past Jeffrey and gasped. "Luther?"

Luther threw his arms open. "Come here and give me a hug before you get stuck on why and how."

Sean and Luther slammed into each other like giants, each trying to squeeze the life out of each other.

"Is it really you?"

"It's really me."

"But I identified your *body*."

"Don't need that body anymore. I kept the blueprint."

"What the hell does that mean?"

Luther looked at Anne. "She might be better for explaining all that.

Anne held out a hand. "Hello, Sean. I've been looking forward to meeting you. I'm Anne Bonny."

Sean shot a look at Catriona. "Like the pirate?"

"Exactly like the pirate. Let's all go to the living room and get comfortable."

"She's been running payroll for the last week without us knowing it," murmured Catriona to Sean. "Well, I *knew*, but I thought you hired her."

His brow knit. "What? Where's Jeanie?"

Anne sent her on vacation and stepped into her shoes.

Sean frowned. "Yikes."

Catriona nodded. "Exactly."

Sean put his arm around her shoulder. "This day is really picking up. Luther's back and you're admitting you're wrong about something."

She scowled. "Very funny."

They gathered in the great room. Broch stared up at the tall ceilings as they entered, so mesmerized by the space he clipped his hip on the edge of a white sofa, knocking it out of alignment.

"'Tis anly ye twa here?" he asked.

Anne nodded and Catriona looked at her. "You understood that?"

Anne chuckled. "I'm good with Celtic accents. I'm Irish, though I've lost most of my accent over the years."

Sean wandered to a collection of photos in frames scattered on a marble sofa table, picking up one to study it. "This is Chuck

Irons' place." He pointed the photo toward them, and Catriona recognized the A-list actor standing with a top director.

"You know Chuck Irons?" he asked Anne.

"He's a friend of a friend." Anne motioned to the large white u-shaped sofa. "Why don't you all sit down while I catch Sean up."

Sean set the photo back in its place and moved to sit.

Jeffrey reappeared with a tray full of ice teas and they each took one. Catriona stared grimly at hers. The little buzz she'd garnered from their Mexican fandango was wearing off and she wasn't sure she wanted to deal with the rest of the day. After all, it was the sangria that had made *any* of it plausible.

"Thank you, Jeffrey," said Anne.

He bowed deeply and backed out of the room. "My only wish is to serve."

Anne rolled her eyes and looked at Catriona. "He gets worse every year."

Anne cleared her throat. "I'm going to keep this as short as possible—"

"Is this fresh peach in here?" asked Luther, staring into his glass of tea.

Anne's face fell slack. "I don't know."

"It does taste like peach, doesn't it?" said Sean.

"Aye. Ah didnae ken that sweet fruity taste...ye ken peach?"

Luther nodded. "Yeah. At first, I thought it was—"

"Jeffrey, is there peach in the tea?" called Anne.

Catriona thought she sounded a little exasperated.

"What's that?" asked Jeffrey pulling an earbud from his head as he appeared.

"Is there peach in the tea?" she repeated at a normal pitch.

"Nectarine. Fresh, crushed nectarine."

"*Nectarine,*" echoed Luther. "I don't know if I woulda guessed."

Anne clapped her hands together. "Well, I'm glad I could clear up that mystery. Can we get back to the monsters coming to destroy your city, way of life, and entire future?"

Luther nodded. "Yup. Apologies."

"All right. Like I mentioned before, you all—except for Luther, who's moved on—"

"*Moved on*?" echoed Sean, looking alarmed.

"I'm an Angel now," said Luther, beaming.

Sean gaped at him. "You *are* dead?"

Anne stomped her foot. "In the name of Boudica's bodice will you all let me get through this thing?"

Sean lifted his palms in submission. "Sorry." He leaned toward Luther to whisper something and Luther released a low chuckle, shaking his head.

Anne took a deep breath and released it. "*Okay*. As I was saying at the lunch you missed, *Sean*—" She emphasized his name loudly enough that he stopped giggling with Luther and straightened. "—you're all *Kairos*. That's what the Angeli call you, anyway. You travel from place to place and time to time, inspiring good in the people around you. You don't always know you're doing it, but it happens anyway."

"What was that word?" asked Sean. "Do you have a pen? I feel like I should be taking notes..."

"Kairos," repeated Catriona.

"How do you spell that?"

"K-A-I-R-O-S." Anne tilted her head, squinting. "I think." She mouthed through the letters again. "I think that's right."

Sean felt his chest. "I wish I had a pen."

"Put it in your phone," suggested Catriona.

Sean pointed at her. "Good idea."

Anne rubbed her temples. "We think some of you have been falling ill with a disease we call *Perfidia*—it makes you act against your nature."

"Some of *us*?" asked Sean, making a circular motion with his finger to encompass the people in the room.

Ann shook her head. "No. Not this specific group. Not that we know."

"Howfur would we ken?" asked Broch.

"Do we get a rash or something?" asked Sean.

"No, there's no *rash*." Anne took a beat and seemed to reconsider. "I mean, your skin starts to rot if it's the same strain the Angels had, but that takes eons."

Catriona raised the right corner of her lip.

Ick.

Anne continued. "Anyway, whereas you currently inspire people to be good and kind, when you're afflicted, you inspire people to be selfish and evil."

Sean finished typing on his phone and looked up. "That doesn't sound so bad. People inspiring a couple of bar fights—"

Anne shook her head. "It might start that way, but think about it—if the wrong people are emboldened for long enough, it's not a bar fight, it's a world war."

"Oh." Sean nodded. "Got it."

"Right. So, how we handled this with the Angeli—"

"That's what I am now," said Luther, patting his chest. "An Angeli."

"An Angel*us*; singular," corrected Anne.

Luther blinked at her a moment and then turned back to Sean. "Check this out."

Luther's body shimmered, like a television losing reception, and then he disappeared, his form briefly replaced by a network of glowing blue light. The others in the room released a low *oooh* as if he were fireworks on a warm Fourth of July evening. It lasted a few seconds and then he returned.

"How 'bout that?" asked Luther, grinning.

"What does it mean?" asked Sean.

Luther shrugged. "I traveled back to the office and then back here. Somethin' else, huh?"

Sean patted him on the back. "That's great, man."

"I know. I know. It *is*."

"Are *we* going to become Angeli?" asked Catriona, pointing to herself, Broch, and Sean with a sweeping gesture.

Anne flipped over her palms like pancakes. "I don't know. I think the number of Angeli is static, but we suffered casualties recently, thanks to Perfidia, *which is what I'm trying to tell you about so it doesn't happen again.*"

Catriona nodded. "Got it. Go ahead."

"Thank you. So, we think Rune is infected and possibly

Fiona, too."

"That makes sense." Catriona felt the same wave of embarrassment she'd suffered at lunch.

What a winner of a family I have.

"We need to reboot them?" she asked.

"We think so. We have to try. Assuming it works the same way with Kairos as it did with Angeli, if you shut them down in a specific way they come back cured."

"Whit dae ye mean by shut them down?" asked Broch.

"In a nutshell, we syphon all the energy out of them until they explode into, uh... glitter lights."

Catriona barked a laugh.

"It sounds prettier than it is. You're killing them, but their energy comes back. Some other time and place."

"Just like us," muttered Sean.

As Anne said the word *killing*, something flashed near her hand. Catriona pointed. "What was that?"

"What?"

"Your hand. A light flashed."

"Oh." Anne held up her arm and a beam of light grew from her fist until it looked as if she were holding a short orange sword made of light and fire. "I've got these."

The four of them gaped at her.

"How dae ah get one of those?" asked Broch.

Anne retracted her sword and her hand looked like any other again. "These are unique to me. They were a gift from a madman." She looked around the room, which had grown quiet for the first time since they'd sat down. "Any questions?"

Catriona couldn't take her eyes off Anne's hand. "How do we do the syphoning?"

Anne grimaced. "That's the thing. We don't exactly know. Michael—he's top brass Angeli—thinks the key might lie with you two."

She pointed at Catriona and Broch.

Catriona slapped her palm to her chest. "Me?"

"Maybe especially you." She pointed at Broch. "His purpose seems to be to protect *you* because you're so darn special."

Luther elbowed Sean. "I told ya. She's a lodestone."

Sean nodded. "All that nonsense in the warehouse is starting to make sense now."

Catriona noticed Broch grinning at her.

"What?"

"Ah ken it. Ah'm here tae protect ye."

Catriona focused on Anne as her cheeks warmed with embarrassment.

"How am I special?" she asked.

"I don't know. We might not know until we get you near Fiona and Rune."

"I've been near them before. Nothing happened."

Anne shrugged. "You weren't *trying* then."

Catriona leaned back. "Here's the next problem—Fiona's gone missing and we don't know where Rune is."

"Michael might know where they are."

"What about us?" asked Sean, motioning to himself and Luther.

"You two can go back to normal life for now. Luther will be your local contact with the Angeli."

Sean slapped Luther on the back. "You're coming back to work?"

Luther smiled. "Aw, you knew I wouldn't leave you."

They high-fived and Catriona shook her head.

"What about Broch and me?"

"You two get a good night's sleep. Tomorrow's a big day. I'm going to start your training."

Suddenly, the pirate seemed very serious.

Sean's smile faded and he pointed to Catriona. "I don't want her doing anything dangerous without me."

Catriona huffed. "I'm *always* doing dangerous things without you. It's my *job*."

"Dangerous things with *normal* people. Stupid actor problems. Not *monsters*. I don't want you involved in all this."

Catriona shrugged. "I don't think you get to decide. According to her, I'm already involved."

Sean turned to Anne. "You're going to watch over them,

right?"

Anne stood. "The utmost safety will be taken at all times." Her expression softened as she looked at Sean. "If it makes you feel any better, I don't think these Kairos-Perfidians are half the threat the Angeli-Perfidians were. You don't have Angeli *power*."

Sean grunted, seemingly unsure whether to be relieved or insulted.

CHAPTER THIRTY-THREE

"I don't know. I don't *know*," said Catriona, flinging open the door to her apartment.

Broch followed her inside.

"Whit dinnae ye ken?"

She spun on her heel. "*Any* of it. It's all too much." She sat on a kitchen island barstool, feeling out of breath.

I'm going to have to calm down before I give myself a panic attack.

She allowed her arms to flop to her sides. "There are too many things. Luther is alive but some kind of angel, a redhead with glowing swords for hands is here to teach me how to kill people, namely my father, who's infected with the same disease as my sister and who might be trying to destroy the world...I'm supposed to kill them..."

She trailed off.

It was a *lot*.

"She said ye wouldnae be *murdering* them..." Broch closed the door behind him and wrapped his arms around her.

"Sweet Cat. Dinnae git yerself in a bother. Tak' it bit by bit."

His voice was soft and it disarmed her agitation.

"But how?" she asked.

He held up his index finger, counting off the ways. "First, Luther is alive. 'Tis a guid thing, aye?"

She nodded. "Yes. It's *great*. But now he's some kind of blue lightning—"

"Does he look lik him? Kin ye blether tae him?"

She considered this. She hadn't had any trouble talking to him. He seemed to be the same old Luther.

"Yes."

"Sae, whofur cares if he looks lik' lightning bugs in a jar? He's *back*."

Catriona giggled. "You're right." She slipped her hands beneath his shirt and rested her palms on either side of his hips, maneuvering him to stand between her legs. Slowly, she slid her hands upward, lifting his shirt to reveal his rippling stomach muscles as if they were actors making a curtain call.

He chuckled. "Whit are ye doin'?"

The sides of his body felt warm and smooth as she eased up his ribs.

"I'm taking off your shirt," she said, her voice falling to a whisper. "Keep talking. You're making me feel better."

"Bit it's hard tae think when yer—"

She banged against the underside of his biceps until he raised his arms and allowed her to pull off his shirt by standing on the foot rail of her stool. Catriona ran her hands across his chest as his tee tumbled to the ground.

"Luther was first. What's second?" she asked, leaning forward to kiss the divot between his pecs.

"Second was Anne," he mumbled. "She's here to help."

"Is she?"

"Aye."

"You promise?"

"Ah promise." Broch took her shirt by the bottom and lifted it over her head before dropping it on top of his own on the floor. He leaned to kiss the spot where her neck and shoulder met as he unclasped her bra and sent it to the floor with the rest of their clothes.

"How did you know how to undo that?" she asked as his palm brushed the side of her breast.

Broch breathed a laugh that tickled her ear and made her eyes flutter shut. "Ah've been dreaming of opening that infernal contraption fer months. Practicing in mah mind."

She chuckled and then sobered. "Anne wants me to kill my family."

Broch's arms encircled her and he swept her off the stool. Her legs wrapped around his waist and she locked her ankles as he shifted one hand beneath her butt, the other steadying her back. He held her chest tight to his as she slipped her arms around his neck and rested her cheek on his shoulder.

"She said thay wilnae be murdered. They'll return healthy n' happy. Juist lik' travelin' through time," he murmured in her ear as he carried her to her bedroom.

She nodded. "I suppose we traveled and it didn't hurt."

"Nae. We're here. Healthy n' happy."

He laid her on the bed and lowered himself down on her, the weight of him sending a jolt of anticipation through her.

"What about us?" she asked.

He stared down into her eyes with an intensity she'd rarely seen in him.

"Yer mine," he said, running his thumb along her cheekbone.

"But the marriage was an accident—"

Brochan placed his index finger across her lips to hush her. "It wasn't a mistake. Ah'm tired o' telling ye, wummin. Nae, ah'm needin' tae prove it tae ye."

He moved away his finger and kissed her, gently at first and then with increasing intensity. Whatever doubt remained in her mind was erased like a sandcastle against the rising tide.

As his lips moved down her body and his hands slid away her jeans, she was struck by a sudden realization.

I know him.

Every move, every touch, felt familiar.

Her mind flooded with memories. They'd kissed a million times. She'd felt his hands on her body a million times. Their flesh young. Their flesh old. Two lovers hopelessly intertwined since time before time. A hundred lifetimes together as friends and lovers.

The relationships she'd known in Los Angeles—the way

things had never felt right with anyone else—suddenly made sense. Her confession to Pete. Her need to run.

She wasn't hers to give.

I was always his.

He was always mine.

Years of blaming herself, insecurities and pain—everything washed away with one racking sob.

He looked at her, concerned, and she smiled to let him know not to worry. She needed him to know her cries came from a place of almost unbearable joy.

"It's *you*," she said, pulling him to her. "It's always been *you*."

He smiled, his eyes, too, already glistening with tears.

"Ah've always been yours, Catriona. Ah live ainlie fer ye. Ah needed ye tae see it."

He kissed her the way she remembered he could.

And always would.

CHAPTER THIRTY-FOUR

On day three, Rune unsnapped the cuffs from Fiona's ankle and allowed her to wander around the house. It wasn't *ideal,* because if she thought the living room was small, dirty, and depressing, the rest of the house only further soured her mood.

Joseph was rarely home. Rune stayed close, but even he had to go to the bathroom, and when he did he insisted she sing to prove she was still nearby, signaling like a cat with a bell around her neck.

In some small way, Fiona felt her singing was payback for her imprisonment.

She sang like a wounded frog.

Still, she could have left. She could have found a way. But she'd become intrigued by Rune and Joseph's plans to rule the world.

Maybe winning an Oscar had been too small a dream. Maybe it was time to think *big.*

This morning, Fiona insisted Rune make them coffee and bacon shortly before Joseph left at his usual time, around ten a.m. She guessed Joseph had a job because nothing about the man implied he was interesting enough to have a life outside the house for any other reason. He'd even reduced recruiting an army to conquer the world down to keeping a spreadsheet, sending out emails, and trolling chatrooms.

Rune appeared surprised she wanted coffee and bacon but

didn't seem suspicious. If anything, he looked pleased. He didn't eat as often as normal people, but he loved his coffee and she'd seen him devour a pound of bacon. Maybe he ate out. Although the last time he'd left the house leaving Joseph to watch her, she'd asked if he'd eaten, and Rune had just *smiled*. He'd been flushed and happy and had a woman's scarf around his neck.

The fact that he looked *younger* gave her hope.

Bacon didn't make him look younger.

People did.

She imagined she had her father to thank for her slight figure, which she was able to maintain with little dieting. Rune never gained an ounce, so she concluded eating people's energy didn't pack on the pounds.

Bonus.

If cutting out carbs and sugar made her lose weight, imagine cutting out *food.*

But her bacon request was less about Keto and more about the effect it had on Rune. The last time they'd had it, he'd stayed in the bathroom much longer than usual. Something about the grease, she suspected.

They made idle taking-over-the-world chit-chat as they sipped their coffee and munched their crispy pork products until Rune set down his plate and stood.

She'd timed it perfectly. Joseph left almost the exact moment her father stood.

"Start singing," he said, heading for the bathroom, a twinge of panic in his eye.

She smiled. "Twinkle, twinkle, little star..."

The moment Rune disappeared into the bathroom, Fiona leaped to her feet and scampered toward Joseph's bedroom. He'd locked the door, but the key hovered above on the trim. She'd seen him stand on his tippy-toes to reach it.

Idiot.

She grabbed the key, raising her volume so it wouldn't be so obvious she'd moved into the hall as she opened the door.

Joseph's laptop sat on his desk, the lid open.

Oh please, oh please...

She tapped the return key and the screen lit. She sat staring at the desktop. She'd caught it in time. The computer hadn't yet gone to sleep and she didn't need to enter the password.

Bingo.

"Up above the world so high…"

Fiona navigated the laptop until she found a spreadsheet filled with the emails, usernames, and real names. The name of the file was *minions*.

Not too obvious.

She emailed the file to herself at her personal and work email addresses and then deleted her message to herself in his sent folder. Poking around, she found a few more files: several drafts of a manifesto, a few to-do lists, and a smattering of other files with names like *kill list* and *enemies*. Things she thought might be important. She sent them all to herself.

After the fifth *kill list* she almost found herself wishing she'd found a cache of porn. *Something* to make the little creep seem human.

He might have been single-minded, but he wasn't bright. It would be a cold day in Hollywood before *Joseph* ended up in charge of herself and the others. Fiona felt a thrill run through her body.

I think I've found my calling.

Rune hadn't been able to *turn* her like he hoped, but he had helped her realize her destiny. She'd all but forgotten about her acting career. For the first time in as long as she could remember, she wasn't worried about her fading looks or the crow's feet beside her eyes.

After all, adoration came in many forms.

Fiona ran back into the hall, pressing the lock on the knob as she slipped through the doorway. She eased the door shut and replaced the key in its lofty spot.

She'd returned to the sofa when she heard Rune flush.

A moment later, he entered the room looking sheepish.

"I wouldn't go in there right away."

She smiled. "No problem."

The back door banged and Joseph appeared, looking

flustered.

"We've got trouble."

Rune's eyes widened. "What is it?"

"My cameras went off out front. People are coming."

"Who?"

"I don't know. The cameras are fuzzy."

Fiona leaned forward to look out the window and spotted movement on the street. A couple was headed for their house. She had to admit, they were much too good-looking to be from the neighborhood. The man had a delectable swagger that made her want to conquer him and take her time doing it. The redheaded woman looked like a model.

A *young* model.

Bitch.

Joseph jumped to grab his key from the trim and opened his bedroom door.

"Was someone in here?" she heard him call.

Fiona pretended not to hear and if Rune heard, he was too busy peeking through the front blinds to answer.

Joseph appeared a moment later wearing a black vest covered in straps and strange pockets with the hilts of silver knives peeking from them.

Fiona couldn't help but laugh.

Joseph shot her a look, his expression darkening. "You won't be laughing much longer," he said, too quietly for Rune to hear.

She snorted a laugh. "Suck it, little man."

Joseph pulled weapons from his wall and slid the smaller ones into the available straps on his jacket.

"You made that yourself, didn't you?" Fiona said, much more loudly, hoping to draw her father's attention to the *loon* he'd hooked his wagon to.

Joseph didn't look at her. "Yes. And I applied for a patent."

"Good luck with that."

Rune turned from the window. "I counted two but there could be more. They're coming this way."

Joseph nodded toward Fiona. "Secure her in the shed out

back. We can use her if we end up in a hostage situation."

Rune nodded and grabbed Fiona's arm, tugging her toward the back of the house.

They burst through a crooked screen door to enter the backyard. Fiona squinted in the sun. It had been a while.

"Dad. Stop."

Rune paused and looked at her.

"Joseph's going to get himself killed. I'm a *hostage*, I'll be fine. And if we get caught I'll vouch for you. I'll tell the cops you were kidnapped, too. They are cops, right? They're coming for me?" Fiona thought about the model couple she'd seen outside Joseph's window.

Come to think of it, they didn't look like cops.

Rune's shoulders bobbed. "I don't know."

Fiona thought hard about what she wanted from the situation at hand.

Do I want to lose Rune yet?

The answer was obvious.

No.

I need him to show me how to get the power.

"You need to go," she said, pushing him toward the back fence.

"What?"

"You need to go. I'll point them in the wrong direction. Run that way."

"But I have to go help Joseph—"

"Joseph is an *idiot*. He's going to get us all killed."

Rune looked pained. "Joseph has our list. We need those people."

"I have the list."

"What?"

"I have the list. I grabbed it while you were in the bathroom."

Rune frowned. "You know, I thought your singing sounded funny but, to be honest, it's hard to tell with the fan on."

"I did it for us. In case something like this happened. You and I have a chance to get out of here. It's you and me, Dad. We don't need Joseph."

Rune stared back at the house. "You have the list? You're sure?"

"I do."

"Okay. Let's go." He grabbed her hand again and dragged her toward the fence.

She dug in as the heel of Catriona's cheap shoes snapped. "Leave me. *You* go."

"No. I *can't*."

"They think I'm a hostage. They won't hurt me. Then I can keep an eye on them and you'll be safe. I'll be your spy."

Rune hemmed and then nodded. "You're right. It's a good plan." He took her by the shoulders. "Be careful, Rabbit."

Fiona gasped. Rune hadn't called her Rabbit since she was little, during the happy times. The times before he fell mad.

She felt tears brim her eyes.

"You, too, Daddy."

Rune kissed her on her forehead and then turned to run, looking like a long-legged spider as he clambered over the metal fence.

CHAPTER THIRTY-FIVE

Broch opened his eyes.

Somethin's different.

He looked to his right and saw Catriona lying beside him, the glow of the morning sun bright enough to highlight the peach-fuzz scattered across her naked upper thigh.

She breathed in slow, steady inhales, a tiny smile across her beautiful lips.

My Catriona.

He held still, barely breathing, unsure whether to wake her and take her again in the glow of a new day, or let her sleep, peacefully, hopefully dreaming of his body against hers.

What was that phrase he'd heard the people at the studio say?

It was a *tough call.*

Before he could decide, her phone rang on the bed stand next to her and her hand reached out to grab it, her eyes never opening. Years of muscle memory ran through a familiar pattern.

"Hello? Hm? Oh."

Catriona's eyes opened and she looked down at her naked body and then at him. He suffered the urge to hide, worrying her expression would flood with regret. Instead, she blushed and smiled.

Happiness flowed in his veins, warming every inch of his flesh.

Then, she scowled, her attention stolen by the voice on the other end of the line.

"Really? Like now? Okay. Okay."

She hung up.

"Whit is it?" he asked reaching out to stroke her hip with his fingertips. He couldn't help himself.

"It's Anne. They found Rune and Fiona. She needs us to go with her."

"Nae?" Dreams of a lazy morning in her kip dissipated like morning fog on a sunny day.

"*Now.*"

She rolled to him and kissed him, pushing him down so she could straddle him.

"That isnae fair," he said, barely, as the breath was stolen from his lungs by a rush of desire.

"Of course," she whispered, rolling toward him. "*Now* is so subjective."

It wasn't long until they arrived at Anne's.

Should have been a wee longer.

His time in Catriona's bed had been too short. But he wasn't the only one unable to resist finishing, so he didn't feel *too* bad.

When Anne answered their knock, she cocked her head, grinning.

"What are you two up to?"

Catriona giggled. "What?"

The sound of her mirth made Broch grin. He couldn't stop, as much as he wanted to appear tough and professional in front of the woman who seemed to be their new boss. He glanced at Catriona and she peeked at him.

Ah juist want tae grab her and steal her away.

Anne laughed. "You two are too much. Follow me."

She walked past them to the garage where a man sat, legs

dangling from the driver's side of a black Range Rover. "This is Con. He's—" Anne seemed at a loss to describe him and let her attempt die on the vine.

"Ready for the big time, boyo?" Con asked Broch, standing to entangle him with a bracing slap of an embrace. His accent was Irish and Broch stood his ground as their bodies bounced off each other's. The Irishman seemed less excited to see him and more interested in testing his strength.

"Ah'm always ready," said Broch.

The glint in Con's eye made him look more like a predatory cat than a man.

Anne slapped Con on the shoulder. "Dial the machismo back a notch, will you?"

Con sniffed, winked at Catriona, and took his place in the driver's seat.

Anne glanced at Catriona. "*Men.* It doesn't matter what species or variation they are. They're all about six years old."

Broch grunted, unhappy to be lumped with Con. Catriona smiled at him and he melted.

Anne motioned to the SUV and moved to take her place in the passenger seat while Broch and Catriona clambered into the back.

"Where are we going?" asked Catriona.

Anne twisted to talk while Con pulled out of the garage.

"Fiona's being held in a house on the edge of West Hollywood. Rune and another man have been spotted entering and leaving.

"We're goan tae rescue her?" asked Broch.

Anne nodded. "Hopefully. That's the plan."

"How do we know she isn't living there with them?" asked Catriona.

"We don't. If she's partnered with them, that'll be plan B. But our scout said she rarely leaves the main living room as if she can't. When she does, she's always got Rune with her."

Catriona grunted and pulled her phone from her pocket to stare at it.

"Whit are ye doin'?" asked Broch.

"Sean said not to do anything dangerous without telling him, but I don't want him trying to join us. You know he will."

Broch imagined Sean's panic at hearing their plans.

"Aye."

"And I don't want him to worry until we're back..." She tapped on her phone and then slipped it back into her pocket. "Maybe I'll hold off."

"Is this dangerous?" asked Broch.

Anne nodded her head from side to side. "It could be. I'll be honest, I was hoping to start your training first."

"Is there anything you can tell us?" asked Catriona.

Anne grimaced. "We don't know the extent of their powers. We don't know much about the man with Rune other than his name, Joseph Almas. But with Con and me both here, it should be more of a learning experience for you than anything else. We should be able to handle the dirty work. I want you to see what we're up against, but stay back."

Broch looked at Catriona and she placed a hand on his knee.

"Just a training exercise," she said.

He nodded, but he could feel his nerves jangling. Not for his safety, but for Catriona's.

To lose her now would be too much for him to bear.

They pulled to the curb on a residential street and Con cut the engine. Broch admired the man's driving skills. The Irishman had remembered to flip on his turn signal at every intersection, something with which Broch struggled.

He still didn't like him much, though.

Seems lik' a troublemaker.

Anne pointed. "It's the sixth house down; the yellow one. Con and I are going to knock on the door. They don't know us. We'll pretend we're lost, looking for a friend's house. You two find a spot across the street behind those cars there. Once we're in, if you want to move in to see better, you can, but be careful. Either way, we'll let you know when it's done."

"When *what's* done, exactly?" asked Catriona.

"We're running with the assumption Joseph is an infected Kairos as well. We're going to see if we can reboot him and Rune and extract Fiona."

Catriona pressed her lips tightly and nodded slowly. "Okay."

Anne frowned. "I know they're family—"

Catriona was quick to shake her head. "I barely know them. What I *do* know of them, what memories I have, aren't good."

"Rune murdered her once," added Broch, making a gun with his hand and pantomiming a shot. "Fiona stabbed me."

"Nice family," muttered Anne.

Whoops. Mebbe she doesnae want everyone tae ken that.

"And I thought my Da was rough," mumbled Con. He looked at Anne and circled his finger in the air. "Let's go, Red. Ah've got things to do."

Anne side-eyed him. "Drinking whiskey by the pool isn't *things to do.*"

"'Tis in my book." Con flashed Broch and Catriona a grin and with another trademark wink, rolled out of the truck.

Catriona looked at Anne.

"Con seems...*fun.*"

Anne sighed. "*Tons.*"

Broch and Catriona exited the vehicle and met Anne outside. Anne tapped Broch on the bicep but locked her eyes on Catriona.

"I'll give you a sign when we have them. Maybe we can hold off syphoning them until we can test if *you're* capable. This could be a great opportunity to explore your powers."

Cat nodded. With that, Broch understood this training exercise was about his wife's powers and not his own.

Mah wife.

He liked the sound of that.

Anne clapped her hands together. "Alright. Let's go."

Anne and Con walked briskly across the street as Catriona

and Broch slipped into the backyard of the nearest house and moved yard-to-yard, closing in on the yellow house.

When they were across from Rune's hideaway, they crept along the side of the bungalow, watching as Anne and Con approached the door.

"This is crazy," said Catriona, squeezing Broch's arm.

He squeezed back. "It'll be fine. They ken whit they're doin'."

"Do they? How do we know?"

"We don't but...ah dinnae ken whyfur they would lie."

"To lure us to Rune?"

Broch turned. "Ah hadn't thought o' that."

Catriona's eyes grew wide. "*Now* you look concerned? I thought you were *positive* she's telling the truth? I thought your Spidey-sense said she was one of the good guys."

"Ah dinnae ken what *Spidey-sense means*—"

"It's the thing you have that lets you sense danger. You said you could *feel* she was safe."

Broch set his jaw and nodded to Catriona so she could *see* how sure he was.

"Aye. Ah did. Ah dae."

She stared at him.

"Bit, ah mean, ah dinnae ken..." He found his words failing him.

Am ah positive?

He felt sure they were safe with Anne and Con, but...

"Mebbe ah kin sense trouble, bit they hae the power tae hide it?"

"Oh come on." Catriona dropped her forehead onto his shoulder and then lifted her chin again, looking concerned.

"Oh no," she said.

"Whit?"

"I just remembered you were in love with Fiona when she first showed up."

He gasped, horrified. "Nae ah *wisn't*. Ah ken she was *ye*."

"Yeah, but you were *wrong*. That's the point. You didn't sense she was evil."

"Mebbe she's nae. Mebbe she's juist an actress. She *did* stab Rune."

"True." Catriona sighed and motioned toward Anne and Con. "They're knocking."

He saw Con raise his hand to the door and a loud *boom!* echoed across the street.

The door of the yellow house exploded into splinters.

Con flew through the air as if he'd leaped backward from the yellow house's tiny porch, landing on his back on the path he and Anne had traversed a moment before. Anne, already standing to the side, spun against the steps' metal railing, her arms raised to protect her head.

Broch jerked Catriona against him, covering her head as he watched Anne's fists explode with orange light.

"Let's go, we have to go help," said Catriona struggling to rise to her feet as he held her down.

"He's git a musket," said Broch, doing his best to keep himself between her and the street.

Another shot rang out and Anne ran through the doorway. Con remained still on the ground outside.

"We have to get Con out of there."

She's richt.

"Stay here."

"Like hell."

Unable to stop Catriona from following him, Broch did his best to stay in front of her as they scurried across the street toward Con. Broch slowed as he saw the pool of dark red blood on Con's chest. The blast had struck him squarely in the ribs. If he wasn't already dead, he would be soon.

"Cat, wait—"

They'd nearly reached Anne's fallen partner when Con's form flickered. His flesh disappeared, replaced by crackling maroon energy that reminded Broch of Luther's demonstration at Anne's house the day before.

A moment later, the Irishman was back in his more familiar form, struggling to rise to his feet. He sat up as they approached, his fist raised and eyes wild.

"Easy. We're here tae help," said Broch.

Con blinked, his fists still poised in the air.

"Annie?" he asked. He jumped to his feet.

Both Broch and Catriona pointed to the house. "Inside."

Without another word, Con ran into the house, his body blurry with speed.

CHAPTER THIRTY-SIX

The man Anne recognized from photos as Joseph Almos fell back from the door, fumbling with his shotgun as she kicked her way into the house. He raised the weapon but Anne was on him by then, knocking it aside before he could fire another blast. The gun clattered to the ground and slid out of reach.

Teeth gritted, Joseph spun away and grabbed a katana from what Anne realized was an entire wall of weapons. He tore the hooks that held the sword from the drywall as he jerked it free and waggled it at her from the opposite side of a sheet-covered sofa.

"Get back."

Anne manifested her glowing orange swords and Joseph's eyes flashed white, his eyes locking on the light radiating from her fists.

Eh.

I don't need these.

The swords took a lot of energy to manifest and she could tell Joseph wasn't like the experienced, powerful Perfidians she'd battled in the past. She wasn't sure they'd even work on a corrupted Kairos. She absorbed the light back into her hands.

"Look. We're here to help," she said, which was true, though she didn't imagine he would see it that way.

Joseph spat a laugh, spittle flying from his lips. He swung at her with the sword, but she was too far away to even flinch.

Anne sensed energy behind her and turned in time to see Con appear at the doorway.

"Find Rune," she said.

"It was this bastard who shot me," he said, glowering at Joseph.

"I've got him. Go find Rune and Fiona."

Con growled and stabbed his finger at Joseph. "Fine. But I've got somethin' for you, Boyo." He shifted into his energy form and ran straight through Joseph, who stiffened and screamed out as if he'd been electrocuted. He dropped his katana before collapsing to the ground.

Anne sighed. She'd been looking forward to a little sparring.

She walked around the sofa and straddled the thick little man where he lay shaking on the ground. Lowering to one knee, she placed one hand on his neck and one on the bare arm protruding from beneath his strange black weapons vest.

"Time for you to start over," she said.

His eyes bulged wide, but beyond his tremors, he seemed unable to move.

She hated to admit it, but Con had created a perfect situation for testing Catriona and Broch's abilities. She'd half-syphon Joseph to be sure he was weak and then—

Anne's thoughts cut short.

Hold on.

I don't feel anything.

Joseph's energy wasn't feeding into her. The rush of power she usually felt during the syphoning process didn't come.

I can't syphon him.

She frowned, trying to think of another way to accomplish what she needed to do.

I guess I'll tie him up. Maybe Con, with his mixture of Sentinel and Angeli power could syphon him, or Catriona or Broch. She could have Michael swing by and give it a shot. There had to be a way...

She looked down at Joseph to find his eyes more focused. He was *looking* at her.

Before she could react, she felt a sharp pain in her left side. He'd recovered from Con's disruption and pulled a small throwing knife from his vest to plunge it into her side.

Stupid. She'd let her guard down.

She tried to disrupt his energy with her own to knock him out, a trick she'd used countless other times against ill-behaved humans, but again, her powers, so carefully provided by the Angeli to help her defeat *their* fallen, failed her.

Anne pushed herself away. Usually, if she was wounded in battle, she'd use the energy of her enemy to quickly heal. But Joseph provided no power. She'd still heal faster than the average human, but at the rate she was losing blood, it wouldn't be fast enough to beat Joseph's next attack. The fireplug was already back on his feet and had produced a large Buck knife from a holster on his side.

He leered at her. "Chica, I'm going to carve you into—"

Something clattered at the door and Anne looked over to see Broch burst into the room with Catriona close behind. She didn't have to say a word. The two assessed her situation and Broch ran forward to catch Joseph's hand in mid-air as he lunged to stab at her.

Joseph grabbed for another knife with his free hand but Broch soon had that wrist in his grasp as well. Though he fought like a bull, Broch's size proved too much for the smaller man. Joseph roared with frustration as Broch pinned him to the floor with his knee.

Catriona ran to Anne's side.

"You're bleeding."

"I'm fine." She could tell by the way Catriona was staring at her wound it didn't *look* like she'd be fine. "I need some time. Try and syphon him while Broch has him down."

Catriona swallowed. "Me?"

Anne nodded and pressed harder on the hole in her side. The pain of the pressure stole her breath.

"I couldn't do it," she said through clenched teeth. "I'm not the right frequency, I guess. Just *try*. Touch bare flesh and imagine his life flowing into you." Catriona was about to move toward Broch when Anne reached out and grabbed her arm. "If it doesn't work go find Con. He can knock him out."

The world around her seemed to spin off its axis, and she closed her eyes.

Don't lose consciousness. Don't lose consciousness. She couldn't leave these two new soldiers alone with Joseph. While it looked as if Broch had him under control, they didn't know—

Suddenly, Broch roared with what sounded like pain, snapping Anne from her thoughts and helping her to refocus. He released Joseph, falling back, nearly crashing into Catriona.

"What is it?" Anne asked, trying to use the commotion to help her focus.

"Pain," said the Highlander, looking bewildered. "It's like he wis ripping the flesh fae me."

Anne frowned. *Joseph was syphoning Broch.* The urgency of regaining her strength returned.

I can't lose these kids. Not on the first job.

Anne struggled to find her feet, but Joseph beat her to it. He lunged for the large knife he'd lost as Broch stood and ran at him, slamming him against the far wall. Broch struck him, hard in the face and Joseph's hands flailed. Broch hit him again and again.

Anne looked at Catriona. "Now! Try and syphon him while Broch has him."

Catriona flew toward the grappling men. She grabbed Joseph's free arm, the one trying to find Broch's flesh to syphon, and wrestled it as if it were an angry whipping python.

"What do I do?" she screamed.

"Concentrate," said Anne, standing with the help of the sofa beside her. "Imagine pulling everything he has into you. Drain him like a battery. *Concentrate* on his power and pull it toward you."

Catriona squeeze her eyes shut.

"Nothing's happening," she said.

Anne took a step forward and stumbled, grabbing Catriona's arm to catch herself.

Joseph stopped thrashing. Anne felt energy enter her body.

Am I syphoning Catriona?

She was about to let go when Joseph screamed.

No. It's Joseph's energy but how—

Catriona jumped and released her grip. "What's *happening*?"

Joseph's energy stopped flowing into Anne. She had her suspicions confirmed.

She and Catriona *together* could syphon him.

"Don't let go," she barked in her most commanding voice.

Catriona grabbed Joseph's bare arm. Anne felt energy flowing into her once again. Joseph wailed as they drained him and Catriona turned her face away, grimacing. Broch struggled to hold the smaller man against the wall as he lunged repeatedly in his attempts to break free, his eyes wild with panic. The Highlander refused to let go, even as Anne heard him grunt with pain as Joseph pulled energy from him to replace his own.

Soon, Joseph's flesh turned the familiar gray of a dying Perfidian. His attempts to escape slowed. Broch stopped gritting his teeth against the pain. Finally, Joseph's features collapsed and he disappeared into a shower of turquoise light.

"That's a new color," mumbled Anne, stepping back. She ran her hand across her side to find the knife wound gone, her flesh smooth again.

Con appeared from the back of the house.

"Nice timing," muttered Anne.

Con was panting. "I found Fiona. She's out back. Rune's gone. Couldn't find him. Did I miss anything?"

Catriona sat on the edge of the sofa, her eyes wide, breathing heavily.

"Are ye okay?" asked Broch, moving to her.

She looked at him. "Are you kidding?"

They all stared at her as she made eye contact with each of them in turn.

"I feel *amazing*," she said.

Anne laughed. She did, too.

Con left the room and returned with Fiona.

"It's about time," Fiona said, her focus on her sister.

Catriona stood. "Oh *bring* it, Fiona. I'm begging you—" She cocked her head. "Wait, is that *my* good black dress?"

Con moved to Anne. "All good?"

She nodded. "We've got a situation with the syphoning, though."

"How so?"

"Let's just say I don't think I'll be going back to New York any time soon."

"No?" Con grinned. "Pity."

He knew that meant she'd be away from Michael. She punched him and he spun away, laughing.

Anne turned to Catriona and Broch.

"So, what did we learn here today?" she asked.

Catriona's hands were still shaking with adrenaline.

"I sucked the energy out of someone until they died, and right now I'm having trouble feeling bad about it."

"He didn't die. He was rebooted," corrected Anne.

She nodded. "And we found out I can't do it without your help."

Anne nodded. "It looks like it takes you and a Sentinel to complete the job."

"*Awkward*," said Catriona, echoing Anne's thoughts.

CHAPTER THIRTY-SEVEN

Anne was surprised to find Michael at her house when the group returned for their debriefing. He stood in the driveway, his arms crossed against his chest. Anne watched Con glower at him from the SUV as they pulled into the drive.

Here we go.

"Con, don't—"

Anne saved her breath. Con was striding toward Michael before she could finish her sentence, let alone get out of the car. He hadn't bothered to open the car door, but phased through it to piss off Michael.

Michael *hated* that Con had Angeli powers.

"Good to see you, Boyo?" drawled Con, as he stopped in front of Michael.

The Angelus arched an eyebrow. "You haven't changed, I see."

Con scoffed. "Why would I mess with perfection?"

Anne motioned for Fiona to get out of the backseat.

"Let's go."

Fiona stepped out of the car, her gaze locked on Michael.

"Who is *that*?" She wolf-whistled without waiting for an answer. "Mama likey. I mean, your driver has that *animal* thing I love when I'm slumming, but that one smells like money from here."

Anne couldn't argue. As usual, Michael was wearing a

manifested suit that, if purchased, would cost as much as a small car.

"What's he do?" Fiona asked.

Anne decided to deflect that one.

"He's here to check you out."

"He's a doctor?" Fiona's eyes widened. She ran her hand through her hair, pinched her cheeks, and gave her armpits a sniff. "Could I get freshened up inside?"

"Sure. Go in. Jeffrey will get you whatever you need."

"Another man? I can't wait to see what *he* looks like."

Anne chuckled to herself.

I think you'll find him a tough nut to crack.

They got out of the car and Anne motioned to the garage. "Go in through there and call Jeffrey. Let him know what you need."

Fiona grabbed Anne by the shoulder and looked into her eyes. "I like the way you roll, Carrot-top. *Deep.* I think we're going to be good friends."

Fiona released her and scurried into the garage.

Anne walked to Michael and Con who remained on the front step, trading barbs.

"Are you Vietnamese?" Con was asking as she approached.

Michael scowled. "No..."

"Really? Because you *Hanoi* the hell out of me."

Con winked at Anne and she rolled her eyes.

"*Terrible.*"

Con scowled. "What? Come *on.* That's *funny.*"

"Why is he here?" asked Michael. He'd never deign to be jealous of her ex hanging around. Not with the ex standing right there, anyway.

Anne shrugged. "I needed someone to cover for the maintenance guy on the lot, too. He was the payroll lady's husband."

Michael arched an eyebrow in Con's direction. "You needed a ditch-digger. Makes sense you thought of him first."

Con scowled. Before he could retort, Anne pointed him toward Catriona and Broch.

"Can you take the kids inside please and get them ready for a debriefing?"

Con smirked and looked as though he had something to add. Anne put her index finger against his lips to stop him.

"If the next words out of your mouth are a play on the word *debriefing*, I swear to *god* I will cut you down."

Con closed his mouth and, with a final sneer at Michael, did as he was told.

Michael watched him go. "You used to date *that*."

She sighed. "He's not like that around me. You bring out the worst in him."

"And it's *so* difficult."

"Shut up. Why are you here? To check out Fiona?"

"Yes. They let me know you'd captured her. You rebooted one?"

She nodded. "Joseph."

"Rune's still in the wind?"

"Yes. And there are other complications. It took both of us to finish him. Catriona and me."

"Both of you? He was that tough?"

"Not that way—we had syphon at the same time. Individually, *nothing*."

Michael scowled. "Interesting. Maybe you have the power and she has the frequency. She's like a power converter for you. An adapter for a plug you don't fit."

"Maybe. But that means we need to work together. That's going to be a process."

"What about the big fellow?"

"Like you said. He'll do anything to keep her safe. He's got skills, too. Good fighter and untapped potential. Possibly some resistance to syphoning. I'd like to work with him, see how far he can go and what he can do."

Michael's face twitched and Anne smiled.

"You're intimidated by him?" she asked.

He scoffed. "The Highlander? What are you talking about?"

"I was thinking you seem a little taller than usual today. Did you give yourself an inch because he's so large?"

"You're ridiculous."

She laughed. "You're no different than Con. Same animal. You just clean up nice."

Michael leaned down and kissed her on the forehead. "That's the most insulting thing you've ever said to me."

CHAPTER THIRTY-EIGHT

Fiona looked up as Tall, Dark and Edible walked into the bedroom where Jeffrey had asked her to wait. She'd hopped in the shower and positioned herself on the edge of the bed, wrapped in a towel, to await him. The side of her wrapped towel had been artfully arranged to expose a fair amount of side-boob. She was delighted to see the doctor enter alone. Sure, she had plans to take over the world, and she could have her pick of young studs then, but for now, a rich doctor who looked like he'd walked out of a high-end cologne commercial would be a *great* backup.

"Fiona, I'm Michael—" He'd started speaking before the door was fully open. As his eye settled on her, he looked away. "I'm sorry, Jeffrey didn't warn me you were changing—"

"*Oh*," she said, pretending to have been caught off guard. "I'm sorry. I've been held captive for three days. I *had* to get a shower. You're the doctor?"

"Doctor?"

"Anne said you were here to check me out?"

He shook his head. "I'm not a doctor. I'll leave so you can get dressed—"

"No—" she snapped. "I mean, I don't have anything..." She glanced around the room, trying to look helpless.

In truth, she'd already checked. The room was Anne's and her closet had plenty of clothes in it. Mostly casual, but high-end, too. She liked Anne more and more.

"I can ask Anne to get you something—" Michael turned his head as if he were about to call for her.

"*No*, I'm fine. I have my towel. Does what you're about to do involve a lot of *activity*?" She dropped a little pause between a *lot of* and *activity*. Just enough to put *active-while-naked* ideas in his mind, but not enough to sound like a tramp. She could tell he liked his women classy.

Good thing I'm an actress.

She chuckled to herself and then sniffed.

I might be loopy from lack of sleep.

Michael released the breath he'd sucked in to call for Anne. "Alright. This won't take long."

Pity.

He left the door open.

"Would you mind closing that?" she asked.

He blinked at her.

She pointed to the door and affected a shiver. "It's drafty."

"Oh." He closed the door.

Yay. Alone at last.

"So..." Michael took a step toward her and clasped his hands together. "Let's see..."

She stood, slithering up his body without touching him.

"Do you need me to stand?"

Michael took a step back. "No. Um, *sit*. I think sitting would work better."

She sat back down.

"Let me ask you, do you feel *different* after spending time with Rune?"

"Different, how?"

"In any way. Did he, uh, do anything to you? Touch you?"

"He's my *father*."

"No, I understand that. I don't mean—" Michael grimaced. "I'm trying to find a polite way to ask you if you feel like he *infected* you. If you feel *sick* in any way."

"Infected me?" Fiona laughed. "I assure you, I am disease-free."

"Maybe I should take this from the top. We believe your people have contracted a disease called Perfidia. Over time, it makes you mad. Makes you act against your nature."

"Who are my people and what is our nature?"

"You're Kairos. And you're here to help people."

She snorted a laugh.

Oh yeah. That sounds like me all over.

"So you *are* a doctor. How do we contract this disease?"

"Not a doctor. And I don't know, exactly. That's what makes it difficult for me to define a course of interrogation."

"Is that what you're doing?" Fiona tilted her head forward and looked up at him. "Interrogating me?"

"In a manner of speaking."

Feeling that he'd failed to glean her intent, Fiona sat back and thought about her time with Rune.

"You said this thing makes us crazy?"

Michael nodded.

That explains a lot.

"Dad did seem out of it. He's been nuts for a long time."

"Okay. Good. So, have you noticed any of that same madness in yourself?"

"No."

Michael nodded. "The problem is, I don't know if you *would* recognize it in yourself. And if you were infected, it would, of course, behoove you to lie about it."

"Why?"

"Because if you were infected we'd have to fix you."

She smiled. "You're going to *fix* me?"

"Not unless I have to."

"But you *want* to?"

"I wouldn't be the one. It would probably be Anne and Catriona."

Bummer.

Fiona looked away.

This guy is a little slow on the uptake.

Maybe it's time to be a little more direct.

"Are you single, Doctor Mike?"

She saw his jaw grit and had to squelch a grin. She'd called him 'doctor' again on purpose.

"I am *not* a doctor," he said in a measured tone. "Nor am I *Mike*, but I would, with your permission, like to lay my hands on you for a moment."

Um, yes please.

"Permission granted," she purred.

Michael stepped forward and put his hands on each of her shoulders.

He closed his eyes. "I'm going to syphon a tiny bit of energy from you. It won't hurt."

"I don't mind. Sometimes a little pain... Ooh!"

Fiona gasped as a blast of pure pleasure ran through her body.

He released her and stepped back.

"What was that?" she asked.

"I syphoned some of your energy to see if I could sense—"

"No, I mean what was *that*? That *feeling*?"

Michael's cheeks colored. "The process can either be painful or pleasurable. I assumed you'd prefer the latter."

She swallowed. "Can you do it again?"

"Hm? No. We're done. Thank you for being a good sport." Michael strode to the door and opened it.

"*Wait*—"

He didn't wait.

Fiona leaned back on her elbows, her jaw hanging slack as she stared at the doorway.

I have got to get myself one of those.

CHAPTER THIRTY-NINE

Catriona sat through the debriefing at Anne's with her legs crossed and one foot bouncing. She felt as if she'd drunk a thousand cups of coffee without any of the heartburn or anxiety. She was pretty sure if she jumped high enough, she would take flight and zoom out the window to parts unknown.

A teeny-tiny part of her still felt shaken by the image of Joseph bursting into a million tiny turquoise lights, but, if you had to 'kill' someone, it was prettier than conventional methods. And Anne assured her she hadn't killed him. Simply sent him to someplace where he could heal and get back to doing his job, inspiring people to be better, not worse.

OMG. I'm a superhero.

She giggled.

"Catriona?"

Anne was looking at her.

"Hm?"

"Did you say something?"

"Hm? No. Sorry."

Michael entered the room and headed directly for Anne.

"How'd it go?" she asked.

He sent a furtive glance in Catriona and Broch's direction and flashed a weak smile. "Fine."

Michael gave Anne a look that Catriona read as something other than *fine*. He seemed confused, and she suspected that wasn't something he was used to feeling.

He doesn't know.

"She's not sick?" Catriona pressed.

Part of her had been looking forward to *cleansing* her sister from her life.

Michael shook his head but didn't answer out loud.

"Hm." Catriona let it drop. She wanted to jump out of her skin. She looked at Broch.

She wanted to jump on *his* skin.

We have to get out of here. I need to do something fun with all this energy...

She turned to Anne.

"Can we go now?"

Anne nodded. "Sure. I'll let you know when the Angeli get a track on Rune. Tomorrow we can set a training schedule."

Catriona sprang to her feet and headed for the door without another word. She didn't mean to be rude, but once she started moving she couldn't stop.

When Broch caught up, she was disappointed to see he didn't come alone.

Hello, Fiona.

Her sister looked clean and fluffy again, her makeup in place, but she still wore *her* best dress. Best *ex*-dress. Now it looked as if it had been left balled-up in the backyard for a week.

Fiona grinned. "Did you hear? I've been declared clean by Doctor Feel-Good."

"We heard." She looked at Broch. "You drive." She was afraid she'd kill them all. She wanted to drive a hundred and fifty miles an hour and jump over an open bridge.

Maybe some sort of canyon leap...

They clambered into the Jeep and Broch headed home.

"What *is* that guy?" asked Fiona from the back seat.

"Who?"

"The doctor."

Catriona shrugged. "He's an Angelus."

"What's that?"

"They're like guardian angels or something."

Fiona made a humming groan of a noise that sounded as if she were a starving woman watching a giant hamburger arrive. "An angel. That makes total sense. Are there more of them?"

"I guess."

"Good. Drop me off at home."

Catriona twisted in her seat to look at her sister. "But Rune is still on the loose."

"That's okay. He's on the run. He won't come after me."

"I don't know..." Catriona didn't know how hard she wanted to insist. While she didn't think it was safe for Fiona to be alone in her apartment, she also didn't like the idea of her coming home with them.

She *hated* that idea.

"Are you sure?" she asked.

Fiona nodded. "I'm sure."

Catriona looked at Broch. "Do you remember how to get to Fiona's?"

"Aye."

Broch made a left and a few blocks later rolled to the curb outside Fiona's apartment building.

"Thanks." Fiona opened the door and hopped out as Catriona lowered her window.

"If you need anything, give me a call. And get my dress professionally cleaned. I want it back."

Fiona looked down at the dress. "You don't think maybe it's time for an upgrade?"

"No."

"Oh, you poor thing. I'll send you something over."

With a final taunting wave, Fiona strode across the street in her bare feet. It was only then that Catriona realized her sister had lost her shoes.

My shoes.

She raised the window. "Let's go home."

She looked at her phone. "I'm going to call Sean and tell him what happened so I can get this chewing out over."

"Aye. Guid idea."

Catriona paused.

"Do you think it's weird that Fiona wanted to go home?"

"How come?"

"Well, after she stabbed my father she was terrified to be alone. Now she's not concerned at all? And he's still out there…"

"Hm."

"*Hm.*" Catriona tapped her phone with her fingernail and then made the dreaded call to Sean, staring out the window as she listened to the ring.

He was going to be *furious.*

CHAPTER FORTY

Rune knocked on Maddie Barbeau's door. He'd run the entire way, far from the little house where he'd felt so at home.

Well, where he'd felt so at home after a good cleaning.

Already, he missed Joseph and Fiona and the world they'd been creating together. Their new world.

Now, a storm of hate roiled his heart—hate for the people who had taken it all away.

They would hear the thunder of his pending approach from miles away. They would feel the crackling lightning of his vengeance.

The door opened and Rune smiled.

"Hey, Maddie, good to see you. How are you?"

In his head, he heard trumpets of doom.

Blood will spill! Pain will rain upon his enemies!

But first, he needed a place to stay. He didn't imagine anyone would look for him at Maddie's. The actress was useful. Maybe she could help him plan his next move.

"You again," she said. She wobbled on her feet as she opened the door. Rune thought he smelled alcohol. Smiling, he walked in and took his usual place on her sofa. "It's been a bad day. I've suffered a setback. I need a place to rest and think."

Maddie flopped onto the chair across from him. "Aren't you wondering why I'm home in the middle of the day?"

He scowled. "No."

She told him anyway. "It's because filming is suspended while they figure out what happened to Dixie."

"Then it will be suspended for a very long time."

"Yeah, well I can't afford that. There's talk they might cancel the show."

Maddie seemed angry. She stared at him until he looked away and then, disgusted by his cowardice, he looked back to glare at her. She didn't blink. His eyes dropped to the bottle of wine and the glass in front of her. Both were empty. He spotted another open bottle on the kitchen counter, that one white, but also empty.

"Are you drunk?" he asked.

Her eyes flared.

"How are you going to *fix* things?" she demanded to know.

Rune lost interest. Drunk people were so *boring*. Joseph only drank beer, and he was always mindful of how much he consumed. He liked that about Joseph.

"I didn't go back and help him," he mumbled.

"What?"

Rune waved her away and returned to his thoughts, mumbling. "I should have gone back in. Joseph could be dead and I didn't help. He was my only friend. He helped me see the possibilities."

"Hey, *Freakshow*." Maddie shifted to the edge of the chair. "You said you were going to help me. You killed my co-star and now I might be out of a job. You need to *fix* this."

Rune bit the side of his cheek, thinking.

Did Fiona trick him?

What if she was lying? What if she had no intention of helping? It seemed as though she'd come around but...

She has the list.

Rune felt his anger rising.

That's it. Fiona had already stolen the list from Joseph. She was never going to tell him she had it. She sent him away so *she* could get away. So she could go *to her friends.* She'd been afraid to send him back in—afraid he'd kill the Highlander and his insipid lot.

Rune heard a click and looked up in time to see Maddie lowering a gun in his direction. The click was her pulling back the hammer on the weapon. She was very close. There was little chance she'd miss him.

"What are you doing?" he asked.

"You help me or I'm going to kill you. I'm prepared this time."

Rune stood. He felt his anger boiling. He heard the lightning crackling.

"Put that down."

She straddled her legs to keep from wobbling. "I will not. Not until you fix things."

"You can't kill me."

She sneered. "Can't I?"

Rune took a step forward and a shot rang out. He felt something strike his chest. The force knocked him back onto the sofa.

He looked down to find blood seeping into his shirt, capillary action spreading an uneven circle across his chest.

He turned his attention to Maddie, who still stood in the same position, gun still pointed at him, her mouth wide with what looked like surprise.

"You shot me," he said. He heard a wheeze and realized she'd punctured his lung. It hurt to breathe.

"Put the gun down."

"I can't." Her hands were trembling now.

"Lower it."

"I can't. You'll kill me."

"I *won't*." He stood, slowly, every breath agony. "I wouldn't. You're my friend, Maddie."

Her lip began to tremble as she lowered the gun. Her eyes were awash with tears, her face twisted in an unattractive mask of sloppy emotion.

"Now I'm going to *jail*," she sobbed, a shiny drip of mucus from her nose running over her upper lip.

Repulsive.

"I need you to listen to me," she whined. "I need you to

fix—"

He lifted his metal arm and held out the hand, hoping it could block a bullet should the need arise. "I understand. I need to lie down. Can you help me? It's very hard to breathe. I think you punctured my lung. I feel so weak."

"Oh my god. I'm so sorry." Maddie glanced at the gun in her hand. Searching for a place to put it, she laid it on her dining room table and then scrambled to him, sniffling.

"You can lie down in my guest room—"

The moment she was near, he grabbed her wrist with both hands.

Her eyes bulged wide. "*No—*"

"Did you think I was going to let you live after you *shot* me?" he asked.

She slapped at him with her other hand, and pulled, trying to free herself. He turned his head so her blows didn't strike his face. Though he didn't feel strong, the grip of his metal hand was nearly unbreakable. She wasn't going anywhere.

The blows to the side and back of his head slowed until they stopped. The skin on her face seemed to melt across her features.

Finally, Maddie collapsed to dust.

Feeling stronger, Rune tore open his shirt and inspected his chest. The wound was healed, a perfectly circular scar dotting his flesh.

For a moment, his healed breast swelled with elation.

He'd still stay at Maddie's. He could hole up—

No.

His mood darkened.

The gunshot.

He couldn't stay. The neighbors might already be calling the authorities.

I have to leave. Now.

Rune ran out of the house and jogged toward Parasol Pictures.

Fiona. He had to find her.

His daughter had told him she'd been living at that girl's

apartment on the studio lot. The girl who looked like her.

She'd probably gone back there after she tricked him.

What was her name?

Catriona.

The name bounced through his head. It meant something but he wasn't sure what.

I'll find Fiona. I'll get the list and I'll kill her.

No.

He needed to think bigger.

I'll kill them all.

He'd found a rhythm jogging. It felt as though he could run forever. He was almost disappointed when he spotted a sign on a wall signifying the space behind it as the property of Parasol Pictures.

Jungle foliage peeked above the fence line.

It wasn't the front gate, but maybe that was a good thing. He could sneak in, undetected, and make his way to Fiona. He leaped up and grabbed the top of the fence, pulling himself up with a rush of strength he didn't know he had.

CHAPTER FORTY-ONE

The moment Catriona walked into her apartment she jumped at Broch, throwing her arms around his neck.

"Take me to bed or lose me forever."

"*Whit?*"

"Sorry. It's from *Top Gun*. But you get the idea."

He wrapped his arms around her waist and she stared up at the gold flecks in his hazel eyes. She felt as if her chest might explode with love for him.

How did this breakthrough happen? Is this what true love feels like?

She'd had crushes before but nothing that made her feel the way she did now. She wanted to *envelop* Broch. Every blink of his eyes or twitch of his lips made her ache with love. Not just *desire*, though there was plenty of that as well.

Thoughts of divorcing him had been stomped to death and thrown out the window into a fiery volcano of *no*.

No. wait.

A *volcane-no.*

She giggled and he peered down at her.

"Whit's so funny?"

"Nothing. Making myself laugh."

"Ye dae that a lot."

"I know. Sorry."

He shook his head, smiling, as she marveled at him.

I want to eat you alive and keep you inside my chest. Is that weird?

"Aye," he said as if he'd heard her thoughts.

She gasped, horrified.

"Did you just read my mind?" she asked.

He cocked his head. "Hm?"

No. She could tell by his expression he hadn't.

Whew.

If he could read every odd thought that ran through her brain he'd run back to ancient Scotland.

He brushed the hair from her eyes. "Bit are ye okay? Ye've been a wee nutty since the *thing*."

She grinned. "Listen to you. *Okay*, the *thing*, you're starting to use all the modern slang."

Adorable. You're like some giant gorgeous Scottish Sasquatch. A Scotchsquatch.

She shook her head.

Stop it.

"Ah'm serious, Cat. Dae ye feel well?"

She stood on her toes to steal a kiss and he retracted his neck.

"Blether tae me," he insisted.

She rolled her eyes. "I'm *fine*. It's just, all that man's..." She struggled to find the right word. "*Power*...lifeforce...*whatever*, flowed into me. I feel like I'm running off of two batteries instead of one if that makes sense."

"It doesnae."

"Oh. Of course not. Um, it feels like I have twice the energy as usual. And I feel almost drunk. Not drunk-drunk. *Giddy*."

"Ah. That doesn't sound sae bad."

"No. Not at all. I've been racking my brain for a way to use up all this energy..."

She hoped she'd said the line suggestively enough.

She had.

She whooped as he scooped her into his arms.

"Ah hae an idea."

She wrapped her arms around his neck. Never in her life had she dreamed a man could sweep her off the ground like that.

"How do you do that? I'm not a tiny girl."

"Ah'm not a tiny man."

She tittered. "No, you are *not*."

He took her into the bedroom and dropped her to the mattress from a little higher than necessary, setting her to laughing all over again.

As she bounced, her phone rang and she pulled it from her pocket.

"I'm unavailable," she announced, glancing at it as she moved to place it on the bedside table.

It was Sean.

"Damn."

"Whit is it?"

"It's Sean. I better answer. He's already furious. Hello?"

Sean sounded annoyed. "We've got an intruder on the *Amazon Death Step* set. Motion alarm went off and the camera's picked up someone."

"Who?"

"It was just a flash. Couldn't see a face. Another one of the lead actor's groupies, more than likely. I'm going to have to do something about that wall along the eastern perimeter. Teenage girls are shockingly inventive when it comes to stalking their idols."

"Maybe it's a jungle cat."

"I don't think so."

Catriona flopped her free arm across the bed. She wanted to scream.

"Send one of the guards."

"There's no one available."

"Where are *you*?"

"Home with Luther. I wanted to talk to him about everything that happened and I owed him dinner. Jeeze, Cat, will you just go check, please? What's the problem?"

Broch had pulled off his shirt and stood beside the bed,

tight and deliciously lumpy in all the right places.

She closed her eyes.

The timing.

"You owe me for ignoring my rules earlier," added Sean. "Oh, and it's your *job.*"

Hard to argue with that.

She sighed. "*Fine.* I'll run over there."

"Take Broch."

"I will. I'll let you know in a bit."

She hung up, grit her teeth, and released a quiet scream of frustration.

"Whit's he want?"

"The security cameras were triggered over on that big Amazon movie set. Someone's out for a jungle stroll."

Broch grunted and stooped to pick up his shirt. "Ah'll gang."

She swung her legs over the bed and put her arms around his butt to pull his stomach against her cheek. "No, we'll go together, get it done, and get back here." She kissed his belly.

"Nae if ye keep that up," he mumbled.

CHAPTER FORTY-TWO

The Amazon Death Step set occupied a good part of the northwest corner of the lot and included an indoor-outdoor jungle area and a realistically sized mountain, complete with a waterfall. A week earlier, Catriona had visited the set during the shooting of a scene using a live jaguar. They'd let her feed it a hunk of meat.

The studio was hoping *Amazon Death Step* would be the next *Indiana Jones*, but she didn't have high hopes. The lead was a singer-turned-actor they hoped would bring in the teeny-bopper audience, but Catriona felt he lacked the chops to play the dashing hero and would lose everyone over the age of thirteen.

"It's probably the kid practicing lines with the fake toucans," she said as they pulled up to the door of the studio.

Catriona typed the code into the lock keypad and they entered a world very different from the desert landscape outside. There was a relatively empty area inside the door littered with cameras, booms, and director's chairs, but beyond the production area was nothing but vines, rocks, and tropical trees.

"Let's check the dressing rooms," she suggested.

They walked to the far wall and opened three doors, one at a time. Each revealed a small costume area, undisturbed and empty of intruders.

Catriona turned to the jungle. "I was hoping we wouldn't have to go tromping through there."

Broch nodded. "Me tae. Feels buggy tae me."

Catriona laughed. "They *do* like to be authentic, but I don't think they pumped in mosquitos."

A mix of real plants and plastic or silk ones created the foliage around them. A few steps into the mess they stopped short to avoid dropping into a pool of indeterminable depth, the bottom painted black to make it seem murky and foreboding. Behind it, a black plastic ramp rose toward the outside portion of the set, which had been raised to simulate a mountain.

"They're using that for a waterfall," explained Catriona, pointing to the ramp. "I saw it running the other day when I came by to meet the jaguar. When they release the tank up there the water rushes into this pool and then gets pumped back up to start again. It cost a fortune."

Broch's eyes scaled the ramp as he shook his head, clearly disapproving. "How come they dinnae just gang tae the real jungle?"

Catriona agreed. "It's hard to imagine it's cheaper to build something on this scale than it is to fly everyone to the Amazon, but apparently, it is."

"Ah ken here they dinnae hae tae worry the star is gobbled by a snake."

Catriona pointed at him. "That might be it."

Something clanged above them and their gazes shot to the top of the artificial mountain. To the left of the giant plastic slide, someone climbed down the metal staircase built to access the tank and plateau above.

"Hey!" screamed Catriona.

The man turned and peered down at them. While he remained partially hidden by the plastic palms, there was no mistaking who that bag of bones was.

Rune.

Broch was already running toward the metal staircase.

Rune turned and started back up.

Catriona made a move to follow Broch and then stopped. The staircase was narrow—she'd be stuck behind him, unable to help should Rune turn to battle him.

Useless.

She eyed the faux waterfall ramp and noticed a staircase had been molded into the plastic. The way was steep and shallow, like the world's most treacherous attic steps, but she *could* climb to the top and maybe cut off Rune on the catwalk above.

Catriona shifted her holster and ran to the stairs to climb them like a dog, using her hands to steady her body against the plastic.

Ahead and above her, Broch turned, searching for her behind him on the stairs. She waved back before continuing to climb.

Rune neared the top. Catriona had half the mountain to scale and was out of breath. She hadn't realized how steep they'd built the mountain.

She glanced at the pool below. There was no handrail or place to grab. She felt a dizzy thrill run through her chest and looked away.

"This was a stupid idea," she muttered.

Rune crested the top level of the staircase. Unless he paused to await Kilty, there was no way she'd reach the top in time to cut him off. She cursed under her breath and tried to pick up her pace, her lungs burning with exertion.

There were better ways to burn off her energy.

Rune ran across the catwalk above her, stopping to peer down. She stopped climbing, hoping he wouldn't notice her, but she could tell by his expression he had.

Damn. There goes the element of surprise.

She expected him to run faster across the catwalk now that he knew *two* people were in pursuit, but instead, he pivoted and headed back toward Broch.

What is he doing?

Rune disappeared from view.

A moment later, an obnoxious warning buzzer blared

through the cavernous studio. Catriona jerked backward and then threw her body against the plastic to keep from plunging to the pool below.

Her heart raced.

What was that?

A grinding noise crunched somewhere behind the waterslide on which she perched.

Oh no.

She knew what the buzzer meant.

Rune hit the pump.

She heard the water before she could see it.

"Catriona!" screamed Broch.

Catriona stared at him, helpless. She scanned the area around her looking for anything to which she could brace, but there was nothing. She looked behind her at the pool below.

How far is that? Thirty feet? Forty?

"Stupid, stupid—"

She'd never dreamed Rune would know how to turn on the waterfall. It never occurred to her he'd even *know* about it. Why would he? The studio must have had the button clearly labeled on the catwalk panel.

Damn OSHA work safety standards.

Above her, dribbles of water cresting the edge, the tank readying to spill, and she knew she only had two choices.

Wait until the water knocked her from her tenuous perch.

Or, *jump.*

The pool below was too narrow to risk being swept off the angled ramp. She'd have to *jump* to clear the steps and have some control over where she splashed.

Catriona took a deep breath and pushed off the wall.

She went airborne.

Now, she just had to pray the pool was deep enough.

She fell, arms flailing and legs parted to keep from hitting the water like a spear and plunging too deep to the uncertain bottom. She smacked the water's surface, wincing, hoping her spine wasn't about to be slammed through her shoulders.

Her feet hit the bottom and her knees bent, absorbing the

landing.

Deep enough.

She would have heaved a sigh of relief if it didn't mean drowning. She launched herself upward.

That wasn't too bad—

The waterfall crashed on her head as she broke the surface.

Catriona spun to the bottom again. Disoriented from the blow, she struggled to find *up*. When she thought her lungs would explode, she felt her hand touch air and gave one last hard stroke to reach oxygen, praying water wouldn't tumble from the sky and into her lungs.

She gasped and felt her lungs inflate.

"Catriona!"

She heard her name as she swam for the side of the pool, Broch's scream muffled by the roar of the waterfall flowing from the top of the artificial mountain.

She waved her arm above her head to let him know she'd survived the drop and dragged herself, sputtering, onto the gravelly bank surrounding the pool. After taking a moment to cough and catch her breath, she stood and scrambled toward the stairs.

Stairs that would have been the better choice the *first* time.

Catriona climbed. Above her, Broch had reached the top. She couldn't see Rune. She doubled her efforts to speed her ascent, wishing she'd spent less time at the gym kickboxing and more time on the Stairmaster.

By the time she'd reached the top, winded and spent, Rune and Broch were nowhere to be seen.

"Broch?"

She called, but could barely hear herself over the roar of the water and the pump. Walking across the catwalk, she stopped to slap the waterfall's labeled red emergency *stop* button. The thunder of the water ceased and she heard voices echoing from somewhere on the opposite side of falls.

She sprinted forward.

Rounding the corner of a crumbling ruin, Catriona saw Broch had Rune cornered against a stucco wall. The metal ladder mounted to it led to the outside world. Rune stood crouched like a wrestler, his hands curled into claws.

"Stop!" Rune screamed at Catriona as she approached. "I'll drain you both in seconds if you touch me."

Broch looked at her. "Ah kin tak' him afore he gets far."

Catriona grimaced. "You probably can, but I don't know if the damage will be permanent." She'd been meaning to ask Anne if being syphoned by the likes of Rune left any lasting damage, but hadn't had the chance. She put it on her mental to-do list.

"Let me handle this," she said reaching for her gun.

She found her holster empty and tilted back her head, groaning.

Arg.

The gun had to be in the pool. She'd never thought to check if she still had it after her tumble.

She huffed and glared at Rune, feeling stuck.

"We're at a stalemate."

Rune placed his good hand on the nearest ladder rung. "No. I'm going to climb this ladder and you're going to stay there."

"We cannae let ye gang," said Broch.

"You can and you will."

Rune's blazing gaze shot from Catriona to Broch and back again as he ascended the ladder. Broch took a step forward and Rune swiped at him.

Broch looked at Catriona. "It tak's awhile," he argued.

She knew he meant he thought Rune wouldn't have the time to drain him before he was able to tie the monster into a knot.

Catriona shook her head. "It took Joseph time. Who knows with Rune?"

Broch clenched his jaw and looked up at Rune.

As she watched her father climb, an image flashed through Catriona's mind of a pile of rubble she'd passed on the way to find Broch. Bolting back down the path she'd traveled, she found the stones. Gathering a few, she tossed one into the air and caught it, feeling the rough surface beneath her fingertips.

Real stone. Not Styrofoam.

Perfect.

In the past, Broch had demonstrated his uncanny throwing accuracy. Collecting five rocks, she ran back to Broch and dropped them at his feet.

"Remember that crazed kid you hit with a rock?" she asked, handing him one shaped like a golf ball.

Broch took the rock and grinned. "Aye."

He looked up at Rune. The skinny goon was almost at the top. He stared down, sneering, clearly feeling cocky now, daring them to chase him up the ladder.

Then he spotted the stone in Broch's paw.

Catriona saw panic flood Rune's expression. He climbed faster, glancing back, again and again, waiting for Broch to throw.

Broch cocked back his arm and tossed the first stone. It shot from his hand like a cannonball. Rune dodged to the right as it crashed against the wall beside him. He raised his arm to block the exploding fragments but remained firm on the ladder.

A moment later he was climbing again.

Catriona raised her arms over her head as bits of rock peppered down.

She gathered Broch another missile and he grabbed a second chunk from the pile. His choice proved more baseball-sized. Catriona couldn't imagine throwing such a large object so far in the air, let alone with any accuracy, but then, she wasn't an enormous Highlander.

Brock cocked back and tossed the larger of the two and Catriona frowned. She could see right away it would end up left of Rune, much like the last attempt. Sure enough, Rune released his left hand again and swung to the right.

By then, Broch already had the other rock launching. When Rune looked down at them, smirking that he had so easily dodged the giant chunk of brick, the last smaller rock hit him squarely in the forehead.

Catriona whooped. "You hit him!"

Rune's body went limp, and his feet slipped from their

rung, but he didn't fall. Instead, he hung from his metal arm like a limp flag.

Catriona's cheer died on her lips. She slapped her hands to her hips and watched as her father slowly rocked back and forth above them.

"You've got to be kidding me."

Broch took a step forward to mount the ladder, but before he could take a step, Rune's body detached from his artificial arm, the fabric of his shirt tearing from his body. The Highlander scrambled out of the way as Rune bounced once against the ladder and hit the ground with a cracking noise Catriona worried would haunt her the rest of her life.

She covered her mouth with her hand, horrified.

"That had to hurt."

Rune was unaware of what bones he might have broken. He remained unconscious.

She moved forward to see if he was alive and saw his chest rising and falling. Gingerly, she touched his neck to feel for a pulse.

"He's alive."

"Dinnae titch him," warned Broch.

She looked back at him. "I have to. I want to try to syphon him."

Catriona closed her eyes and endeavored with all her concentration to pull energy from her father. Nothing happened. No rush of power entered her body. She felt deflated.

"It isn't working." Her shoulders slumped. "What if he comes around?"

"Ah'll bind him," suggested Broch.

Catriona nodded and jerked a fake vine from the underbrush around them. It felt very much like a rope.

"Use this."

Broch took the vine and stood there, staring at Rune, seemingly puzzled.

"What are you waiting for?" she asked.

"Hae am ah supposed tae tie him with one hand?"

She scowled.

Good point.

It was like a Buddhist koan.

What is the sound of one hand being tied?"

Broch perked. "Och, ah'll tie his hand to his *foot*."

Catriona watched him bind Rune's remaining arm to his legs. When he was done, he lifted the boney man over his shoulder like a shearing sheep, careful to keep Rune's bare flesh from touching him, just in case.

"Let's get him tae Anne afore he wakes up."

Catriona pulled her phone from her pocket, pleased to find it still worked after her plunge. She dialed the number Anne had given her in case of emergency and the Sentinel answered.

"Catriona?"

"We have Rune."

"You do?"

"He was lurking on a movie set. We have him tied up."

"That's great. Did you try—"

Catriona sighed. "I did. My darndest. Couldn't drain him. Not even a little."

"Okay. Shoot. Michael just left or I would have had him pop over there and take him."

"We would've had to get Michael a pass to get him on the lot anyway. It's a pain. We'll just bring him to you."

Anne chuckled. "He could have gotten on the lot just fine, but, okay. Bring him here and I'll call Michael back from New York. He'll want to see this."

"He's on his way home?"

"He's already home."

"But it's only been two hours—"

"He doesn't fly commercial."

"But even—" Catriona let it drop, suspecting Michael didn't fly in planes at *all*. "Okay. We'll be there in a bit."

"Great. Be careful. We don't know what he's capable of."

Catriona glanced at Rune, flopping against Broch's back as he headed back toward the catwalk.

"I think we've got things pretty well wrapped up."

She glanced up at the ladder and saw Rune's arm swinging

there.

I guess I better get that.

CHAPTER FORTY-THREE

By the time Catriona and Broch arrived at Anne's house, Michael was, once again, standing outside the house like a handsome impatient gargoyle.

Broch rode in the back hatch area with the back seats down, Rune bundled at his feet. He crouched poised, ready to smack Catriona's father back into unconsciousness should he awaken.

The gangly man never moved a muscle.

As the Jeep rolled to a stop, Broch opened the hatch and hopped out. Michael strode up to him as he moved to pull Rune from the back.

"I have him," said Michael. He eyed Broch's hairline and straightened to bring his parallel.

Broch had seen men do similar things before.

He guessed next to him Michael came up a wee short.

He glanced at Rune and then turned back to Michael.

"Are ye sure? He's heavier than he looks."

Michael reached into the back of the Jeep, his arm morphing into a network of thin blue lightning. When he came in contact with their captive, Rune disappeared, his form disappearing into the same sapphire web.

Michael smiled. "I've got him."

A moment later, Michael had disappeared completely,

along with Rune.

Broch grunted.

Ah may be taller, bit ah cannae dae that.

Catriona came around the back of the Jeep, Rune's metal arm in her hand. She looked into the Jeep.

"Where'd he go?"

"Michael took him."

She looked around. "Where?"

Broch tapped his fingertips together and then exploded them outward. "He flew away, ah ken."

Catriona held up the arm. "He forgot this."

Anne arrived and winced at the arm.

"What the hell is that?"

"Rune's arm. Michael took him but he forgot this."

Anne rapped on it with her knuckle. "Some kind of bionics? I don't think it's important, but I'll have one of the other Angeli take it to him."

Catriona handed the limb to Anne. "Where did Rune go? I thought we were going to *fix* Rune together. You and me."

Broch noticed Catriona looked disappointed. It was cute.

She might lik' that power rush a wee tae much.

"Michael took him to a holding facility," said Anne. "He wants to understand what happened to Rune so maybe they can stop it from happening to others."

"He's going to keep him like a laboratory rat?"

"Something like that, I guess. He won't torture him if that's what you're worried about." Anne smiled. "Have you eaten? It's just me and Jeffrey here. Might be nice to have some company for dinner."

Broch nodded. It felt like he hadn't eaten in a week.

Aye. Please.

He loved many things about Catriona, but her cooking wasn't one of them. And the snacks Jeffrey made them during their last visit...he was still thinking about them.

Catriona notice how much he wanted Anne's food and flashed him a lopsided smile.

"Sure. I guess we have plenty of time to get back to what we were doing."

"A lifetime," said Broch, putting an arm around her. He kissed the top of her head.

Anne started back to the house with Catriona and Broch following.

"Maybe you could tell us more about you," suggested Catriona. "If this keeps up, we might be spending a lot more time together."

Anne nodded. "Sure. I'll make sure Jeffrey has some dessert."

Broch made a little fist pump with the arm not draped around Catriona.

Anne opened the door and ushered them inside.

"I warn you," she said. "It's a *long* story."

~~ THE END ~~

WANT SOME MORE? FREE PREVIEWS!

If you liked this book, read on for a preview of the next Kilty AND the Shee McQueen Mystery-Thriller Series!

THANK YOU FOR READING!

If you enjoyed this book, please swing back to Amazon and **leave me a review** — even short reviews help authors like me find new fans! You can also FOLLOW AMY on AMAZON

ABOUT THE AUTHOR

USA Today and Wall Street Journal bestselling author Amy Vansant has written over 20 books, including the fun, thrilling Shee McQueen series, the rollicking, twisty Pineapple Port Mysteries, and the action-packed Kilty urban fantasies. Throw in a couple romances and a YA fantasy for her nieces...

Amy specializes in fun, exciting reads with plenty of laughs and action -- she tried to write serious books, but they always ended up full of jokes, so she gave up.

Amy lives in Jupiter, Florida with her muse/husband a goony Bordoodle named Archer.

Books by Amy Vansant

Pineapple Port Mysteries
Funny, clean & full of unforgettable characters

Shee McQueen Mystery-Thrillers
Action-packed, fun romantic mystery-thrillers

Kilty Urban Fantasy/Romantic Suspense
Action-packed romantic suspense/urban fantasy

Slightly Romantic Comedies
Classic romantic romps

The Magicatory
Middle-grade fantasy

FREE PREVIEW

KILTY AS HELL

CHAPTER ONE

Fiona entered her apartment building's private garage.

That's when she saw the boy.

She had no idea how old he was. She wasn't good at guessing kids' ages. He was small, so... Two? Six? Eight?

Who knows?

His age wasn't important. The important part was that the little brat was sitting on the hood of her car.

"Hey!" she snapped, speeding her step. "Get *off* of there."

"Watch your tone, young lady," said the boy.

Fiona stopped.

Oh no.

A seed of dread grew in the pit of her stomach.

It can't be.

She took a few steps forward, squinting at the boy in the dim light of the garage. He stared back at her with icy blue eyes.

Shit.

"Dad?" she asked.

The boy scoffed. "Yes. Of course, it's me. Who else would it be?"

His cadence mimicked that of her ever-irritable father, Rune, but his tone had a higher pitch—as if someone had sped Rune's voice like a chipmunk's.

She motioned to him as if she were lassoing him with her index finger.

"Is it me? I remember you taller."

The boy scowled. "I had to start over, and I miscalculated the year. I wanted to return to *this* year as an adult but...I was reborn six years ago instead of twenty."

He sighed.

Fiona noticed something. The last time she'd seen her father, he had one metal arm. He'd lost the original to her sister Catriona's adoptive father, Sean, in some modern-day sword fight.

How he managed to get himself roped into that...

She didn't care. To say Catriona and she had a complicated relationship with their father was like saying police had a *complicated* relationship with serial killers. To be fair, *complicated* was the only relationship anyone *could* have with Rune.

"You got your arm back," she said.

He glanced at his little hand.

"Yes. Look, I don't have much time—"

"There you are!"

A woman entered the garage and made a beeline for baby Rune. Fiona's elderly lobby attendant, Teddy, hustled behind her, chugging like a locomotive.

Rune swore. "That's my mother," he muttered. He raised his arms. "Help me down?"

Fiona's lip curled. "What?"

He gritted his baby teeth. "Help me down and *listen.*"

Fiona stepped forward to slide her arms under the boy's armpits, grimacing as if he were made of snot, yellow poo, and common cold viruses, which she assumed he *was.*

"I've regained my consciousness," he said as she pulled him from the hood of her car. "I'll be back the next chance I get, and we'll plot our path going forward."

She held him as he dangled in front of her. "Plot our path forward? What? You want me to help you fill out pre-school applications?"

Rune scowled, which would be an *adorable* expression on such a tiny face if Fiona didn't find children, in general, repulsive.

"For your information, I start first grade next week," he said.

He seemed genuinely proud. Fiona assumed his adult memories and child's mind remained jumbled.

"Congratulations," she said.

He glanced over his shoulder. His mother was closing in on them.

"Look, I'll be able to get away—"

Fiona laughed. "And then what? You're going to throw diapers at people until they make you king?"

"I am fully potty-trained!" Rune roared. He kicked at Fiona, and she dropped him. He landed on his feet, but his little legs collapsed like noodles, and he ended up on his butt, red-faced and furious. Fiona stepped back for fear he'd lunge forward to bite her ankles.

"Oliver!" yipped his mother as she swept in and scooped the boy up from the ground. She glared at Fiona. "Were you trying to kidnap him?"

Fiona barked a laugh. "*Kidnap* him? Lady, I don't want your stupid kid. The little ass was sitting on my car."

The woman held Rune to her chest, rocking him back and forth as he hung like a ragdoll. "Oliver, what were you thinking? Why would you run away from Mommy like that?"

"Yeah, *Oliver*, what were you thinking?" asked Fiona.

"My name is *Rune*," said the boy, glaring at his mother as he tried to push away from her.

A flash of embarrassment crossed the mother's face as she caught Fiona's eye. "His name's Oliver," she explained. "A few months ago, he told us he wanted to be called *Rune*. Refuses to respond to any other name." She chuckled and threw in an overly-dramatic eye roll. "*Kids.*"

Fiona nodded. "Hey, just spitballing here, but did you ever consider *Oliver* might be a time traveler reborn as your child, who recently remembered who he *really* is and wants to get back to his nefarious plan to take over the world?"

The woman's jaw dropped open, her gaze locked with Fiona's, her hand tight around Rune's wrist.

"What is wrong with you?" she asked.

Fiona shrugged. "Just a thought."

The woman glanced at the doorman and dragged Rune back the way they'd come.

Rune glanced over his shoulder at Fiona as he tried to keep up with his stupid little feet.

"I'll be back," he called.

"Don't hurry," Fiona returned.

She glanced at Teddy, who remained standing dumbly beside her.

"Sorry about that, Miss Fiona," he said, looking sheepish.

Fiona pointed in the direction mother and child had disappeared.

"You keep that kid away from me," she said. "You see him again, you call the police."

Teddy nodded. "Yes ma'am."

Fiona turned and continued to her car.

It was official.

Daddy's back.

She flopped into her seat and shut the door.

This is not good.

ANOTHER FREE PREVIEW!

THE GIRL WHO WANTS

A Shee McQueen Mystery-Thriller by Amy Vansant

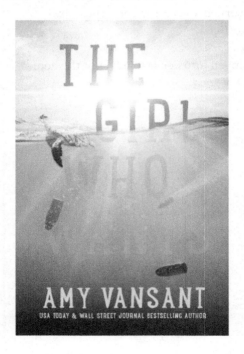

Chapter One

Three Weeks Ago, Nashua, New Hampshire.

Shee realized her mistake the moment her feet left the grass.

He's enormous.

She'd watched him drop from the side window of the house. He landed four feet from where she stood, and still, her brain refused to register the warning signs. The nose, big and lumpy as breadfruit, the forehead some beach town could use as a jetty if they buried him to his neck...

His knees bent to absorb his weight and *her* brain thought, *got you.*

Her brain couldn't be bothered with simple math: *Giant, plus Shee, equals Pain.*

Instead, she jumped to tackle him, dangling airborne as his knees straightened and the *pet the rabbit* bastard stood to his full height.

Crap.

The math added up pretty quickly after that.

Hovering like Superman mid-flight, there wasn't much she could do to change her disastrous trajectory. She'd *felt* like a superhero when she left the ground. Now, she felt more like a Canada goose staring into the propellers of Captain Sully's Airbus A320.

She might take down the plane, but it was going to *hurt.*

Frankenjerk turned toward her at the same moment she plowed into him. She clamped her arms around his waist like a little girl hugging a redwood. Lurch returned the embrace, twisting her to the ground. Her back hit the dirt and air burst from her lungs like a double shotgun blast.

Ow.

Wheezing, she punched upward, striking Beardless Hagrid in the throat.

That didn't go over well.

Grabbing her shoulder with one hand, Dickasaurus flipped her on her stomach like a sausage link, slipped his hand under her chin and pressed his forearm against her windpipe.

The only air she'd gulped before he cut her supply stank of damp armpit. He'd tucked her cranium in his arm crotch, much like the famous noggin-less horseman once held his severed head. Fireworks exploded in the dark behind her eyes.

That's when a thought occurred to her.

I haven't been home in fifteen years.

What if she died in Gigantor's armpit? Would her father even know?

Has it really been that long?

Flopping like a landed fish, she forced her assailant to adjust his hold and sucked a breath as she flipped on her back. Spittle glistened on his lips, his brow furrowed as if she'd asked him to read a paragraph of big-boy words.

His nostrils flared like the Holland Tunnel.

There's an idea.

Making a V with her fingers, Shee thrust upward, stabbing into his nose, straining to reach his tiny brain.

Goliath roared. Jerking back, he grabbed her arm to unplug her fingers from his nose socket. She whipped away her limb before he had a good grip, fearing he'd snap her bones with his Godzilla paws.

Kneeling before her, he clamped both hands over his face, cursing as blood seeped from behind his fingers.

Shee's gaze didn't linger on that mess. Her focus fell to his crotch, hovering a foot above her feet, protected by nothing but a thin pair of oversized sweatpants.

Scrambled eggs, sir?

She kicked.

He howled.

Shee scuttled back like a crab, found her feet and snatched her gun from her side. The gun she should have pulled *before* trying to tackle the Empire State Building.

"Move a muscle and I'll aerate you," she said. She always liked that line.

The golem growled, but remained on the ground like a good dog, cradling his family jewels.

Shee's partner in this manhunt, a local cop easier on the eyes than he was useful, rounded the corner and drew his own weapon.

She smiled and holstered the gun he'd lent her. Unknowingly.

"Glad you could make it."

Her portion of the operation accomplished, she headed toward the car as more officers swarmed the scene.

"Shee, where are you going?" called the cop.

She stopped and turned.

"Home, I think."

His gaze dropped to her hip.

"Is that my gun?"

Get *The Girl Who Wants* on

Amazon!

Vansant Creations, LLC / Amy Vansant
Jupiter, FL
http://www.AmyVansant.com

Copy editing by Carolyn Steele
Proofreading by Effrosyni Moschoudi, Meg Barnhart & Connie Leap
Cover by Lance Buckley & Amy Vansant

Made in United States
North Haven, CT
01 July 2024

54302735R00153